HERE YOU ARE

By Jo Fletcher

2023

Butterworth Books is a different breed of publishing house. It's a home for Indies, for independent authors who take great pride in their work and produce top quality books for readers who deserve the best. Professional editing, professional cover design, professional proof reading, professional book production—you get the idea. As Individual as the Indie authors we're proud to work with, we're Butterworths and we're *different*.

Authors currently publishing with us:

E.V. Bancroft
Valden Bush
Addison M Conley
Jo Fletcher
Helena Harte
Lee Haven
Karen Klyne
AJ Mason
Ally McGuire
James Merrick
Robyn Nyx
Simon Smalley
Brey Willows

For more information visit www.butterworthbooks.co.uk

CATALOGING INFORMATION
ISBN: 978-1-915009-44-9
CREDITS
Editor: Nicci Robinson
Jacket Design: Nicci Robinson & Jo Fletcher
Production Design: Global Wordsmiths
Cover Illustration: Caroline Harroe (@carolineharroearts)
carolineharroearts.co.uk

Acknowledgements

First of all, I want to give a huge thanks to Nicci Robinson, my editor. She has really helped me sharpen my writing, showed me how to craft a better story, and gently nudged me on my bad habits.

Big thanks to my dear friend, Iona Kane, who pushed me to get my jumbled-up ideas down on paper and start my writing journey. Iona has been at my side through this entire process.

My amazing wife, Rachel, also deserves a big thank you. She has gifted me the time, space, and energy to make this dream a reality. She's been reading my work-in-progress with her eagle eyes (even when she forgot her glasses!) and giving me honest feedback. That support means the world to me.

To my son, for chatting to me about character names and ideas and indulging my trips to Paris for—ahem—research.

I also need to give a special shout-out to my cover artist, Caroline Harroe. I can't thank her enough for her patience and creativity; she really brought my characters Elda and Charlie to life.

And speaking of characters, I'm constantly inspired by my fellow writers of sapphic literature. Their amazing characters, plots, and worlds keep me motivated day in and day out.

And finally, a huge thanks to Mr Camish, my old English teacher. You gave me such valuable feedback, and I'm realizing now how much I've forgotten your voice over the years. I hope you don't read this book though. It's probably not what you had in mind when you sent me on my way with pen and paper in hand.

Dedication

To my mum.
My first and loudest cheerleader.

To R and R.
For everything.

To Sue
Thank you for
your support.
Enjoy the read.

Jo x

CHAPTER ONE

"Miss Mason, your case files." Charlie's clerk dropped a stack of bulging manilla folders onto her desk with a thud. She stared at her laptop, ignoring his shadow looming over the desk, and pulled at the ribbon on the top file.

"What've we got?" She didn't have time to look up.

"It's a Section 20. A pretty complex case of neglect. There's possible crossover with criminal court and the in-house solicitor wants you."

"Who?" Her fingers hovered over the folder.

Joshua Pinkman put his hand in his pocket and shifted onto one leg. "Jude." He cleared his throat.

"For fuck's sake." Charlie's jaw hardened, and she swallowed her frustration. She and Jude had an arrangement which had worked for years. Pleasure, not business. A smirk spread across Joshua's stubbly face. Tension gathered between her eyes. "Don't start, I'm not in the mood."

"Well, you are the best. Jude wants to win the case." He bounded towards the door, turning back with a wide smile. "I thought you were always in the mood, miss."

"Joshua," Charlie called after him.

"I've done my job," he said, glancing back. "Look over the file and see what you make of it."

Charlie edged back in her seat. The leather was worn by the bodies of her predecessors, most of them heavy men. Joshua had been her clerk for years at the chambers. He knew her well, and they respected each other. He also knew which solicitors she'd dated and who she preferred to avoid. He was discreet, and

Charlie needed that. But this time, he was pushing her.

She rubbed at her tight forehead and picked up the phone.

"Can you get me Jude Oswald?" She swivelled on her chair and looked out of the window.

The city's sky was thick with cloud, as if it could rain at any moment. Her gaze fell to the mill building on the horizon. She wondered what happened behind those leaded windowpanes.

"Jude, you don't need me for this case. Get someone cheaper."

There was an intake of breath and a giggle. "Hey, Charlie. How are you, darling? I've been meaning to call. How are you fixed tonight?"

Charlie tried to resist the temptation of Jude's voice, but its deep, familiar melody sent a shiver down her spine.

"Did you get my little gift?"

"Yes, I did." Charlie sighed. Jude had form for pulling this kind of stunt and embroiling her in a case which would have them both tied up for months. "Listen, Joshua will find someone else to try this case for you. It doesn't need me." Charlie took a breath. She needed to keep her head down at work and avoid any distractions. "And tonight, I can't do." She held the phone away from her ear, putting a little distance between them.

"Just look at the file, Charlie. You'll find it stimulating, I promise. I saw it and thought of you."

Charlie gripped the edge of her oak desk. She was busy and could do without Jude's sales pitch. But she knew how to press Charlie's buttons, and she was irresistible, as well as convenient to have around. They enjoyed a mutual understanding that neither of them wanted anything other than occasional, no-strings satisfaction. So why was she pitching this work? Maybe it was worth a look.

The silence drew out a moment too long.

"Darling, let's meet for coffee, and I can talk you through it. It'd be nice to catch up in the daylight, like normal people. Maybe cocktails at that place you like?"

"Fine, I'll fix a date with your office." Charlie hung up.

Keeping the phone against her ear, she called Joshua.

"Can you get me an hour with Jude Oswald before the weekend? Case prep. Cheers."

A couple of days later, they looked like every other pair of suits around them, talking shop and nailing down a deal. Charlie clocked her own reflection in a mirror and pushed her cropped hair back into place. Jude sat opposite, her face flushed with lunchtime wine. She was wearing the cashmere jumper Charlie had thrown onto her bedroom floor last month.

"I don't mind where you go with it, darling. You're the one with the talent for words." Jude's eyes widened and she smirked. "Among other things."

"We said we wouldn't work together. I thought that was clear." Charlie sipped her water, desperately trying to ignore the cut of Jude's skirt, inching up her thigh every time she moved. The woman was annoying as hell sometimes but really got under Charlie's skin.

"I get it, I do." Jude raised her hands. She sighed and tipped her head to one side. "I just need you on this case, Charlie. All jokes aside, it calls for someone with your blend of perfection and compassion."

Charlie knew she wouldn't be breaching their agreed code without good reason. Play together, work apart. It had been that way for more than two years. Charlie had made it clear that she had no time for a relationship, especially one which might trip her up in the courtroom.

"Charlie, you're a bloody tease. Just take the case, and we can finish these drinks and head somewhere more comfortable."

A group of clerks from her chambers had gathered at the bar, and Charlie wanted to avoid their attention. The last thing she needed at work was any speculation about her personal life ruining her chances of another promotion. The boys would love to get one up on her any way they could.

"Are you listening to me? Let's go and have some fun." Jude

leaned across the table and held Charlie's fingers in her own.

Charlie pulled back, avoiding her touch. She wanted to say no, but it had been a couple of weeks since they last saw each other, and Jude looked delicious across the table. *What's the harm?*

"Okay, I'm bored, so let's go to your place. But I haven't made a decision on the brief. Joshua might need to get another barrister onto it. I don't like mess at work, you know that." Charlie used the broken-record technique with clients when she had boundaries to enforce. She also used it with people she loved, even liked, when she wanted to protect herself from difficult feelings.

She stretched her legs and enjoyed the sharp tailoring of her designer two-piece.

"Settle the bill and put it against the case. I'll meet you at the door."

A few blissful hours passed, and Charlie stretched against the hotel sheets, while running her fingertips across Jude's shoulder blades.

"Kiss me."

Jude's command made Charlie throb with a yearning that had only just been satisfied. She complied, guiding Jude's lips to her own. She brushed her hands across Jude's bronze skin, teasing the smooth surface beneath her fingers.

She ran her tongue along Jude's jawline and tasted the sweat from the last few hours they'd spent in the king size bed.

"If you're trying to soften me up to take that case, it's not going to work—"

Jude clamped her mouth on Charlie's nipple, and the vibration coursed through her breasts.

"I have no doubt, Charlotte Mason, that you will take that case based on its legal merit and your burning desire to," Jude looked at Charlie and ran her tongue across her lips, "do the right thing."

Charlie's back arched, her muscles contracted, and her thoughts evaporated under Jude's lips. Being together was a sort of stress relief for them both.

Jude's thigh nestled between Charlie's legs, and she couldn't still the pulsing which started. Her breath came quicker, and her lips parted. Jude planted kisses along Charlie's stomach. She gave in to Jude's expert touch, relishing the moment. She parted her legs, guiding Jude to her centre. Her breathing was heavy and rhythmic. She craved this feeling of abandonment, where there was nothing else in the world but her body responding to the touch of someone else.

Charlie raised her hips, and she fought the urge to clamp her legs at Jude's caresses. Her need was building, and she couldn't hold back much longer. She was desperate to flip Jude and take control.

It seemed like Jude read her body, barely touching and then pushing harder, and harder again. The combination of Jude's tongue and her fingers were too much; Charlie bucked and curved towards the ceiling of the hotel room. "Yes." She clutched Jude's head against her.

"Fuck." Jude played with Charlie for a moment longer before they relaxed into one another's arms.

Charlie pictured the pile of manilla folders on her desk. She got up and walked around the room, collecting her strewn clothes.

"I have to go," She struggled with a button in her haste to leave and left it undone.

"Really? Stay for a while. I have the good champagne in the fridge." Jude propped herself up on two pillows and crossed her arms above her head.

"I have work to finish. And I bet you do too." Charlie laughed, adjusting her trousers. She liked being with Jude, but she also liked having the freedom to leave. "You clearly have no intention of seeing me to the door."

"True. This was gorgeous, as ever." Jude stretched and the covers fell to reveal her breasts.

Charlie averted her gaze. She really did have work to do and didn't have time for round two. "Sure."

"Charlie?" Jude turned onto her side and hooked her leg out of the white sheet. "Let me know about the case."

Charlie stepped out and closed the door behind her. She ran her tongue over her top lip and tasted Jude, recalling the pleasures of the last few hours. She relished the thrill of hungry bodies that didn't come laden with emotions. Heading into the cold air, she was thankful to Jude for dragging her out of the office in the middle of the day. Sure, she got lonely, sometimes, but work kept her mind busy and when she was in the mood, Jude was just a phone call away.

Maybe taking this case wouldn't be such an awful idea? Jude would do the heavy lifting and it would be a favour, for a friend. That's what they were, wasn't it? Friends, with benefits.

CHAPTER TWO

"SHIT." ELDA BROWN RUBBED her head where she'd just cracked it on the corner of the desk. She was on her hands and knees, picking up paperclips scattered over the frayed carpet. She slumped into her chair and set the refilled pot of clips on her scuffed desk. If she lifted her head, she could see endless copies of her cubicle, stretching in rows towards tall windows. At one time, the panes of glass would have glimmered, but now they were covered in greasy handprints and dusty raindrops. Her heart sank for the fiftieth time that day. It wasn't just the monotony of her day job. Her love life was a disaster. When was she finally going to have her own happily ever after?

Swallowing a yawn, she carried on pasting numbers from one screen to another. Her back ached. She'd never bothered to adjust her chair. That would have meant accepting this temping job was getting kind of permanent. So, she'd perched on the edge of her seat since finishing art college.

Without looking away from the screen, Elda reached into a tub of chocolates and popped another mini Mars in her mouth. She pulled at the cuffs around her wrists and rubbed her arms to warm herself up. Her eyelids drooped, and she squinted at the numbers in green, scanning for the line she was working on. She had three more hours to get through.

"Are you out tonight, El?" Jack Reynolds deposited a mug of beige tea on her desk. The steaming liquid was still making waves when he collapsed into the cubicle next to her.

Elda bumped back in her chair and gave her best friend a wide smile. Jack was one of the few reasons she'd stuck this job out. "I'm heading to the studio tonight. I need to catch up."

Jack leaned in. "Rubbish. We're off to that new place on Cromwell Street for cocktails and pizza. It's Friday night... Why don't you come after you're done with your creations?" He gestured with his hands. "People will be out, Elderflower."

"Yeah, if you like. I can meet you afterwards."

"Will you bring your new hot girl too? What's her name? Becky?"

"Rebecca. She hates people shortening her name."

"Okay, bit weird. How was your romantic weekend in Paris?"

Elda looked away. She didn't want to relive the disappointment of last week's trip, but Jack stayed put, clearly wanting all the details. "It was a bit of letdown, to be honest."

"Oh no, why? I thought she'd swept you off your feet?"

"Me too." She looked to the ceiling and drew a breath. "We just ended up in a shitty bit of the city, wandering the streets while bars closed around us. It was grim."

"Not exactly guidebook perfect then?"

"The worst part was that Rebecca was oblivious. She spent most of the time either drunk or hungover. I don't know, it was an anticlimax. I thought it would be dreamy."

"Did you even make it to that fancy museum you wanted to go to?"

"Musée d'Orsay? I went on my own. Can you believe that? She wouldn't even drag herself out of bed. She said the queues would be too long. It just wasn't what I was expecting it to be."

"I get it. You know, it might be time to adjust your expectations. Everything will be a disappointment if it's all in your head." Jack delved into the box of chocolates.

"Well, she's invited me to her parents' house at the coast for her mum's birthday this weekend, so it's not a total write-off."

Jack raised his eyebrows. "Really? You've only been going out a couple of months?"

She caught his meaning, and she knew, deep down, he was

right. Her flirtation with Rebecca was already showing signs of rising damp. Maybe it was time to cut and run. "Don't start. It might work out." She wasn't convincing herself, never mind Jack. "Her family sound lovely. Normal." Which is more than she had, so it was worth a go. She trusted Jack more than anyone and needed him to tell her it would be okay.

"She might not be the one you're searching for. Something feels off to me."

She blew out a breath. How many times had they had this conversation? And every time, he'd been right.

"Don't bother if you're unhappy, El. You're too special. Don't waste time."

She gave his hand a quick squeeze. She'd get through it without making too much of a fuss and come up with a plan. Elda looked back to her screen and signalled the conversation was over. She loved Jack, but sometimes she hated that he knew the depths of her desperation to find love.

Jack lingered. Elda heard him curling his lanyard but avoided his gaze. She'd unravel if he questioned her too much about the weekend. The truth was it was awful. She'd realised in the dirty backstreet hotel room that there was no way she was ever going to fall in love with Rebecca. But she'd gone through the motions of a romantic weekend in Paris in the hope of finding some sort of connection. Apart from Jack, she was alone, and lonely.

"Thanks for the tea, Jack." When Elda looked up, he'd gone.

At the end of her shift, she scanned her pass and exited into the night. Her shoulders dropped a couple of inches. It was such a relief to have time to herself. Her breath formed clouds, and she wrapped her scarf tighter. The cool air cleared her head of the boredom of the office, and she half jogged with excitement across town towards the large mill building.

Elda loved this place. At the entrance, she punched a code into the frame and yanked down a heavy lever. Down a corridor, she reached a battered old door marked "Studio eight." She eased the brass key backwards when it stuck, until it released with a deep clunk.

She flicked the switches and fluorescent tubes burst with light above her. She dropped her bag and dragged a couple of oil heaters towards the centre of the room.

Ready to get going, she stepped on the back of her shoes and kicked them off, then shed her layer of office wear. Her hairs stood on end with the cold and the anticipation of the evening ahead. She stepped into a boiler suit and secured a fistful of hair on top of her head.

Elda tapped a switch on the floor, and the room was bathed in white. Every contour had a different hue. Three canvases leaned on wooden frames, each begging for attention.

The mill was home to dreamers and makers, and Elda had rented this studio since she'd left art college five years ago. Making art was part of her, and although she struggled to make money, she wasn't ready to give it up. She'd stumbled into her office job, and it paid the bills. But here, in this space, she was herself.

Elda approached the window and peered down towards the murky canal, all but invisible in the darkness. She imagined the flow of water beneath and her neighbours cooped up in colourful narrowboats. She could hear the hum of the city beyond, and laughter from the bars nestled along the canal. Life was happening to someone else out there.

Elda turned away and braced herself. After weeks of painful indecision, she had to make progress tonight. As usual, she'd been doubting herself. That little voice in the back of her mind telling her she wasn't good enough.

She stood back from her three canvases and adjusted the floodlight. She took in a breath that travelled all the way to the pit of her stomach, and she smiled.

While she worked with her paints, cloths, and brushes, the outside world faded away. Her heart beat faster and sweat gathered at her brow. The depths she reached inside her body when her mind was focused on the palette in her palm and the brush between her fingers were exhilarating. She could rely on herself with a canvas at her fingertips. There was no doubt, she was connected to something, and everything was whole.

Elda became frantic, absorbed, and soon, she was shrugging off the sleeves of her boiler suit and wrapping them around her waist. Beads of moisture began to form at her lower back beneath her crop top. Adrenaline was pulsing through her veins, giving her the hyper focus she needed to channel every ounce of imagination into her work in progress.

There was nothing, except for her and the colours she was mixing. Her racing thoughts stilled, her constant chatter muted. The helicopter of catastrophes that accompanied her everywhere was silent.

She reached for water and took three gulps. Hunger stabbed at her, and she became aware of the time. She'd worked for two hours without a break. Her phone rang and broke the silence.

"El, are you coming out or what?"

Jack. She'd completely forgotten her promise to go out. Her heart sank, and she looked across to the unfinished canvas. It would have to wait.

"We've got pizza and alcohol. Come down and we'll feed you."

"I'll be about twenty minutes. Where are you?"

***

Elda twisted the volume control, and the music faded as Rebecca drove onto a short gravel driveway at the edge of suburbia.

"You look hot." Rebecca cut the engine and stroked the back of Elda's earlobe.

Elda's shoulders hunched towards her neck, and she forced them down. She wasn't sure why her body tensed up so much, but she hoped Rebecca hadn't noticed.

She imagined this was her family home, with her mother and

father waving from the doorstep. Perfect family fantasies often played out her mind, usually starring her absent father.

The curtain twitched and brought her back to the present. A woman flashed behind it before the front door swung open and an older and fatter male version of Rebecca galloped towards them.

"Hello there. This must be the famous Elda. I'm Philip."

Before she could step away, she was suffocated in a brief embrace, his round belly thankfully preventing him from getting too close. "Thank you for having me." Elda bristled at the unwanted touch and peeled herself away.

"Dad, grab that other bag from the boot for me."

"Gotcha." Philip disappeared behind the car.

Rebecca led her inside and they settled in the kitchen. "Elda, this is my mum, Sue."

"Happy birthday, it's lovely to meet you." Elda brushed at imaginary creases on her jumper.

"Thank you so much for coming. It's wonderful to have you both."

Sue disappeared into her daughter's hug, and Elda couldn't quite place the jab to her belly. It wasn't regret. Was it envy? She rested her eyes on the wooden cabinets and china plates. They seemed safe enough not to trigger any emotions.

"Do you like those plates, Elda? They're family heirlooms."

Elda smiled. She'd seen most of them at the department store in town. Perhaps Sue wanted them to be *future* heirlooms.

"Rebecca doesn't often bring her girlfriends home."

"Mum, Elda doesn't need any back stories."

If Elda had spoken to her mum like that she'd have got a mouthful back. Visits home were rare, and they always ended in some sort of row.

Philip hovered close by. His face was quite repulsive; his eyes sat too close together and his chin disappeared into his neck. His lips turned up into a half-smile half-sneer, as if he could see something no one else could or like he was about to tell a dirty joke.

"Go on into the lounge, and I'll bring you some treats." Sue ushered them out with the soft whip of a cat-patterned tea towel.

Sinking into an oversized armchair, Elda cursed herself for agreeing to another awkward social engagement with someone she wasn't that into. It was the story of her life, saying yes to things she'd rather not do. She scanned the chintzy living room and settled her gaze on Rebecca, whose face was similar to her repulsive father's. She'd never noticed the downturn of her mouth before. Elda glanced up at a wooden grandmother clock ticking on the wall, wishing the time away.

At eight o'clock, Philip poured himself a fifth glass of wine, almost to the brim. He smiled and revealed dark red stains on his teeth. Sue stacked plates and ferried them into the kitchen. Rebecca yawned as she rose to help her mother.

"Nice meal inside you. Bet you two starve on your own." Philip turned the dimmer switch, and the bulbs crackled.

Elda adjusted her eyes to the fuzzy light. He screeched his chair closer and poured more wine into her glass.

"I'm fine. Thank you," she said, trying to keep her voice light. She'd had enough alcohol to get through the awkwardness of dinner but didn't need any more.

"It's nice to spend time with you, Elda."

His gaze moved across her jumper, and she looked down to see if she'd spilled her dinner. When it was clear her jumper was perfectly clean, she pushed her chair away from him and looked to the doorway for signs of Rebecca or her mum. She struggled against the urge to run.

Philip reached behind her neck. It took a split second to realise what was happening, then her body took over. She jerked away, toppling the glass of wine. "I'm sorry." She jumped back, red wine leeching into the fabric in slow motion.

Rebecca stood still in the doorway.

"You've got paint on you. That's all!" Philip sat back in his chair and laughed, thrusting out his stomach.

Elda caught Rebecca's eye and without uttering a single word, she begged her to understand what was happening.

"What are you two up to?" Rebecca moved the remaining dishes. "She's always covered in paint, Dad."

Sue reappeared, fussing her away, to take over the cleaning duties.

The grandmother clock ticked, every second pounding in her ears. Doubt crept through her body. Had she imagined it? Had she misread Philip's creepy moves? "I'm going to head up for tonight." She didn't wait for a round of well wishes and rushed up the stairs.

It was dark when the bedroom door opened.

"What the fuck, Elda?" Rebecca's silhouette appeared in the landing light.

"I don't think I should stay tonight." She was being impulsive, but there was something about the dynamic in the house that didn't feel right. If there was one thing Elda could spot a mile off, it was a dysfunctional family.

The ceiling light illuminated the room. Elda stayed on the bed and brought her knees to her chest.

"What does that mean? You don't like my parents? It's an overnight visit and one dinner. Maybe small talk over poached eggs. You can't just throw wine around and storm upstairs. My dad is just drunk."

She blinked in the light. Rebecca knew what had happened. Maybe it had happened before, and Philip was actually a bit of a pervert. "I feel uncomfortable." Elda scanned Rebecca's face for a sign that she understood. "I know you see it."

"I see you acting weird. And I see him trying to make you welcome," Rebecca said. "Look, you're embarrassed. That's okay. We can just go downstairs and enjoy the rest of the evening. My parents will be fine with it."

Her pulse thundered in her ears, and her palms were clammy. She stood and began to fold her clothes into her overnight bag. "No." For once, she wasn't going to back down just to please the people around her. "This isn't really working. You're nice, but this isn't for me." She walked to the door.

"Please." Rebecca gripped the handle and a look of panic moved across her face. "Don't go. We're here now. Just get back into bed."

"Rebecca," Elda's chest tightened, "this isn't working. I would like to leave, please."

Rebecca stepped aside, and Elda took the stairs two at a time to reach the front door. Air rushed at her hot cheeks as she cracked the door open. She turned at the end of the drive and continued along the main road, barely able to make out what was in front of her through the tears in her eyes.

Streetlamps huddled together for the first fifty yards, and then nothing, not a beam, for a couple of miles. She looked up at the blank sky above her, no idea where the hell she was heading.

Car headlights flicked up and down, blinding her, and she stepped to safety into the wet grass. She'd been walking for a mile or so when her thoughts slowed down. She pulled out her phone and called Jack. "It's me."

"Lucky you. I don't answer my phone for anyone."

"I've just left Rebecca's parents' and I'm walking down a country lane. I don't know where I am."

"Is she with you?"

"No. I've just left her. I told you." She stumbled on the uneven ground.

"What happened?"

"It all just felt wrong. I can't explain over the phone, but can you come and get me? I can get to the A61, I think. I'll meet you on there."

"Are you joking? It must be freezing out there."

Elda hung up so she could concentrate on her footsteps. The verge was overgrown and slippery. It'd be just her luck to trip and get mown down by a speeding bus.

Why did everything have to be so hard? Why couldn't she

meet a nice, normal human? Why did she have to get herself into so many uncomfortable situations like this one? She sighed. Finding someone to share her life was proving an impossible task.

CHAPTER THREE

THE WIND HOWLED ACROSS the beach, throwing dusty sand clouds under the moonlight. Charlie closed her eyes and listened to the waves crash outside her parents' house.

"You look tired, love. Are they working you too hard?"

"No, Mum, I'm just relaxed." Charlie bit her cheek. She was drowsy, and her muscles still ached from the game of sex-twister with Jude.

Her head rested against the deckchair, as she breathed in the salt buried in the weave. The long drive lingered in her bones, and she was dreading the journey back. But it was worth it. This wasn't her childhood home, but it was as close as she was going to get after her parents had retired and uprooted.

"I'm so pleased that you came today. Your dad perks up when you visit. The poor man gets bored with just me." Her mum chuckled.

Charlie reached for her mum's gloved hand, like she'd done so many times as a child. She took a gulp of briny air and looked across the inky water.

"It's getting late. Will you stay the night?"

Charlie rolled damp sand between her fingers, and the shards pinched her skin. She loved spending time with her folks, but she rarely managed more than a flying visit. "I'll head back soon. It's Theresa's anniversary tomorrow, and I want to be home."

"Goodness, is it? Has it been, what, fifteen years?"

"Seventeen. She's been dead longer than she was alive." Charlie studied her hands, stretching and gathering the skin at her knuckles. She'd been growing older, while the girl she'd loved remained sixteen forever.

"How are you this year, darling?" Her mum shifted in her chair as a cloud drifted, revealing another cluster of stars.

Charlie watched a shadowy wave break into white foam, fizzing at the shoreline. She struggled to smile. She wanted to spare her parents from the hurt she still felt but sharing it would lessen the pain. Heaps of therapy had taught her that much. "Up and down." She met her mother's eyes again and leaned in. "But at least I'm here to remember her."

Her mum ran her hand through Charlie's hair, making her wriggle.

"Charlotte, you've got so much bleach in this hair of yours, it's like straw." She shifted in her chair, still holding Charlie's arm. "I'm proud of you, little one."

Charlie broke into a grin. She'd towered above her five-foot-nothing mother since she was a teenager, but she was always her little girl, no matter what strife she brought home. She was cherished. They held her when she fell, and they held her when she stood tall, and she loved them for it.

"Are you still seeing that girl, what was her name?" her mum asked.

"Jude? We're just casual." Charlie shivered and pulled her jacket around her against the chill.

"I worry about you. Aren't you lonely in the city on your own?"

"Not really. People are messy."

"It can't all be about working, Charlotte. There's time to find someone special, sweetheart." Her mum squeezed her leg. "Don't leave it too long though. I want grandchildren running around before my knees need replacing."

Their laughter rippled into the sea air. Charlie didn't want to think about settling down with anyone's baggage. She had a case to argue and that was complication enough. "Will Dad be back by now? I want to say goodbye before I head off."

"I should think so. Let's go and bother him."

They walked towards the backlit windows of the house and entered through the kitchen door.

"Time for goodbyes already, Sherbert?" Her dad swept Charlie into a hug. "Call me soon with tales of the city. I miss it a bit." He laughed.

"I have no tales, Dad. I stay in like a good girl." She smiled widely.

"Ha, I doubt that, missy. Don't let those tricky cases leave their mark. You work far too hard."

"Thank you for lunch." She looked out the window towards the jet-black sea. "I needed some fresh air and a decent meal."

"Glad to have you, sweetheart."

He wrapped her in his arms, and she lingered for a few seconds, enjoying the warmth of his embrace.

"What's your mother been chewing over?" He drew back and started to empty the grocery bags onto the kitchen counter.

"She's worried about you."

"I'm fine. Your mother worries about me too much. She frets over little things."

"I worry too. Aren't you bored out here?"

"Of course! That's the point of retiring. Slow down, tinker, embrace the silence, have a glass of something, and start again tomorrow." The lines of his face creased a little deeper. "I'm okay though. I enjoy it. The peace is quite restorative."

This time, Charlie wasn't convinced by her dad's usual optimism. He'd retired at the top of his academic career and that had to sting. She'd feel like she'd lost a limb if it was her.

"Mum said you'd been feeling a bit down. Have you seen the doctor?"

"I see the doctor all the bloody time. Blood pressure, cholesterol, sugar. It's all through the roof." He laughed and patted his smooth palm on her cheek. "Trivial. Nothing to be concerned over. You, or your mother."

Charlie perched on a stool to tie her bootlaces while her father unpacked a rainbow of fresh vegetables.

"Tell me. Are they treating you well at the chambers?"

"I'm getting decent briefs. I won an award last month for upcoming talent or something." Charlie made a half-hearted attempt to downplay it, but she'd gone after that accolade, and she knew he'd be proud.

"You did, you clever thing. Mum showed me the photo. Very good. Did you have to prop up the old guys at a fancy awards dinner?"

"Yes, it was unpleasant. But the wine was free."

"That always helps."

"The Capri still going strong I see." He nodded towards the driveway to her car.

"She is. I look after her," Charlie said.

"You always have done."

She and her dad had spent hours together in their old garage, tinkering with his modest collection of classic cars. She'd been over the moon when he'd handed over the keys to the Ford Capri when they'd moved to the coast.

"Dad?"

"Mm?" He pottered around her, filling the kettle and lighting the stove.

"Kim's been calling me." She'd been avoiding the subject all day but needed her dad's advice. "She needed my help."

"Again, love? Didn't you put her off the last time?" His eyes narrowed.

"I thought so. But I'm all she has, really. And every time it gets a bit tough, she has nowhere to go. I can't imagine what it must be like to support the children with no one else."

"I thought there was a new boyfriend on the scene?"

"He's not much use. I don't think he gives a shit about the kids because they're not his. He's just interested in Kim."

"You have no obligations there, Charlotte." He frowned and deep ridges etched his forehead. "I know you want to do the right thing. But it isn't down to you. It never has been."

"I know."

"Sherbert," he said softly. "You love to fix things for people but in this case, that's a role that you simply can't fulfil. You've got your own life to live."

"I know I have a life, Dad." It was like he could read her mind. *I have a life.*

"Sweetheart, what is it?" Her mum came back into the room and set her sewing on the worktop.

"It's Kim. She's been in touch again." Charlie rubbed at her face.

"Oh, why? It's all in the past. You were just a child when all that happened. She should focus on raising her own children."

"Mum, please don't make it worse. I shouldn't have mentioned it." Charlie swallowed back the lump in her throat and gathered her bag.

"I just don't know why that Kim is dragging it all up. Theresa has been gone for a long time now."

Charlie stared at the watercolours on the kitchen wall, her mother's words washing over her. *It wasn't the same for you.* "It's tough at this time of year, Mum."

"I'm sorry, I know you loved her, and it brings it all back." Her mum pulled her close and Charlie welcomed the hug.

"It's good to be here," she said, "and if I can support Kim and the children, in some weird way that helps me too. Listen, I'd better head off. It's getting late."

Most days, Charlie kept her mask in place. The strong, professional woman who demanded respect in both the office and the bedroom. But no matter how much therapy she had, the grief never lessened. Maybe she'd carry it forever. She wished she could shrug it off and move on, but the calendar would turn again, and she'd wake up to fresh agony, as if time hadn't passed at all.

Her parents waved her off, and the lights from the porch faded to nothing in the rear-view mirror.

Charlie gripped the steering wheel and squinted. The lanes between her parents' house and the main road were narrow and winding.

She had been just fourteen when Theresa moved into the house across the road. Charlie hadn't known the family, but they were foster carers, and kids would come and go. Sometimes they'd only stayed for a night or two but now and then, they'd stick around.

Theresa had stuck around, and Charlie was drawn to her like no one she'd ever known. Remembering it now, Charlie rubbed the goosebumps on her neck. Theresa had been everything.

Together, they'd been a force to be reckoned with. Theresa wasn't just her neighbour; she was her classmate, and they were inseparable. They'd huddle in Charlie's room, sharing a pair of headphones, listening to music. More than once, they stole booze from the cupboard under the sink and spent the night under the stars.

Charlie gritted her teeth. She didn't want to think about their nights under the stars. It hurt to remember Theresa's kisses. But even now, she could bring to mind the touch of her fingers beneath her T-shirt.

But she'd lost her. And now she faced the burden of Theresa's birth mum and younger siblings to look after. *Dad's right. What am I trying to fix?*

She reached the main road and straightened her shoulders. She needed to keep her mind on the journey. The roads were pitch black, and it had started to rain. She fiddled with the windscreen wipers but struggled to settle on the perfect speed. She loved her Ford Capri. An oldie and a goodie but at times like these, it showed its age.

Rounding the bend, she blinked at two full beams straight ahead and knocked her own lights down. As her eyes adjusted in the darkness, something appeared on the side of the road. It took a second to register, but the shape was in the road, and she was going to hit it. She swerved the steering wheel, slammed the brakes, and the car screeched. Charlie closed her eyes and braced for the impact, but it didn't come.

Scanning the darkness, she couldn't see a trace of the shape. She grabbed at the car door and forced it into the night. Panicked, she clambered across uneven ground to the spot behind her that she'd swerved to avoid. Lying in the depths of a grass verge was a woman.

"Shit. Are you okay?"

The woman groaned but rolled over and moved to get up.

"Hold on. I'll come and help you."

"Don't worry, I'm fine," the woman said.

"Christ, I'm so sorry. Are you hurt?"

"No. Please, it's not your fault." The woman was on her feet, and although she was leaning into Charlie's arms, she looked intact. "I was walking along a main road. You didn't hit me. I just jumped out of the way and lost my footing."

Charlie stood her in front of the headlights and tried to check her over.

"Ah." The woman winced. "I think I might have done something to my arm."

"I'll take you to the hospital." Charlie guided her to the passenger seat. "I'm sorry, I don't even know your name."

"Stop apologising. It's Elda."

Charlie paused and looked at the woman's face for the first time. "Hi, Elda. I'm Charlie."

It took half an hour to get to the nearest hospital and Charlie made the journey on autopilot. Inside the emergency department, her stomach churned. She closed her eyes for a moment to block out the overhead lights and passing trolleys. On top of the emotional day she'd had, tonight had all been a bit much. She wanted nothing more than to be in her own bed. Instead, she turned to study Elda, the stranger next to her. She felt somehow grounded by her presence despite the terror that rose in her chest every time she thought about what could have happened out on the road.

There was a scratch above Elda's cheek and mud in her hair

but otherwise, she was beautiful. She scanned Elda's petite body for signs of injury and saw grazes on her forehead and a rip in her coat. Charlie had a fleeting thought that if she'd seen Elda in a bar, she would've wasted no time in trying to hook up. She glanced away, embarrassed at the thought.

Elda massaged her head. "Listen, I really am wasting your time. I'm fine. Why don't you just get off? It's getting late."

"Elda," Charlie repeated the name in her head so she'd remember it, "I just ran you off the road. You're not fine." She rose to her feet, wanting something to happen. Lack of control wasn't something she was used to. It made her twitchy.

"I'm sorry, I just didn't see you." Elda stared at the floor, deflated.

"Likewise." Charlie's pressed at her knuckles. "That road is awful. I've never liked it."

"Why were you there?" Elda turned towards Charlie, her movement stiff.

"On the road?" Charlie closed her eyes for just a second, and the sharp bend blazed behind her eyelids. She forced them open. "I was coming back from my parents' house. They retired on the east coast."

Elda started to fidget, her face crumpling.

"Are you in pain?" Charlie stretched to see any signs of movement at the desk.

"It's just my arm; I'm fine. At least I'll be able to work."

"What do you do?" Charlie's own head pounded, but she was determined to keep Elda talking.

"I paint. I'm an artist. I mean, I've got an office job too." Elda took a deep breath. "But at least I still have a good painting arm. I'm trying to get a piece accepted in an exhibition at the docks."

"In the city? I know the docks. I work across the road."

A nurse came around the corner. "Elda Brown?"

"Here." Charlie stood to supervise Elda's handover to the medical staff. *Good. Something's happening.*

Elda eased into a wheelchair. Charlie kept watch, not sure what to do next. Before the curtain was drawn closed, Elda hunched her shoulders, and she let out a dry sob. Shock and shame pulsed through Charlie's body. She tried to work out what had happened. It was a near miss, but she couldn't shake the thought of Elda's body looking so broken in the ditch.

This weekend had been a complete roller-coaster, and Charlie needed to get a grip. She thought back to the simple pleasure of Jude's bed just a couple of days ago. Part of her wished she could turn back the clock and stick around for some uninterrupted physical exertion. She frowned, the thought of Kim and the children still nagging at her. Now, Elda had stumbled into her path, and Charlie had another crisis on her plate. Hunger jabbed her in the ribs. It was late, but she couldn't leave Elda alone. There was something about her that kept Charlie right by her side.

CHAPTER FOUR

ELDA NEEDED TO CLEAR her head. The last week had been a series of disasters. She'd called in sick at the office to nurse her physical and emotional wounds. She laid back against her pillow and patted the space next to her in bed. Just a few nights ago, Rebecca had been dribbling on the sheets with half her clothes on, the stench of her breath making Elda's stomach roll. She was glad to be rid of Rebecca but hated the idea of being alone again.

Squeezing her eyes tight, Elda pushed at the doubt flooding her thoughts. Why was she so blinded by the thought of someone being attracted to her? The sadness weighed heavy. She'd been so eager to be with someone that she hadn't really thought about whether she even liked Rebecca.

She opened her eyes and took comfort in the empty space that was hers. She'd drawn blood sanding the floorboards and cried tears over making the rent. She'd poured herself into this flat, transforming a tired wreck into her hideaway. It was lonely, yes, but it was all hers.

She dragged herself out of the warm bed and headed to the kitchen, adjusting her sling around her arm. She flicked on the kettle and set a mug down in the round coffee stain which branded the work surface. It was the only mark that Elda couldn't shift when she'd scrubbed the place till her hands were cracked. She left it, eventually, as a reminder that she couldn't scrub everything clean; she had to live with imperfection.

She steadied herself at the fridge, wrinkling her nose in pain. Maybe she should go back to bed. The doctors had told her to rest. She tried to ignore the chatter in her mind. The burden of finishing her work at the studio had been whirring through her thoughts before she fell asleep last night, and she'd woken up under the same pressure.

Letting her fresh coffee cool, Elda walked towards her small bathroom. She closed the door and tipped her head back against the panelling. *Why do I get myself into these situations?* Showering in her cast was too much hard work, so she settled for brushing her teeth, splashing her face, and pulling on last night's jeans and jumper. She tipped her coffee into a flask and set out.

As the pink sun bathed the waking city, the fresh air did her good. She managed to shrug the thought of Rebecca and her weird family from her mind. But someone else filled her daydream—the girl from the ditch. Well, hardly a girl. She was older than Elda, but there was something curious about her. The way she held herself. The confidence with which she'd scooped Elda to safety, and how she commanded attention at the hospital. Everyone had listened to her. Her voice had been like steel wrapped in velvet. Elda had memorised her side profile at the hospital, studied the angle of her cheekbones and the razor edge of her hair against the bar in her ear. She was gorgeous, with blond, barber-cut hair standing high, and Scandinavian features. She was perfect. Totally out of Elda's league.

Her fantasy kept her company all the way to the mill and once there, she became absorbed in the silence, moving to the beat of her breath. The canvases each spoke to her, willing her to come to them. She stood back, considering her next steps. It wasn't easy, bringing together three pieces simultaneously, knitting the threads of her narrative together across the three acts.

An hour had passed without her looking up from the canvas when she was disturbed from her trance by the creaking of the studio door. She looked across at the man standing in the doorway. He was older than her, with thick, brown hair falling across his forehead and a few days of stubble. A jumper hugged his taut stomach, and Elda admired his vintage jeans before she bristled at the interruption.

"Sorry, I didn't want to disturb you." He looked hesitant. "I'm Francis Paul."

Elda couldn't place his soft accent. "Elda." She set down her brushes. "Can I help you?"

"I'm working on the launch of the new exhibition. The private viewing. I wanted to introduce myself to some of the artists here." He smiled widely.

"Wow, okay. Good to meet you." Elda moved too quickly, and pain jolted through her arm. The annual show was a flashy event, and she wanted to make a good impression. This year was a big deal. If she could get on with it, she might have three pieces to submit and wanted a decent space. "Sorry, I'm just finishing up. Can we have a coffee and chat through your plans?"

"I'd like that. Do you know somewhere? I'm new here, and I'm lost just getting around this building. So please, take me under your wing."

"Well, I only have one good wing at the moment. But it's all yours." She held up her cast. Elda liked this new guy. She wasn't a fan of surprises, but he seemed genuine, and with any luck, he'd be a good contact.

Ten minutes later, Elda strolled alongside him to the waterfront café. She took her usual corner table, with her back to a brick wall. She'd skipped breakfast, so she added toast to her order and fiddled with a cushion.

"So, where are you from? I've been trying to work it out all the way here."

"I'm from Turin in Italy. But I lived in France just before I came here. I have family in the south and spend a little time in Paris, working in galleries."

"Wow, Parisian galleries. That sounds amazing." Elda tried not to let her nerves show, but the more she heard from her new pan-European friend, the further she fell into the depths of her own inadequacy. "I've just spent a weekend in Paris. Any places that I'd have heard of?"

"Maybe. They were small, independent spaces, off the tourist trail. My best work has been in London. I studied there." Francis settled opposite. "Elda, tell me, what do you plan to show this year? Your threesome?"

She chuckled at his turn of phrase, but he held her eye contact and looked serious. "I'm flattered that you think I'm able to exhibit. Isn't there a selection process?"

"Yes, of course. But I've pre-selected you."

"Really? How do you know my work?" Confusion raced through her mind. How was it possible this guy knew anything about her?

"I do my homework before I start a new job." He straightened his cutlery. "Tell me about the paintings."

Elda wasn't sure what to make of this development. She was expecting to chat through the plans for the exhibition and make the right noises about being part of it. Stuff like this didn't happen to her. She was bottom of the pack, average at best. She always had to fight for a win. It didn't land in her plate.

"Are you surprised? I was given access to the artists' work before I came to England. I already know who I want to feature. Now, tell me what you're working on."

"Well, the *trio* is important to me. I started them a few years ago to explore emotional states. They're almost finished." She couldn't remember a time when the three paintings weren't part of her work in progress.

"They're not finished?" Francis smiled, his eyes hinting at something he left unsaid. "What's your vision for them?"

"I don't like talking about work in progress, and I wasn't expecting to meet the actual curator tonight, so I don't have my pitch ready." She tried to laugh it off but hoped he would still take her seriously.

"You don't need to be worried, Elda. I've seen your previous pieces. I want you in the exhibition, so there's no need to sell yourself to me." He edged closer. "You're going to get them finished though, right?"

She examined the contours of his face. He seemed genuine. He didn't look like he was mocking her or trying to provoke a reaction.

The waiter brought teapots and mismatched cups to the table. Elda sighed, relieved to distract Francis from his interrogation. She poured milk into her cup and waited for the leaves to brew.

"Of course I'm going to finish them. They're almost done."

"Good," he said. "Then we can work together."

She had a feeling Francis could really turn her disastrous week around.

***

"I COULD MAKE IT, with his help." Elda sipped her tea.

"Let me just play this back, so I understand." Jack tied an apron at his middle. "Some handsome, kind, mysterious country of origin guy wants to show your paintings."

"Yes. And he's Italian. It's not that mysterious." Elda drummed her fingers. "He's an exhibition curator who came out of Goldsmiths and has done some great stuff in London and Paris. God knows why he's here, but the mill studios have brought him in to run the annual show."

"Well, if he sees something in your work, then I'm a fan. What's next?"

"He's put me on the programme, and I need to finish the trio of paintings." Her gut wrenched. She'd been stalling for months and now she had a very firm deadline approaching.

"Shall we add chocolate chips or raisins to the cookies?" Jack held two packets in the air.

"Chocolate. Anyone who says they like raisins is lying, really." Elda drifted off while Jack sifted flour. Francis had dangled a huge career carrot in front of her. Making a splash at a private viewing would catapult her onto the next exhibition and from there, who knew where?

"You know, obsessing over an art show is also much healthier than obsessing over your love life," Jack said.

"I'm with you there." Elda smiled. "This could be the break I need. And it's a welcome distraction from the breakup. I might go home at the weekend to see Mum and Nan. You never know, Mum might even be proud of me."

"Elda, you don't need your mum to be proud of you. *I'm* proud of you, and you should be proud of yourself. You're doing this. That guy walked into your studio and wants to put *your* paintings on display in the city's main exhibition." Jack tipped his cookie batter onto the surface with a flourish.

"You're right." Elda sat a little higher and raised her mug in a toast. She flinched as pain shot across her shoulders, reminding her that she still had some healing to do even though life was looking more hopeful. "Onwards."

Elda yearned for the thrill of an exhibition, to see her name on a programme, to feel pride in her work. Creating something from nothing filled parts of her that were empty. She wasn't sure why, but something was different about this time, and she wanted to give it everything she had.

There was something in the air, and she was buoyed up with pain relief and optimism. Even the thought of sharing the news with her mum didn't dampen her spirits.

CHAPTER FIVE

CHARLIE STEPPED DOWN THE moss-covered path, the stones slippery from the overnight rain. Grateful for her sturdy trainers, she picked up the pace. The walk from home to the office was short, but she shivered in the early chill. Her shoulders ached from the weight of her rucksack.

She took a lungful of cold air, tipped her head up towards the blue sky and opened herself to everything. She had a few papers to file and had blocked some time in the afternoon to spend alone. Work had been consuming every drop of energy lately, and she had to take a breath. She couldn't shake the thought of driving home from her parents' the week before and what would have happened if she'd fallen asleep at the wheel.

As she walked across the city park, Charlie noticed a familiar shape coming towards her: Maureen, the only female KC at the chambers.

"Charlotte, good to see you. How are you?"

"Maureen. Good morning."

"On your way in? Nice day to walk." Maureen wore sturdy but shiny boots which were entirely appropriate for both the walk through the park and the office.

Charlie cringed at her own filthy runners.

"Yes, it is. I walk most days just to get some exercise." The breach in her routine irritated her. She wasn't a fan of small talk, and they were still a way off from the chambers.

"I'm glad I've seen you actually. You need to know you're being considered for bigger and better. It's a good thing," Maureen said. "You should prepare yourself, your finances. There'll be lots of conferences and pro bono work to do before you can be nominated. And you'll be put forward for the Chambers Awards this season."

Charlie bit her lip and waited for more.

"Just tidy up your personal circumstances," Maureen said.

"What?" Charlie's footsteps faltered for a second and her temper flared.

Maureen kept up her pace and looked straight ahead. "Charlotte, if all goes well, in a decade or so you'll take silk, and that comes with certain responsibilities. Clients want stability and family values. Just get your house in order before they start to ask difficult questions, otherwise... It's okay to be different. Just have a nice story to tell. No one wants it shoved in their face is all I'm saying. And you can't bring a different plus one to all the client dinners, it's not the done thing. Get it sorted now, and you'll reap the rewards later."

Charlie stopped walking. Had she crossed the park into the fucking fifties? "Maureen. It's a pleasure to see you this morning. I appreciate you giving me the heads-up on the whole career situation. But I can assure you that I won't be editing myself to get a seat at the top table."

They'd made it to the entrance to the chambers where the clerks were gathering. Maureen took a step backwards, and the corners of her mouth quivered. Charlie wasn't sure whether she was trying to suppress laughter or fury. In the end, she shook her head.

"I haven't made my point, Charlotte. I give the boys this advice as well as the girls, so it's not just you." She laughed at something Charlie didn't understand. "I hope you reflect on what I've said and if you'd like to talk further, you know where to find me. Just make an appointment with my assistant." With that, she turned her perfect block heel and made her way into the building.

Charlie's head was boiling over with questions. The last couple of weeks had taken its toll on her ability to compartmentalise the hard stuff from the easy stuff, and she was suffocating. Theresa's anniversary, the run in with Elda on the way back from her parents' house, and a pile of case notes to read was weighing heavy on her mind. Her rucksack slipped from her shoulder, and she stiffened with rage and humiliation.

This is fucking bullshit. She knew who she was, and she wasn't going to have Maureen or any other high-up tell her she wasn't the right fit. But her job was everything. It defined who she was. She couldn't risk slipping off the career path just because she couldn't fit in every now and again. She'd played the part of the career-minded barrister perfectly. Work was a performance most of the time, and she could surely keep it up for another few years. Then the likes of Maureen would be long gone, and she could run the show.

The interaction with Maureen put her in an awful mood for the rest of the day. By four o'clock, Charlie was beyond ready to have Joshua hold her calls. She decided to head across to the mill building. It had been more than a week since she'd run Elda off the country road, but she couldn't shake it off. It was so unlike her not to be able to detach from the emotion of a situation, but she hadn't been able to stop fretting about it. Coming here was sure to put it to rest. She just had to check in on her.

For years, it had been derelict. In the dusk, she saw the flicker of lamps behind each gridded window, inviting her in like candles in an old church. She walked towards the main door and scanned the list of rooms for a clue to Elda's whereabouts.

Someone burst through the exit and held it open. She took a chance.

"Long shot, but do you know where Elda Brown's room is?"

The trendy chap, dressed in double denim, narrowed his eyes. "Think it's eight. Down the corridor, turn left. Keep going."

As Charlie approached, she saw a door ajar and heard a scratching sound. *What if she's not even here? What am I doing?*

Inside, Elda was scraping red paint from a scalpel. Her left arm was strapped up and getting in her way.

"Knock, knock," Charlie said.

"Charlie!" Elda jerked and her face screwed up, obviously in pain. "Why are you here? How'd you find me?" She took a breath, and her expression settled. "Sorry. Hi, come in."

Charlie studied her black boots and wondered why she'd come. It had seemed like the right thing to do, but now she was conscious of invading Elda's space. "I don't want to disturb you. I just wanted to see how you were—after last week." Charlie shuffled her feet, trying to resist turning back the way she came. It was weird feeling like she wanted to get out of her own skin. No one had ever made her feel unsure of herself. "You said you worked in the mill, so I thought I'd come and see if I could find you."

Charlie picked at a thread on her coat and tightened her scarf, wishing she could disappear beneath it.

"It's fine," Elda said, almost shouting. "I'm glad you came. I was totally out of it that night and didn't get the chance to thank you for looking after me. And for staying with me. Thank you." She brushed her hands down her overalls. "I was in a bit of a state."

"No thanks required. I nearly ran you over." Charlie forced herself to blink. She'd been struggling to make sense of the chaos in her mind for the last few days. She kept playing the accident back, seeing the shape in the road and bracing for impact. But more than that, she couldn't stop thinking about Elda's delicate cheekbones and kissable lips. "How about a coffee?" she asked. "As an apology. With me, at some point, not now. And also, I brought you this." She handed Elda her phone. "It was in the footwell." She should've led with that. Returning someone's phone was a normal thing to do.

Elda checked the battery was dead and twisted her mouth in what looked like curiosity. "Thank you, I ordered a new one when I couldn't find it. Off-grid for a few days has done me good." She placed it in a drawer. "Yes, let's get coffee. I'll sort stuff here and get out of this." Elda waved at her boiler suit.

Charlie tried to adjust to this spontaneity. She looked around for the first time and took in the full studio: three canvases standing tall in the middle of the room, surrounded by paints, brushes, pots of water, and empty mugs. She hadn't been sure where this afternoon would take her, and now they were off out together. She had a pile of case files waiting in the office and that should take priority.

Typically, she avoided Elda's type. Dishevelled and creative, with drama following her around like a strong perfume. But she had to admit she was intrigued. She could catch up on work. Her stomach rumbled, reminding Charlie she'd skipped lunch. "I could eat, too."

They wandered to the coffee shop. Charlie stared at the cake display. Choosing food for someone else wasn't really her thing. She wasn't even a coffee and a chat kind of girl. Even pillow talk was short and sweet and ended with directions to the door.

Elda dropped two painkillers between her lips. Guilt nagged at Charlie.

"I couldn't decide, so got us a selection. We can swap, or share," she said as she reached their table.

"Everything is delicious. I come here all the time."

"It's not far from my office, but I've never even noticed it. I don't get out from behind my desk once I'm there."

"Where do you work?" Elda licked the coffee froth from her spoon.

Charlie had to look away. "I'm at the Elliott and Hall Chambers, on East Street. My office looks over to the mill building."

"I hope you've not been spying on me." Elda laughed.

"No comment!" Charlie pretended to look outraged. "But I have always wondered what's behind the façade. Now I know."

They were interrupted by Charlie's phone ringing. She rummaged inside her jacket. "Hi, Jude. Can I call you back?"

"Sure, that's fine. Wondered if you were free tonight, for another catch-up."

Heat rose to Charlie's cheeks. Jude's voice was dripping with sexual intent, while Elda looked adorable, sat opposite. It was a juxtaposition Charlie couldn't handle. "I can't tonight, Jude, I'm busy. I'll call tomorrow...about the case." She hung up and returned the phone to her pocket. "Sorry about that. Work stuff. No one special."

Elda frowned, and Charlie wished Jude hadn't interrupted them.

"Is there someone special?" Elda raised her eyebrow. There was a hint of flirtation in the smirk that accompanied it.

"No, not really." She fiddled with the teaspoon, tempted by the direction Elda was taking her. Charlie was drawn into her green eyes, the flick of her eyelashes, and the contours of her jaw. The lighting was softer than it had been at the hospital. She was attractive, and Charlie had to look away.

"So, there's no one waiting for you at the end of a long day in court?"

Charlie laughed. "I don't really do relationships."

"Me neither." Elda's smile fell. "Well, I try to. But I never seem to pull it off. The night we met I'd just walked out of a brief relationship with a pretty awful woman," Elda said.

"Really? I'm sorry."

"I was in a bit of a state that night. It had all been a bit bonkers. But it was the right thing to do. I'm free, single, and looking forward." Elda sipped her coffee. "I imagined courtrooms would be full of eligible bachelors, even if they do wear funny wigs."

"I don't really do eligible bachelors, either." Charlie met Elda's gaze, hoping she'd understand that Charlie was into women too. "And don't knock the wig. With the right pair of heels, it can be quite sexy."

A few crumbs of chocolate cake escaped from Elda's mouth as she giggled.

"I'm changing the subject. I wasn't expecting to be discussing legal fetishes so early in the evening."

Grateful for the change in direction, Charlie nodded her

consent with a broad smile. It was unusual, but she wanted to get to know Elda.

"You'd been at your parents' that night? Do they live out in the sticks?"

"They have a house along the coastal road. My dad retired a year ago. He was a law professor. No wigs." Charlie winked. "Their place is lovely. I don't see as much of them as I'd like."

"Are you close? Is it just you?"

"Yeah, just me. An adored only child. Don't get me wrong, I had a few rebellious teenage years, but I think we're closer now than ever." Charlie frowned, thinking about the pain she'd felt when she was a teenager. "How about you? Your folks local?"

"No. I grew up with my mum and Nan down south. Mum struggled with holding down a job and my nan ended up looking after both of us. There was a lot of fish fingers and oven chips." Elda sniffed. "Dad had buggered off. It was, you know, pretty miserable."

"I'm sorry to hear that."

"Don't be. He left when I was six, so I never really knew him."

"You haven't seen him since?" Charlie leaned in. She was used to stories of broken homes—they always came with broken hearts.

"He tried a couple of times to reach out, but my mum was adamant that he was bad news. She told me he left us almost destitute and if it wasn't for my nan, we would've had nothing." Elda took a sip of coffee. "I don't really remember what he looked like."

Charlie remained silent, unsure what to say.

"Feel free to change the subject again." Elda laughed, graciously relieving the tension.

"So, you're an artist?"

"I am. I was accepted for that exhibition I ranted about at the hospital."

"Congratulations. I saw a bit of your work back in the studio; it's really impressive. I wish I could be creative."

"You don't feel creative?" Elda asked.

She bit her lip in a way that made Charlie want to run her

tongue over it. "I have a photographic memory for facts, a way with words—"

"You look good in a wig?"

Charlie laughed. "Maybe. But I don't have an artistic bone in my body."

"You must have to get quite creative in court."

"I work in family law. It's not like the courtroom dramas on the TV." Charlie rubbed at her eyes. Talking to Elda felt easy. "I like rules and conventions. Life gets messy when there are too many variables."

"A bit of chaos can be good for you. It can be spontaneous and energising. That's what art's all about really. Capturing what's messy about life and sometimes making sense of it." Elda fiddled with the salt shaker.

"Tell me about your paintings." She wanted to hear Elda's voice, slow down and drink in the conversation.

"I don't talk much about my work. It's difficult to explain. Even when I've had tutors or mentors, I struggle to find the right words, and then people don't get it. It can be awkward, you know?" Elda wriggled in her seat.

"Try me." Charlie locked her gaze, hoping she'd open up. There had been a hint of something so powerful in the canvases she saw back in the studio.

The clatter of forks and hum of conversations hung in the air. Charlie scanned the room, breaking the eye contact she'd been sharing with Elda. She'd been so engrossed by their conversation that she hadn't realised the café was full of people.

"It's a trio of paintings. Each about six feet by five. You saw them just now. They're taller than me." She reached above her head and her cheeks coloured.

Charlie nodded, and Elda frowned for just a second, as if she doubted herself.

"The first is full of shadows. Threats. Fear. Things that hurt you and make you feel small." Elda rubbed her temple. "The second is about shame. Hiding from the truth. Believing lies about yourself. Lies you tell yourself." She sat back in her chair and folded her arms.

"Go on." Charlie wanted to reach over but drew her hand back. It was weird to feel compelled to touch Elda. She'd never had any problems keeping a physical or emotional distance from others.

"The third is about light. It's sort of joyful. It's about unconditional love with no strings and no expectations."

Charlie wasn't expecting the wave of sadness and optimism that crashed through her body. She was honoured that Elda had shared the detail, and her reaction caught her off guard. She let out a long, whistling breath and laughed as Elda's eyebrows lifted. "Wow, Elda. That's powerful. A real story of despair and hope. Can I see them?"

"Well, you already got a sneak peek at them. They aren't finished yet, but you can see them when they're done." She protected her cast as two plates of cake arrived.

"Pop them in the middle. We're going to share," Elda said and directed her perfect smile at the waitress.

Charlie had no idea where this chance connection was going, but she wanted to find out. Elda had appeared out of nowhere on a dark, miserable night, but now Charlie revelled in the light ease between them. Out of habit, she thought for a moment about asking Elda to come home with her. There was no doubt in her mind that a night together would be blissful, if a little awkward around Elda's cast. Simply sitting across from her set Charlie's insides on fire. She could imagine peeling off those autumn layers and warming away the goosebumps on her naked skin.

But for once, she didn't want to ruin this with a one-night stand. She wanted to uncover Elda's depths slowly, which was a first in a very long time.

CHAPTER SIX

"I'M HERE TO VIEW the third floor," Francis said.

Elda pinched herself to make sure she wasn't dreaming. Things were moving fast. She was about to see the exhibition hall and take her pick of the hanging space. Her brain buzzed with anticipation as her new curator advanced through the atrium.

At the end, a bright opening led to an expanse of smooth concrete. The walls were brilliant white, and they beamed with potential. Elda looked up to the ceiling rig. It was perfect. A space like this was too good for her. She was used to scrabbling together a few pieces for a back room showing at the local arts centre.

Her phone buzzed in her pocket.

I have a work thing on Friday. The launch of the new art gallery in town. Fancy going? C

A shiver of curiosity ran through her. She'd love to see Charlie again. Plus, it'd be really special to see the new gallery before it was open to the general public.

Yes, that'd be lovely. Where and when? E

"Elda, follow me," Francis said.

"Sorry." She shoved her phone away and caught up.

"I'd like to have welcome drinks here." He scribbled in the black leather book he'd produced from his pocket. "Let me show you something. I think you'll like it."

He led her to the middle of the vast room. The space was empty, and she giggled with anticipation. This week was really looking up.

"I want to build a huge structure here. Imagine three walls rising from the ground." He moved his hands in the air, and his coat flowed behind him. "It'll be a triangular centrepiece. During the private viewing, the speeches will happen right here." He pointed at the floor and mimed a small stage, his eyes sparkling along with his smile.

Elda pieced together the meaning of his broken sentences. "My trio? A feature triangle? Wow, Francis that's a lot of effort for me. I'm not a big enough name."

"You underestimate yourself." He held his finger in the air and grinned.

"You're going to make me the headline artist..." For a moment, Elda didn't recognise the feeling in her chest. It was panic. The paintings weren't even finished. Not that she was going to mention that right now.

Francis stepped towards her. "You're brilliant. More than you realise. And you can do this, Elda. I know it."

He hadn't touched her, but his words embraced her with a cloak of confidence. She returned his smile and let out an embarrassed laugh. He thought too much of her. She was just an office bod with a mediocre back catalogue from art school. But she couldn't admit that to Francis. His enthusiasm filled her with an energy she'd never had before.

"I've seen those pieces," Francis said. "I can see what they'll be, and I think they'll be a major draw for this exhibition. People will want to see them. Trust me."

He took her right hand in his, and she shivered. He turned her around, so they stood toe to toe. She stepped back, creating some distance between them. Tension hung in the air while she considered what was in front of her. Was there anything to lose? It wasn't like she had any sort of professional reputation to damage.

"I want you to be the centre of this." He pressed his hands together. "Please say yes. For me?"

"Okay, I will," Elda whispered. Maybe she could pull this off. She shook her head and tried to make sense of what was happening. The white walls, which had been so far away, were now closing in. It wasn't unpleasant, but it was surprising that this big shot curator had walked into her life and was giving her an opportunity to show her art. What could she do other than accept?

But there was something about his tone and body language that suggested he might want more from her. She'd have to put him straight on that. There was no denying that this would be great for her career. He'd already placed her centre stage. She ignored the nagging doubt and the thought that everything would completely implode if this all went wrong, which it likely would, given her track record.

She hardly knew this guy. *I don't know Charlie either, but I like her*. Why was Charlie crashing into her thoughts? This was a serious artistic opportunity, and she didn't need any kind of distraction.

***

Jack's foot slipped on the rung of the ladder, and Elda grabbed his ankle with her good arm.

"Steady on, Elda. I'm fine."

"I thought you were falling. Be careful." She bit at her thumbnail and glanced at the door, worried someone would hear them hiding out in the office storeroom. "Sorry, I'm a bit edgy. I can't switch my brain off."

"Well, chill out. You'll end up breaking the other arm if I land on you." He groaned and dragged a cardboard box off the top shelf. "Grab this."

Elda braced herself, not knowing whether the box was full of paperclips or paperweights. "Is it heavy?"

"Light as a feather. Stop fretting." Jack made his way down the ladder.

He opened the box, and she peered inside at bubble wrap and shredded paper.

"Here it is." He passed her half a bottle of vodka. "This should lift our spirits."

"You'll get us into trouble."

"Hope so." His eyes twinkled with mischief. "I'm in charge tonight, and I'm on a break. If anyone catches us, we'll say you were bringing in your sick note, and I was tidying the stationery cupboard."

"That's a likely story."

"It's more believable than us having a secret romantic rendezvous in here."

"True. No one would swallow that." Elda chuckled, twisted the screw top and tasted the burning liquid. She lowered herself to the ground and sat cross-legged.

Jack followed and leaned against the racking. "Tell me more about this morning. Where did Francis whisk you off to?"

"One of the mill buildings. He's got the top floor for the exhibition. It's going to look so good."

"And, what's the plan? Did he offer you a space?" Jack nudged her in the ribs.

She loved him for rooting for her. "Not just a space. The highlight of the whole show." Elda took another swig. "I'm still not sure whether I believe it. Or believe I can do it."

"Have a bit of faith in yourself. Fancy Francis wouldn't have asked you otherwise. This is it, Elda. Just take the chance while it's there. Beats tapping your keyboard in this place forever."

"I don't think it's going to lead to anything major. But it would be great to have the three paintings displayed properly for people to see." Elda jumped to her feet, excitement coursing through her veins now the alcohol had numbed her self-doubt. "Francis knows what he's doing, so it'll be beautifully lit, and there'll be flow to the whole space. I can't get my head around it."

"I can't wait, chick. You deserve some good stuff. How's your arm feeling?"

Elda glanced down at the cast. "Bit better. Not as painful. It just gets in the way."

"Could've been your painting arm though, El. That would've

been a nightmare."

"Don't. I couldn't have coped." She sat and leaned her head against Jack's shoulder. "That woman from the other night came to see me at the studio."

"What woman?"

"Charlie. The one who took me to the hospital. We went for coffee."

"The one who ran you over?"

"It wasn't like that, but yes. We had a really nice chat."

"Uh oh. I know what your nice chats lead to." Jack grinned.

"Don't wind me up. She just wanted to check in with me and bring my phone back. It was good of her."

"Okay, I've seen that look before." Jack sat up and looked Elda in the eye. "You've only just given repulsive Rebecca the heave-ho. Don't jump straight in with the next woman who happens to buy you a latte."

"That's offensive." She avoided his gaze, doubt creeping through her. "I thought Rebecca was great to begin with."

"Oh yeah, Rebecca was marvellous. So was Penny before her. And Michelle before her. You see the pattern here, don't you? All I'm saying is, don't let history repeat itself. Slow down, and you might save yourself some heartache."

Elda sulked, annoyed that Jack was holding a mirror up to her behaviour. He offered her the bottle. "No, thanks, I've had enough." Elda knew her limits. Her mum's battle with alcohol had taught her to have them securely in place.

"Sorry." Jack looked away, as if he could read her mind. "Hey, you called your mum yet?"

"Yes, I have." She bristled at his nagging. "As usual, she was at the club with her latest fling."

"Gross. At least you made the effort." Jack kissed her forehead. "I'd better get back to work soon. Phone calls to monitor, tea to make, you know?"

"Such responsibilities."

"You have no idea, Elderflower. I can't just swan in and out like you. I have timesheets to check and cupboards to lock."

They fell together, laughing. Just like old times, they could find the joke in the ups and downs of their daily grind. "I've got pins and needles." She took a deep breath and lifted herself off the floor.

"Stamp your feet. But don't make too much noise, or someone will find us." Jack shoved the vodka bottle back in its box. "I'll come and clear that away later."

Elda hushed the voice in her head telling her that she was still a bit of a mess. A broken love life, a broken arm, and almost-finished paintings weren't really a huge selling point in her career—or life—pitch. She ignored the fact that she was slumped on the storeroom floor of her office, chugging vodka from a bottle with her childhood best friend like she was stuck in her dysfunctional teenage years.

"I'm really excited for you, El," Jack said.

"Me too. I just need to finish those canvases. Then who knows what might happen?" Elda bumped her fist against his bicep and followed him out into the corridor, stifling a giggle.

Whatever happened, Jack would have her back. She just had to be brave enough to look life in the eye and fight her demons. She was worthy of this attention from Francis. Maybe, she was even worthy of some attention from Charlie.

CHAPTER SEVEN

CHARLIE SAT IN THE driver's seat of the Capri, picking at a loose thread in the fabric. She closed her eyes. The rhythm of the bouncing tyres on the flyover above helped to slow her thoughts. She pulled up to a block of flats curved like a half moon, climbed out, and made her way to a ground floor entrance.

She knocked at the door, tracing the bumpy glass with her fingertips. This place shouldn't remind her of Theresa; she'd never even lived there. But it was full of people who brought her to life. A hazy figure approached behind the glass and the door opened, releasing a blast of heat.

"Charlotte, thank you for coming. Come in. I've got the kettle on, and the kids want to see you."

This was the last thing that Charlie wanted. She'd already turned away, ready to escape, but Jacob pulled at her sleeve.

"Charlie, come and see."

She bent down to pick him up and almost buckled. "Wow, you're heavy! Piggyback then." She hooked her arms over his legs. "Look at you, fella. You've grown so big! You must be fourteen by now."

"I'm only four."

He giggled into her hair, and warmth flooded her body. Maybe a few minutes out of her day wouldn't hurt. "I can't stay too long, Kim." Charlie noticed the deep shadows under her eyes. "I've got to get to work."

She carried Jacob through a narrow hall into the cramped kitchen, just big enough for a pine table and two benches. A strip of light from the low ceiling made her blink. Dishes flowed over the sides into the sink and the start of breakfast was still on the table. She regretted disturbing their routine. The shapes of two sleepy teenagers came towards her.

"Hey, you two," she said, as she placed the youngest back on the floor.

They grunted, while Jacob handed her a remote-controlled car and a bag of dinosaurs. The kettle came to a crescendo, and all three children clambered across the benches.

Without speaking, Charlie handed Kim an envelope, which she tucked up on a shelf next to a tree of mismatched mugs. They exchanged a look before Kim's gaze fell to the floor. Charlie hated that she might feel bad for taking the money. "Chloe, how's school?"

"It's all right. I've got a Geography mock this week." She scooped cereal hoops into her mouth. She looked so grown up next to Jacob, wobbling on the bench like he was sitting on jelly.

"Mock exams already? I haven't seen you for such a long time." Charlie gave Jacob a squeeze. "I've missed you all."

"Come over more often, Charlotte. We'd love to have you." Kim leaned against the worktop.

A familiar barb of guilt pierced Charlie's chest. *This isn't my family. This is Theresa's family.* "I know, but work keeps me busy, and you guys have got your own stuff going on. How's football, Sam?"

The elder boy fiddled with his school tie. "Not bad. Ended last season third in the league."

"Tell her, Sam. You've been playing in defence and don't let the buggers past you. He loved that England shirt you bought him last year. Not had it off, except for school." Kim scraped butter onto some toast. "And even then he sneaks it underneath sometimes." Kim tutted and handed out hot tea.

"Sometimes he goes to bed in it." Chloe's laughter echoed off the walls.

Kim settled against the counter. "Sam, Chloe, take Jacob into the living room while me and your Aunty Charlotte have a chat."

Charlie's shoulders tensed at the undeserved title. "You shouldn't call me that. You're confusing them."

"We both know that if Theresa was still alive you'd be together. You're still part of this family."

Charlie stepped back. She'd been tangled in this web before. Kim's expectations were too high. "Even if Theresa was still here, I wouldn't be their aunty." She gritted her teeth. "She was their older sister, not yours."

"Don't get legal with me, young lady. You know what aunty means. It means you're part of this family. Blood or no blood. And Theresa isn't here anymore, but you are." Kim sniffed and took a seat at the opposite bench. Her white blouse was stained down the front from cooking. Close up, she had faint lines around her lips. She looked her forty-six years and more. "I wanted to talk to you about stuff. I know I'm a pain, but you're everything we've got at the moment."

Charlie raised her hand. She couldn't stand being responsible for the small family she'd inherited through shame. "You know I think the world of you all. Theresa would be so proud of you and how settled the kids are. You know that." She faltered. Who was she to pass judgement on Theresa's mother? *Jesus, why am I stuck in this kitchen?* She rose to her feet.

"I need more, Charlotte. Just a bit more to get us through the next few months. I can't go to work, not with Jacob. I can't get him into the nursery. But next year, he'll be at school and then Chloe can watch him, so I can start paying you back."

"You don't need to pay me back. I never want anything back. Put that out of your mind." Charlie took a long breath. "There's more in the envelope. I need to get off to work now." She looked up at the shelf and walked into the living room to say goodbye to the children. "I love you. You are all so special," she said, kissing Jacob. "Be good for your mum, and I'll see you soon. You can tell me about school and football again."

Outside, at the end of the path, she looked back. Jacob was waving through the window, and Kim stood behind him, wiping her cheeks.

***

"I found you." Charlie placed her hand on Elda's shoulder.

"Hey, I was just about to call you. This place is busy. I didn't know if I'd be able to spot you," Elda said. Someone bumped Charlie from behind and closed the distance between them. "Let's get inside, where it's quieter." She took Elda's hand and drew her towards the stone steps of the imposing gallery. It proudly looked over the city's main square while the hustle and bustle of the Friday commute played out.

She dropped her hand, her palm clammy with nerves. Elda left a void that she hadn't expected. "Thanks for coming."

"I appreciate the invitation. I've been dying to see what they've done with the building." Elda's cheeks flushed. "So, what kind of work thing is this?"

"We have to do all kinds of corporate networking, often to keep favour with the big clients. I usually keep my head down and decline most of them, but this one caught my eye, and I thought you might like it."

"Well, aren't I the lucky one?"

There was a cheeky glint in Elda's eye that Charlie had never noticed before. Not that a hospital visit and a coffee shop had given her much chance to catalogue Elda's body language. She banished the tempting thought of Elda's body. This was just a casual night out with a new friend. Charlie hadn't fostered any new friendships for a long time. She kept her circles tight. Work was work. Play was usually cocktails and sex. But something about Elda made her want to talk to her, get to know her more, spend time together.

She followed Elda's gaze towards the white walls of the gallery.

"I'll get us a drink, and we can get straight in there."

"Do you mind? I'm itching to see what they've hung."

"Go on, I'll catch you up." Charlie took Elda's coat and dropped by the cloakroom. She plucked two glasses of champagne from a tray and lagged behind, enjoying the sway of Elda's hips. Elda's face lit up as she approached the first canvas.

"What's the verdict?" Charlie dragged her attention from Elda to the huge canvas looming over them both.

"I like this guy. He explores being trapped in your own body. Whatever the reason, physical, emotional. You see anything in it?"

"Mm." Charlie bit her lip, pondering. She could give Elda an educated guess, something vaguely academic. But she didn't want to dish out stock answers. She wanted to be more honest with her. "I'm not sure what I make of it."

Elda laughed. "That's okay. You don't need to have an emotional response to every piece. That's not how it works."

"Are you sure? I feel like I've failed my first art assignment." Charlie grinned, leaning into Elda's teasing.

"You brought me here. You haven't failed. You've given us both an opportunity." Elda looked up again. "What can you see? Just tell me what's there."

Charlie swallowed. She tore her gaze away from Elda's exposed neck, focused on the painting, and tried to form an intelligent sentence. "There's nothing delicate about this one. The brushstrokes are thick and heavy. I can see scratches and lumps. Is that deliberate?"

"Yeah. Everything is deliberate."

Elda flashed a smile that made Charlie's blood pump a little faster. "Why is that?" The question slipped from Charlie's lips. She didn't mind sharing her ignorance with Elda.

"Why do you think?" Elda raised her eyebrow.

"I don't know. I'd just be putting my own interpretation out there."

"That's all anybody does when they look at art."

A silence hung between them as they turned towards the

canvas. Charlie sipped her champagne. "Okay, I'd say it looks heavy in its style because being trapped is stifling, suffocating, hard. Do I pass the test?"

Elda raised her glass. "You've passed with flying colours."

Charlie took Elda's elbow and steered her further into the room. "Of course, the real test is how many of my colleagues I can avoid before the evening's out?"

"You don't like your workmates?"

"I love work, don't get me wrong. But I don't relish this kind of thing and, to be honest, I'd much rather be talking to you." Charlie held Elda's gaze, wanting to follow the moment and discover where it could lead.

"I see. Well, let's keep our heads down and not draw any attention to ourselves." Elda smirked.

They found a corner sofa in a breakout space and set down their glasses. Charlie patted the seat next to her. The weight of the day made her shoulders sag.

"You okay? You look a little tired." Elda tipped her head, looking worried.

"It's been a long day. I'm sorry." She didn't want the stress of the last few hours to spoil this evening.

"Work stuff?"

Charlie went to gloss over the truth but decided against it. "Family stuff, kind of. I went to see an old friend today. She needed help with money. She's like part of the family. Her and the three kids."

"Sounds tough. Is she all right?" Elda shifted, giving Charlie her full attention.

"She'll get there. Her name's Kim. The kids are Chloe, Sam, and Jacob."

"How old are they?"

"Honestly, I can't keep up." Charlie brushed her fingers through her hair, flicking back through the years in her memory. "The two older ones are teenagers, and Jacob is about four. He's not at school yet."

"Big age gap. Must be hard."

"Yeah, massive age gap, really. Kim's eldest daughter, Theresa, was my friend actually. So, she'd be thirty-one." Charlie stopped, forming her next sentence. "She died when we were younger."

"I'm so sorry." Elda's hands pressed together in her lap.

"No, I am. I didn't mean for this to get so depressing." Charlie clapped her hands together and stood up. "Let's go and see some more art."

They wandered through the next room, in sync with each other. It was easy to be with Elda in a way that Charlie hadn't noticed with anyone else. She was hot and sexy as hell, in a dishevelled kind of way, but there was something else about her that made Charlie bask in her presence. A sort of unique authenticity that rarely crossed Charlie's path. Her train of thought was broken by the appearance of Maureen in the foyer.

"Shit. Follow me," she whispered, guiding Elda into a narrow corridor. "I spotted someone from work. Bit of a cow, and I'd rather not have to make small talk."

Elda ducked, then craned her neck to see who Charlie was pointing to. "She looks a bit scary. Quite cool though. Not many people can pull off a scarlet trouser suit."

"That's Maureen. She's a KC—King's Counsel. She likes to make an entrance. Who wears head-to-toe velvet?"

Elda's laughter burst into the narrow space, and Charlie couldn't help but join in.

Maureen was on the move. Frowning, Charlie took Elda's hand and ventured further into the gallery. "This is turning into a bit of a farce. Let's talk about you. How's your week been?"

Elda dusted her shirt off and looked flustered at the attention. "It's been a good one. I saw the new curator again, and he's offered me top of the bill in the exhibition I mentioned."

"That's such good news. I'm really pleased for you." She beamed, wondering where this feeling of pride had come from.

"Yeah, I'm just going to go for it. It's been a real turnaround week actually, given that it started with a broken arm. Hey, there's a sculpture room next. Show me around?"

"I'd love to."

Elda's energy was infectious. She might be someone that Charlie needed in her life: a contrast to all the stifled lawyers she was surrounded by. She reminded herself that jeopardising their potential friendship with a one-night stand would be a real waste. She was fast approaching her mid-thirties, with no real friends to call on in a crisis. Sure, she was driven, successful, and a shit-hot lay, if Jude's response was anything to go by. But maybe there was more to life than dream careers and dreamier orgasms.

CHAPTER EIGHT

ON CHARLIE'S SECOND VISIT to the studio, she brought steaming tea and chocolate biscuits. She looked like part of the loosely arranged furniture, laid back on the sheepskin rug that Elda had installed to make the room more cosy.

"I don't want to disturb you if you're in the zone," Charlie said, pulling an earbud out so she could hear Elda's reply.

"You're not disturbing me. Which is weird because I've not painted around someone else since college."

"Really? You like to work alone?"

"I've never really thought about it. I like solitude, but you're not in my way. Just sit and be with me." Elda caught herself right in the moment. With others, even Jack, she played an internal monologue of things to say next, wondering how her face looked, how to make someone laugh. But with Charlie, she was just there, listening and leaving everything else to instinct. "Anyway, I'm almost there with these."

"They're finished?" Charlie propped herself up on her elbows. "How do you know when you're done?"

"Good question. I struggle with that, I guess." Elda turned back to the canvas. "Something in my gut. In my heart. When I'm no longer compelled to lift the brush or spread the paint." She stood back from the three easels. Charlie joined her and their shoulders touched, sending a rush through Elda as if someone was tickling her ribs. "This is it." She blinked, the sudden clarity hitting like a freight train.

Charlie squeezed Elda's right arm and wrapped her in a hug. Her body softened into Charlie's curves like she belonged there.

It was too brief. They broke away, and she left a yellow smudge on Charlie's neck where her thumb had rested. Elda fought the temptation to touch her.

"You did it." Charlie brushed away a tear.

"Yeah, I did it." She'd never had anyone mirror the pride she felt when she'd finished a piece. Every part of her filled up with joy.

"Stay here. I'll be back." Charlie put her jacket on and disappeared out of the studio.

"Where are you off to?" Elda whispered after her, but she was grateful for the respite. The tension in the room was simmering. Tears of relief threatened to stream down her face, and she didn't want to melt in front of Charlie. She hadn't really believed that she could finish the canvases in time for the exhibition, and now that she had, a burden lifted from her shoulders. She distracted herself by cleaning her tools and packing away her paints. She could take a break now and focus on the hanging space and promoting the exhibition.

Ten minutes later, Charlie returned, holding two mugs from the mill's kitchen and a bottle of champagne. She popped the cork with a flourish. "I'm so excited for you. This is it! You can relax now."

"I know. I'm bloody knackered. And so over making excuses to Francis. He's been at me all week." Holding out her mug to Charlie, she swallowed the relief at the back of her throat and wiped away a tear. "Thank you for being here with me."

"It's a privilege. I know that." Charlie had looked at her feet and then back up to Elda. "Anyway, I needed to carry your bags and make your tea. It's my fault you've only got one arm."

Somehow, she'd allowed Charlie into her innermost thoughts and had explored her most vulnerable, creative depths with Charlie sitting on a rug, sipping tea from a mug that she'd made her own. She thought back to Jack's warning and promised herself that this couldn't go any faster. If she rushed into something with Charlie, she'd fall flat on her face just like every other time.

Once again, Elda found herself as a passenger in the Ford Capri that had forced her off the road. There was no denying the vintage sex appeal of the car. Almost as sexy as its owner. Charlie changed lanes through tunnels without slowing down, undertaking tourists in the city. They turned into a tiny multi-storey that Elda had never noticed before.

"This is the chambers' car park. I have a space." Charlie made a corkscrew ascent to a roof top with views across the skyline. Even with its grey, autumn cloak, it was beautiful.

"Fancy." Elda poked her in the ribs, and Charlie shot her a humble but gorgeous smile.

"It's convenient. We can just cross the road over the bridge."

Elda was desperate for something to wear for the private viewing on Friday night. She'd spent the last couple of weeks obsessing over the final strokes of her paintings and hadn't given the actual exhibition and its mechanics much thought.

Charlie took her free hand, sending a jolt of excitement through Elda. She was thrilled to be featuring in her first proper, grown-up exhibition and grateful to have Charlie's advice with the wardrobe choices. But the pressure was on, and every moment reminded her of the literal pedestal Francis had built for her. Elda wanted the event to be a success but her anxiety about looking good and living up to everyone's expectations threatened to overwhelm her.

Charlie led the way into a trendy-looking boutique, and Elda shrunk into her coat. It wasn't her usual kind of place. She squinted at a sea of fabrics, textures, shapes, and sizes all in the same black and grey palette.

"How about this?" Charlie lifted a black jacket off a rail. "You'd look stunning."

Elda touched it gently, and the leather moved under her fingertips like silk. She stroked its high collar and folded darts. "I need something underneath it first," she said.

"Do you?" Charlie's eyes wrinkled as she laughed.

"Be serious, you." Elda pulled her away, and her cheeks flushed. She was glad the store was so dimly lit.

"Try this." Charlie passed her a charcoal silk shirt and a pair of wide leg trousers.

"I don't know if I've got the height for those."

Charlie ushered her into the fitting room, and she changed without fuss, avoiding her reflection in the mirror. She drew back the heavy curtain and met Charlie's waiting gaze.

"You look beautiful," Charlie said.

Elda's stomach flipped. "Do you think it'll do?"

"Yeah. It's perfect." Charlie fidgeted with her buttons. "I'll wait out in the shop while you get ready."

Charlie looked more flustered than her usual cool self. But now wasn't the time to be misreading signals. She was just being a good friend.

Purchase made and bags in hand, they marched arm-in-arm through the city.

"Mission accomplished," Elda said. "Shall we go for a cheeky cocktail to celebrate?"

"But I have the car." Charlie wrinkled her nose.

Elda didn't want their time together to end yet. Apart from Jack, she'd never wanted to spend so much time with the same person. "You could get a cab and leave it till the morning."

Charlie tilted her head. "Okay, but it's a school night, so no leading me astray, Elda Brown."

"Scout's honour." Elda beamed. "I'll be on my best behaviour."

They turned up a cobbled street towards a row of white Georgian buildings. Behind the backlit windows, Elda envied the couples starting their romantic dinner dates. She glanced across at Charlie and imagined sitting opposite her at a candlelit table for two. She bit her lip, fighting the urge to let her fantasy unravel in her mind, while a warm excitement filled her belly.

They carried their drinks and settled into a snug booth at the back of an upmarket cocktail bar. Most people were shouting over their mates at the bar, but Elda leaned in so she could hear Charlie's voice.

"A toast. To you." Charlie tipped her glass in Elda's direction. "It's exciting, your first exhibition."

"I'm not sure I've reached excitement yet. I'm shitting myself, to be honest."

"Why?" Charlie frowned. "You've put the work in. Sit back and bask in the glory of showing it all off."

"You're braver than I am. Putting a piece on show is like walking onto a stage naked. Imagine being in court with your trousers down."

"When you put it like that, it sounds fucking horrendous." Charlie laughed, revealing the appealing length of her neck.

Elda shrugged. "It's not that bad, I suppose. I'm winding myself up a bit."

"What's the worst that could happen?"

"No one likes the paintings. I'm slated in the trade press. I never work again." Elda put her head on the table with an operatic groan.

"Or people like them. They fall head over heels in love with you, the artist. You're celebrated as the top billing of Francis's famous mill gallery. Curators all over the country flock to see your work. You have to fight off agents."

"I'm fragile. Don't mock me." Elda peered at Charlie through her fingers.

"I'm not! Good things might happen if you give them half a chance."

Were they still talking about the exhibition? Elda fidgeted.

As the waiter dropped off their third round of cocktails, Elda shuffled closer and rested her thigh against Charlie's. Knowing there were just the two layers of denim between them sent a thrill down her spine.

"Have you convinced your mum to come to the private viewing?" Charlie asked, raising her voice over the dance music.

"She hasn't mentioned it since I asked." Elda sighed. She longed to tell a story of a loving family, who took interest in her life and celebrated her success, but there was no point in lying. "I think my nan is too frail for the journey, and she can't leave her alone." Elda papered over the truth, because she wasn't ready to admit to Charlie that her mum was probably drunk when she asked and might have instantly forgotten.

"Remind me, does she live far away?"

"It's a couple of hours. She'll get the train, which she hates because of all the people."

"I hope she can make it. I love it when my mum visits."

"I can probably count on one hand how many times she's come to me since I left for university." Elda rubbed at the frown gathering across her forehead, a battle raging in her thoughts. "How have you got such strong arms?" Desperate to change the subject, Elda spoke the first thought inside her head.

Charlie gripped her own bicep with mock pride. "I don't know. Lifting heavy files up and down court steps?"

Emboldened with rum and sugar syrup, Elda stroked the silky skin on Charlie's arm. Her body trembled, and she hoped Charlie didn't notice. "Let's go dancing at that place in the basement of Jimmy's." Elda's leg twitched. She was jittery and wanted to distract herself.

"It's Wednesday night. I've got case files to review in the morning, and I'm already a bit buzzed." Charlie put her hand on Elda's knee. "You've had too much sugar in your mojitos. Your legs are going be jigging all night. I'm glad I'm not sharing your bed."

The image of Charlie *sleeping* next to her in bed crashed Elda's thoughts, making her want to lean in and put her head into the crease of Charlie's neck. She wanted to kiss the line of her jaw and taste her mouth. Fuelled by booze, her insides were on fire, and she was burning for Charlie's touch.

Charlie's hand was still on her bouncing knee, and Elda covered it with her own. They connected, and Elda's stomach did a somersault. Charlie looked at Elda intently, like she was begging her to kiss her. There was nothing Elda wanted more than to fill herself up with Charlie. Her mind raced with possibilities. In a few seconds, she saw the future and catalogued all the things that could go wrong. Was she misreading Charlie's body language? Would this ruin their friendship?

She sat fixed to the spot, no idea what to do next. She shifted on her seat to relieve the deep ache in her groin, growing with every unsatisfying moment. Without warning, she moved from under Charlie's touch and tipped the dregs of her glass down her throat.

"Let's go."

***

"Did something happen between you two last night?" Jack asked.

Elda shook her head.

"So, you're just thinking about kissing the woman who ran you over?"

"You don't need to call her that." Elda covered her ear with the hand that wasn't strapped up in a cast.

"I thought you were making serious career moves on Francis, not sexy moves on Charlie. He's the one who thinks you're an amazing artist."

Elda wriggled under Jack's stare. "That's just work. Charlie —"

"Charlie makes your pants tingle."

Elda wrinkled her nose. Jack repulsed her with his real talk sometimes. But he was right. Francis was perfect for her career, and Charlie was setting her body alight. She looked at Jack and couldn't form any words. She nodded.

"Why are you fantasising about Charlie, who frankly is a bit weird for hanging around you like a stalker because she ran you over?"

"She's not weird, Jack. She just wanted to see how I was, and then we..." Elda hadn't really found the words to describe what their relationship was. "We became friends and like spending time together. It's not a massive deal. I wish I hadn't told you now."

Jack's shoulders relaxed, and he released his grip on the worktop. Elda turned away from him. It was easier to wrestle with tricky subjects when she didn't have to look someone in the eye.

"Do you really like her?" His voice softened as he moved to Elda's side and put his head against hers.

Elda had been going over the same thing in her head since finishing the trio. "Yes, I do like her," she said out loud for the first time. "I think I'm going mad a bit. But I can't stop thinking about her, and I make so many excuses to see her. I end up going for lunch with her, even if I've just eaten. And I engineer things to invite her to. And actually, she's also told me I'm an amazing artist."

"When?"

"At the studio the other night, when I finished the trio."

"You finished those paintings with Charlie in the room? You don't even let me in that bloody studio." Jack laughed. "Oh shit, this is bad. Do you think she feels the same?"

Elda wasn't sure which answer would be more of a mess. She had no idea what was going on in Charlie's head. Was she just kidding herself that Charlie liked her? "Maybe. I don't know. What if I've just made it all up in my head?"

Jack was still chuckling as Elda elbowed him in the ribs. He straightened. "Have you told her?"

"No way. She'll think I'm mad."

Jack stood at her back, and she leaned into him.

"I'm not sure she will. She might feel the same. Why else would she be hanging around? You just need to work out what you want."

His sharp bones pinched Elda's skin. She let it sting for a bit, just to take her mind off the whirring thoughts. This was too hard. Francis was opening up a whole world to her. He was turning into her agent, and her career was really taking off. She might not have time to devote to a new relationship.

No. She couldn't trust herself. Falling for someone and creating a fairy tale in her head was classic Elda. Was she so desperate to love and be loved that she'd fall for her new friend? Someone who was turning into a solid gold friend. It was too much to risk, given her track record. But there was something about Charlie that she couldn't shake off.

CHAPTER NINE

THE LAST CLIENT OF the day ran over, so by the time Charlie made it across to the third mill building, she was out of breath and skipping over her undone bootlace.

"Careful, you'll go arse over tit like that," said a slender young man hovering in the foyer. "You must be Charlie? Elda told me to look out for a tall, handsome blond. You're obviously the bombshell in question."

"I guess that's me. Not sure about that description!" She knelt to tie the offending lace. "And you're Jack? I've heard lots about you." Straightening up, she gave him her best smile.

"Here we are, in the flesh. Listen, I'm Elda's oldest friend, so you can never usurp me in that category, even if you are fast becoming her favourite."

He offered her a grin which was so warm, Charlie couldn't be offended.

"From the stories I've heard, you're irreplaceable. It's lovely to meet you at last." Charlie extended her hand. She already liked Jack and had no intention of getting in the way of his friendship with Elda. If anything, she was curious about what made their friendship tick along after all these years. Keeping people at arm's length was her usual playbook. "Is Elda inside? How is she?"

"The artist herself? Terrified. But looking gorgeous, as ever. I fashioned her a black sling to go with her outfit." He clapped his hands together, as if directing the proceedings. "Let's go and lend our support. She needs a couple of extroverts to hold her up."

"Have you been to any of Elda's shows before?" Charlie followed him through the wide reception area and into the lift.

"I'll have you know, I've followed her career all the way from Mrs Beecham's classroom to her final graduate show."

So it was going to be hard to know if Jack was ever serious about anything then.

"But tonight is special to her. It's the first proper gig she's had as a professional artist. That curator guy really knows his stuff."

"Yeah, I got that impression." Charlie tucked in a loose tuft of hair. She desperately needed a cut, but her spare time had been filled lately by spontaneous opportunities to catch up with Elda. "Have many people turned up?"

"Loads more than I was expecting. The Francis Paul PR machine has clearly been working overdrive. Even the local news has turned out."

"Blimey, no wonder Elda is feeling nervous." Charlie's urge to protect Elda was strong and unexpected. A little voice inside her head reminded her to stop trying to fix everything.

The doors opened to reveal the exhibition space just as Elda had described. The large room was bustling with an array of colour. Loud, flamboyant outfits clashed with life-size paintings, and everything stood starkly against the bright white walls.

As Charlie's eyes adjusted, she craned her neck to scan the crowd for Elda's familiar figure. She spotted her holding court with a small gathering of people. "Is that her collection?" Hanging perfectly from six suspended wires, they looked better here than she'd ever imagined from Elda's description.

"That's it. He had three walls rendered, and that copper cable isn't cheap, you know? Just for our girl." Jack filled the room with pride, and Charlie quietly matched his energy. "Go, disturb her. She'll be glad of the interruption, especially from you."

A flutter of nerves caught Charlie off-guard. She wasn't used to her body betraying her. She hesitated for a moment longer, enjoying the view. Elda held her space with elegance, and the silk shirt they'd chosen together caressed every movement of her petite frame. Her small audience was captivated, and though

Charlie was too far to hear the words, she studied Elda's lips, imagining how they tasted.

When Elda caught her eye, adrenaline shattered Charlie's stillness. Here she was, across a crowded room, bathing in the presence of a woman she really liked being around. What was it about her? She certainly transcended the physical transactions she'd shared with others. But Charlie wasn't sure she could handle anything more than casual. What if it all went wrong, and she was left alone again?

There wasn't time to dissect her feelings when Elda broke from her group and strode across the polished concrete floor. Charlie stiffened her spine, glad of the firm surface beneath her feet. She'd never thought about swooning over anyone, but if challenged in court, she wouldn't be able to think of another way to describe the sway overcoming her as Elda approached.

"Why are you smiling like that?" Elda tilted her head.

"Nothing. I'm just pleased to see you here." She gestured to the room. "Look at all this, and your pieces right in the middle of it. It's phenomenal."

"I'm so glad you're here. Is Jack here too? Have you met him? I told him to come and look for you. I couldn't bear the thought of you wandering the corridors trying to find the entrance, and –"

"He found me. Are you okay? Let's grab a drink." Charlie touched the small of her back, and they walked to the bar. She picked up two glasses. "To you, and your continued success."

Elda took a deep breath. "Thank you. I'm grateful that you came. I know you're busy."

"There's no way I would've missed this. I want to brag to all these people that I was in the room when the last stroke was brushed across the canvas." Charlie avoided Elda's eye contact, hoping her flimsy humour would hide the fact that her heart was beating like a drum. "Has your mum made it?"

"No." Elda's shoulders hunched.

"Have you called her?"

"No way. She could get herself to the train station if she really wanted to make the effort. She'll probably have forgotten all about it."

"What do you mean? She wouldn't have let something as big as this slip her mind."

Elda smirked but couldn't hide the sadness in her eyes or the tremble of her bottom lip.

"She'll have lost half the day at the bottom of a bottle. It's classic behaviour. I don't know why I expect more from her." Elda's volume dropped. "I'm sorry, I should have told you before about her drinking. It's been a problem for years. Tragic, but true."

"I'm so sorry." Charlie hated that Elda's mum had let her down. She thought of her own parents, who stood by her at every milestone, no matter how big or small. She started to wrap her arm around Elda's shoulder, wishing the pain away.

"You're here. I've been looking for you everywhere." Another man took Elda's elbow and steered her away.

Jealousy pierced Charlie's train of thought. From his accent, and his arrogance, she assumed he was the celebrated curator.

"Yep, that's Francis." Jack had appeared, glass in hand. "He's bossy, isn't he?"

"Where's he taking her?"

"Who knows? Maybe some hot investor wants to buy all her pieces tonight. Look out for the red dots."

Jack's optimism jarred with Charlie. Francis had been rude.

Elda returned before she could stew too long. "He wants me to do a bloody TV interview with the local news. What am I supposed to say?" Elda bit her nails, clearly petrified by the suggestion.

"I don't know. I've only been on TV in the audience on *Saturday Night Takeaway*. It was before my braces, so I try not to think about it. But you'll be fab, Elderflower. You always are." Jack raised his glass to show his support.

Charlie stepped forward, not content to leave Elda floundering. "They'll just ask you about your work and how you feel about exhibiting here. It'll be a good opportunity to tell your story."

"Don't talk to me with your barrister voice. You're making me even more nervous."

"Do you have a barrister voice?" Jack asked. "Sexy."

"No, I don't." Charlie laughed off the tease. "Sorry, I was just trying to help calm your nerves. You have all the answers to their questions." She laid a hand on Elda's good shoulder and gently squeezed. As they met each other's gaze, the busy room faded away. She wanted to scoop Elda into her arms and tell her to be brave and enjoy every moment. "Do it. You'll be great."

As she watched Elda cross the room back to a waiting Francis, her jaw clenched. She didn't like the way he spoke to her. Was she misreading his impatience? It must be stressful for him too. But he seemed possessive and controlling. Charlie fought the urge to follow and defend her.

"She'll be fine. Let's get another drink." Jack led the way. "Hey, I'm glad you came tonight. Elda won't shut up about you, and I was beginning to think you were an imaginary friend."

"Imaginary?"

"You know, too good to be true." Jack scratched his head. "But you're all right, actually. I like the look of you. Elda calms down a bit too when you're around. You're okay." He winked.

Charlie's brow furrowed. What had Elda said about her? She wasn't even sure she knew how to describe their relationship. Was she just a new friend that came to Elda's rescue when things got a bit difficult? Deep down, Charlie knew that her feelings for Elda were growing into something much more complex than a friendship. This was new territory, and she'd never proven herself in a proper relationship. The type where you liked being around each other beyond the bedroom. Was it worth risking their friendship to find out?

CHAPTER TEN

ELDA HAD JUMPED AT the chance to see Charlie again. But this wasn't exactly what she had in mind. "Why are you taking the kids for the afternoon?"

"It's not all of them. It's just Jacob. He's only four. Kim has a job interview at the industrial park. She won't be long."

"What are the older ones up to?"

"I expect Chloe will have her head in her books. She has her mock exams soon. And Sam will be off out with his mates. They tend to look after themselves now. But Kim worries about leaving Jacob with them."

"Sounds like she couldn't cope without you."

Charlie kept her eyes on the road. "I'm more dependable than most people around her, I guess." She drummed her fingers on the steering wheel. "Listen, Kim's life is messy. Sometimes I think she's sorted herself out, but then she blows in with another crisis."

"Sounds chaotic." Elda didn't want to jump to conclusions, but Kim was starting to remind her of her own mum: unreliable and needy.

"It can be. But they're like family, you know? When family need you, you do what you can to help." Charlie's jaw went rigid.

Elda stared out the passenger window. The streets had become narrower, the shops dishevelled or closed. Her chest tightened when she thought of her own family. Since her mum's no-show at the private viewing, she'd avoided her phone calls. She wasn't sure she could forgive her for not being there this time.

The car came to a stop underneath a flyover, and Charlie cut the engine. "Stay here. I'll be back in a minute."

Elda sighed and watched Charlie walk towards the block of flats. She thought they'd shared a moment at the exhibition. Charlie had seemed more open to her than she ever had. When she'd called to ask her out this afternoon, she'd hoped something would happen. She hadn't expected to be babysitting a pre-schooler.

When Charlie returned, a cute little boy walked beside her, gripping her hand. Joy radiated from Charlie's face as they chatted to each other. She looked happy, and sexy, in a mum-at-the-school-gates kind of way.

"Here he is. Jacob, this is my friend, Elda." Charlie popped him onto a booster seat and fixed his seatbelt.

"Hello, Jacob. Nice to meet you."

"Hello." Jacob studied her through his blond eyelashes. "What's that?" He pointed to her sling.

"Oh, I hurt my arm, and it's just making itself better. I have to keep it very still while it heals."

His eyes twinkled, as if he was taking in every word. "I hurt my finger. It was ouch but Mummy made it better."

"Yeah? Mine was a bit ouch-ey too." She couldn't remember the last time her mum had made anything better. "Are you looking forward to going to the park with us?"

He squeaked his response and swung his legs against the back of the driver's seat.

"I have a surprise for you when we get there."

Charlie's sing-song lilt was new to Elda, a whole different side to the sexy lawyer vibe she gave off most of the time.

"What is it? What is it?" Jacob wriggled with anticipation.

"Wait and see. We'll be there in five minutes."

Charlie shot her a conspiratorial grin, which tugged at Elda's heart. She warmed under Charlie's attention and unzipped her jacket.

By the time they got to the park's gravel entrance, Elda was more upbeat about the afternoon. Charlie hopped out first and helped Jacob down from his seat. As she opened the boot, Jacob clapped his little hands together with glee.

"A scooter!" He jumped on the spot and created dust beneath his boots. "Is it mine?"

"Yes, it's all yours. You need a helmet on before you can try it." Charlie beamed at them both.

"What a brilliant gift. He's so happy." Elda stepped closer to Charlie and nudged her arm. "You really know how to make people's day, don't you?"

Charlie wrinkled her nose, as if she couldn't take the compliment. "I don't know. All kids love riding around, don't they? I thought it'd be easier to teach him to scoot than to ride a big bike."

"Yeah. It's perfect." Elda bit her lip. She wanted to hug her right there in the car park. Charlie was so much more than she'd first assumed.

"Can we go yet?" Jacob tugged at Charlie's hand, pulling her out of Elda's reach.

"Yes. Let's hit the trails." Charlie grabbed a tiny red helmet from the car. "Safety first though. Pop this on your head."

He complied before he was off again, leading them to the park's entrance. Swinging the scooter under her arm, Charlie looked into Elda's eyes, and they shared a moment of deeper connection than ever before. Maybe it was the innocence of the situation. Perhaps being chaperoned by a small child wasn't such a killjoy after all.

Elda had known Charlie had a caring side. She'd been on the receiving end of it that first night at the hospital. But seeing her with Jacob had brought out a whole new level of nurturing. And maternal Charlie was seriously hot. Charlie skipped after Jacob, holding her hands at his side to protect him from a fall. Elda tilted her head, glimpsing a version of a future that made her heart skip.

Jack's voice rang in her ears. But he could no longer accuse Elda of rushing into anything. She and Charlie had spent weeks getting to know each other as friends. Could they have something more together?

***

Elda finished her shift at the office and thought about doing a stint at the exhibition. Artists were expected to cover the opening hours when they could, to draw visitors in. But she couldn't face the glare of an audience. Tonight, she craved time alone to digest the last few days and create.

She'd been caught in a whirlwind. On the outside, she'd been darting from work to the mill, flashing her smiles and playing the part of enigmatic artist. She'd barely slept between shifts. Inside, she'd been tossing and turning over her growing attachment to Charlie. Every time she closed her eyes, she conjured a new, more enticing fantasy of them together. After yesterday afternoon's jaunt to the park, she had a fresh vision of them creating a family.

Daydreaming her life away while the reality drifted past was typical. But this time, the drift was more of a rush. The pace of the exhibition and the demands from Francis were coming thick and fast. She'd done three more interviews with trade magazines since the TV station collared her at the launch. Part of her relished the opportunity. But it drained her energy levels, and she needed to retreat for a while.

She flicked the kettle on in the studio and pondered the space before her. It had been a long time since her easels had been empty. With the trio gracing the walls of the mill gallery, she was left with a void to fill. Elda found her sketch book under a pile of rags and newspaper. With a full mug of tea, she settled on the sagging sofa.

Allowing her pencil to drift across the page, she took a slow, deep breath into her diaphragm. The past few weeks had carved familiar paths in her wandering mind. They all led to Charlie. Curved, soft lines appeared in graphite on the white paper, tracing the sweep of Charlie's brow, the cut of her cheekbones, and the fullness of her lips.

Elda closed her eyes, imagining Charlie's face within reach of a kiss. The fiction was disturbed by a knock at the studio door. Elda looked up to see Francis in the doorway.

"Hi, do you have time to talk?"

"Sure, is everything all right at the mill? I wasn't expecting to see you here."

"All is well. I just wanted to see you."

Elda's heart sank. She'd been ripped from an enticing reverie and now had to give Francis her full attention. "What can I do for you?"

Francis stepped into the space with what she now recognised as his usual swagger. "I got talking to someone important last night."

"Really? At the exhibition?"

"Yes. He'd come to see your work, among others."

Pride fluttered across Elda's chest, making her sit up straighter. She bit her lip.

"He knew my work from London and Paris before that."

"Okay, that's exciting. What does he do?"

"His name is Claude Pelleterie. Have you heard of him?"

"No." Elda admitted her ignorance, irritated that Francis seemed to like showing her up.

"He's an academic in Paris. At one of the best universities." Francis took another step and pulled his hands from his pockets. "He offered me a position as a senior curator, along with a professorship."

"In Paris? Congratulations. That's fantastic." She twisted on the sofa, and he took up the space beside her.

"There's more. He'd like me to build a team." He gripped her arm. "You could be a practising artist and have a teaching position in the faculty."

"Goodness, that's a lot to take in. Would you like a cup of tea?" she asked, feeling somewhat ambushed.

"Why not?"

He was offering her a dream job. She knew it. But her thoughts whirled like a tornado, and she swallowed back the taste of fear. Right in the eye of the storm was Charlie. She thought of the previous day at the park. She cherished the time she had with Charlie, like she finally belonged somewhere. Could she abandon that feeling for the career opportunity of a lifetime? She stroked the fragile edge of a teabag as the water reboiled. "I've never thought about working in Paris."

"Every artist wants to work in Paris."

Ouch. "Yeah, I know. I suppose it's all come as a bit of a shock." She stumbled, not wanting Francis to think less of her. She stood taller, nervous energy pumping through her muscles. Art was her dream career. Until now, that's all it had been, a hope that she tended to every now and again. She'd never expected for it to bloom into something so real and living.

"You need to sit down and then we can sort it all out," he said.

Nausea rose through Elda's chest, and she touched her clammy cheeks, pinching colour into them. Frustration bubbled in her stomach. She wanted to cut her own path. But Francis could sweep her along with his career, and she would let him. She'd been following him around for the past few weeks, not knowing what was going to happen next. Elda had no plan of her own. She never really had. It was why she'd drifted at college and followed Jack into a terrible office job. Now, following Francis seemed like the obvious choice, but the thought of not having Charlie in her life was crushing, as was the thought of saying goodbye.

CHAPTER ELEVEN

"CAN WE WIN THE case?" The man peered at Charlie over a pair of silver-rimmed spectacles.

She breathed in and looked away from the spots clustered under his stubble. "No one really wins these cases. These are the nasty ones, where children are taken from families, and everyone takes a lifetime to recover from the trauma."

"Yeah, but will we win?"

"With me as your barrister, and with a reasonable judge, yes." Charlie's ribs contracted as she hid her impatience. Her client rose to his feet, but she stayed rooted to the chair. She wasn't going to grace him with her finest manners.

The door opened, and Joshua led him away. A few minutes later, he returned with a fully loaded bagel and a steaming mug of tea.

"You lifesaver." Food tumbled from her mouth, and she wiped it with the back of her hand. "I need a break from child protection. Can you line up a couple of custodies next?" She was joking, but he'd work his magic with her caseload. She wanted to carve out more free time in her schedule.

"A palette cleanser? Yeah, no probs." He took a seat by her side and scratched at his short hair. "You all right, boss?"

Charlie swallowed. She liked her clerk; he'd been solid for years. "It's been a hectic few weeks." Charlie brushed off his query, but her mind had been whirring with questions about Elda since the launch night at the mill, wondering why she hadn't gone in for a kiss.

"You've not been yourself this past month."

She followed his line of sight to the painting of a horse, a relic of the previous barrister, and she wondered why she kept it in the office. *Why do I shrink into this place? Why can't I be myself?* "Maybe we should get some new pieces in here. These old prints are so dated." She wasn't convincing anyone, but she didn't have the energy to unpick what was happening. She thought of her cold, silent three-bedroomed house. She had once loved the sanctuary it provided but recently, it felt empty. Unscrambling her feelings for Elda was unsettling.

"Well, if you fancy bending my ear over a couple of drinks, you know where I am. It wouldn't go any further. Clerk's honour." He tipped an imaginary cap towards the horse.

"This job takes its toll, doesn't it?" She was talking to herself as much as Joshua, pondering how she'd prioritised her career over her life for so long.

"Well, I've seen people work all hours, if that's what you mean. And sacrifice things. Parents' evenings and dinner dates are the first to go. Yeah, it takes its toll." He faced Charlie, his shirt sleeves stretching around his biceps. "People put up walls, I think. You have to with the kind of stuff you see. But I don't think it's healthy to keep it all inside. You need to talk, if you can."

It wasn't the most eloquent of points, but she understood what he was getting at. She'd built a ten-foot wall around herself over the last few years. People were allowed in a night at a time, but just into her bed, never into her head.

Elda appeared in her mind's eye. She could hear the gentle tone of her voice and almost feel the soft, downy hairs on the top of her forearm. "You're right. People in this place keep everyone at a safe distance. Maybe it's time to take a chance."

Joshua tilted his head, opening his mouth as if to speak then shutting it. A shadow appeared at the door, and they both turned. It was Clarissa, a third junior from the front desk.

"Sorry to interrupt. There's a lady for you at reception, miss."

"Who is it?" Charlie asked while Joshua leafed through the

paper diary searching for an appointment he'd forgotten.

"She just said to tell you that Kim was here, if you're available."

She let out a long sigh.

"You okay?"

Charlie was brought back into the room by Joshua's fingers on her forearm, and she snapped a smile on her face, even though her chest grew hot with alarm. "Yep. Clarissa, please show Kim into meeting room three. It'll be free; I had it booked for case prep. I'll be there in two minutes." She rose, grounding herself. "Don't offer her a drink. We won't be long."

She shrugged off the feeling of Joshua watching her every move and strode the ten steps down the corridor to her own office. Charlie perched on her chair and tugged at a heavy drawer. She picked out a small dusty mirror and inspected her flushed cheeks before returning it to the drawer. Her gaze rested on the photo of Theresa and her younger self, a teenager fixed in time, her arms draped around the girl she loved. Memories of their laughter flooded her vision, and she blinked her tears away.

A shiver ran across her shoulders and brought her back into the present. She lifted her head and walked towards room three. She gripped the cold steel of the handle and took a breath to brace herself for whatever state Kim would be in this time. It had to be bad for her to come to the office.

Kim looked tiny in the expanse of the conference room. She sat in a corner, hunched over the table, massaging her temples. "Charlotte. Jesus, I thought you weren't coming. The girl at the desk seemed a bit dithery, to be honest, and I had to practically beg her to come and find you. Before you say anything, I'm sorry. I didn't want to come and bother you, but I've got no choice this time."

"Sit down, Kim. This can't take long." She stood behind a chair.

"Yeah, but you don't understand, things are really bad, and I can't think of what to do. I need your help to figure it all out again. Work out what's going on, and how to straighten it." She fell silent and rested her head on the table.

"You can't come to my work. You know that." Charlie controlled the pitch, speed, and volume of each word. She sat down and leaned back into the chair. Kim's face was so like Theresa's, she could trace it with her eyes closed. But this was a softer version, baggier around the cheekbones, grey not pink, drawn not flushed. The eyes in front of her were sunken, but the ones in her memories sparkled with joy. She shook away the story playing in her mind and gripped the table in front of her. "Tell me exactly what's wrong. But be quick because I don't have much time."

"I can't cope. It's the kids. They're all over the place. I didn't get that job. It was too much, because they needed me to work shifts, and I've got no one to look after Jacob. Darren's working all hours, so he can't help. And the money's gone, and it wasn't enough. We just haven't got enough. Chloe needs a new school skirt and a pair of shoes. The girls at school are bullying her for it." Her voice broke, and her face etched in pain.

"Okay. I get it. How much?" An itch crawled across Charlie's chest.

"Just enough to get us to the end of the month, love. You know, a couple of hundred or so."

"Right. Let's leave it there, shall we? I'll drop it through the door." Charlie flinched as Kim's cold hand rested on hers. A part of her was used to reassuring people in the hardest moments, and she gave Kim's skinny fingers a squeeze. "It'll be fine."

Kim's eyes brimmed with tears. "You're a good girl. The best. I'm lucky to have you."

"I don't mind helping out, but please don't come to the office again. I have to work and can't have people turning up unexpectedly."

"I know. It won't happen again." Kim stood to gather herself. She pulled her coat tight to her neck and pushed buttons through their holes. There were two missing. "Thank you, love. I'll see you tomorrow?"

"I'll sort it this week. It's a busy one, but I'll drop it off."

There was a knock at the door and Joshua's head poked in. "You have a personal engagement at six o'clock, miss."

"Yes, of course. Thank you." She was grateful for the interruption, and she guided Kim to the open door. "Can you show my visitor out, please?" Turning away, it occurred to her that ghosts of the past showing up was the last thing she needed right now. She had to keep her head down and her sheet clear. If only she could crack on with work and drown out the thoughts that played on her mind at night. She went back to her office for her bag so she could meet Elda at a pub around the corner.

An hour later, Charlie twisted a beermat at the bar and checked her watch. Elda was late, gifting her time to stew over Kim's money troubles.

"Hey, you."

Elda's voice tickled her neck, and she swung around, almost touching her lips.

"That was close," Elda said.

Charlie's laugh was more high-pitched than she'd have liked. "Hi." She gained enough control to dispense a brief hug. Elda leaned into it further than usual. Charlie liked it. "Have you been drinking somewhere else without me?"

"I had a couple after work with Jack." Elda's cheeks flushed. She fidgeted with her backpack and grinned. "Let's sit. I need your help with something."

God, she was beautiful. Charlie gripped her own fist to avoid any further physical contact. She couldn't be trusted not to pull Elda to her lips. "Sounds intriguing." Charlie cleared her throat and picked up two glasses of wine.

They settled in a booth, shoulder to shoulder. Charlie leaned away, forcing some distance between them. Her head was still spinning from her run-in with Kim. "How was the studio? Did you get into something?" Charlie asked. She tipped the glass against her lips, letting the alcohol burn the back of her tongue.

"Not really. I didn't have time to get into the zone. But something else happened." Elda wrinkled her nose.

Charlie's stomach flipped inside out, possibilities ticker-taping through her mind. "Tell me. What is it?"

"Francis offered me a job." Elda pressed her palms to her cheeks. "It's a teaching post, but it comes with a studio, so I can work."

"Really? Where?" She dreaded the response.

"In Paris." Elda dropped her chin. "I don't know what to do."

Charlie's breath stuck in her throat, and panic rose beneath her ribs. Elda couldn't go—she'd only just found her. "Is it what you want?"

"I don't know if I want to live in Paris. I'm not sure I want to... not live here." Elda shifted against the leather seat. "But it could be amazing. I can't begin to think about what it might lead to. And I can't stay working in Jack's office for the rest of my life."

The inevitability of their separation crept into Charlie's stomach. The emptiness could've been hunger, but she recognised it as something more. Elda was slipping away, and she had no right to stop her. How could she ask Elda to prioritise their friendship over a dream job? That was all they had so far, wasn't it? Friendship. She couldn't offer Elda anything more because she didn't trust herself to be that person.

"What do you think I should do?"

Charlie swallowed the truth with a gulp of wine. She wanted to scream at Elda to stay. Wanted to kiss her. To discover how she tasted. But the words wouldn't come. She'd never asked anyone for anything. How could she forgive herself if she thwarted Elda's career for what might only be a few nights of amazing sex? "You should go. It's an unbelievable opportunity. Working in Paris," her voice strained, "being able to create and paint... It's all you've dreamed of, isn't it?" It wasn't a question. "Francis will be there to support you too."

Charlie's bones ached for Elda to reject the suggestion. She closed her eyes with an unspoken plea that Elda would hear something beyond her words, beneath the bravado she kicked out into the world.

"You're right." Elda broke the silence, crushing Charlie's hopes. She took her own glass and lifted it in celebration. "A toast? To new beginnings."

"To new beginnings." Charlie forced her glass towards the ceiling, as her shoulders dropped, defeated. "This calls for something fizzy." Charlie rose to her feet and walked to the bar, steadying her breath. She couldn't bear to look Elda in the face. She was losing her, even though Elda wasn't hers to begin with.

Blinking back tears, she thought about her own career. She had to put work first to get anywhere in the chambers. She had so much potential; wasting it wasn't an option. She'd been coasting with her cases ever since Elda had jumped in front of her car. Before that, she'd been happy with work and play. Maybe she'd call Jude for a hook-up. The idea stung.

She snuck a look over at the booth. Elda's hair fell onto her slim shoulders, and she dusted it away. Even wearing a frown, she sent sparks through Charlie's body. Rolling back to life before Elda was unthinkable. But she had no choice. Elda was leaving for Paris, and Charlie could be nothing more than be a good friend about it.

CHAPTER TWELVE

"You're early, miss." Joshua scrambled up off his chair. "I'll get you a cuppa."

"Thank you, that'd be good." Charlie had been up since four a.m., tossing and turning over the conversation with Elda at the bar. She went over every syllable, looking for signs that Elda wanted her to say something different. Maybe she'd missed something.

In the end she couldn't trust her reading of the situation. If she had pushed Elda away, there was no going back now. She just had to move on with her life. They could still be friends, couldn't they? She could visit Paris. Slumping into her chair, she closed her eyes and pinched the tension between her brows. The sleepless night was catching up with her.

Joshua entered and placed a cup and a pastry on her desk. "Thought you might need some sugar too."

"You're a mind reader."

"So I've been told, miss." He faltered at the desk. "Anything I can do?"

"I just had a rough night. Nothing to worry about." After he left, she grabbed her mirror and inspected the dark circles under her eyes. She looked a state. There was a knock on her office door, and she shuffled back into position. "What've you forgotten?" She looked up to see Maureen at the door. "Sorry, I thought you were Joshua. Please, come in." Charlie stood to receive her visitor, her mind racing. It was unusual to have a KC grace her office, even as a senior barrister.

"I won't stay long." Maureen sat in the chair opposite. "Are you working on the Kendrick case?"

"I am." Charlie's shoulders relaxed. At least this was about work.

"Watch out for the solicitor. He's a creep. As well as being a bit of a know-it-all."

"I got that impression yesterday. We met to discuss the brief."

"Just take care with that one. Have your clerk with you and keep records."

"Understood." Charlie furrowed her brow, grateful for the concern. "While you're here, can we discuss something else?"

"I don't have much time." Maureen stayed put, giving permission to go on.

Charlie shifted her weight. She wasn't sure what to say, but this was an opportunity she had to take. She blocked the thought of Elda from her mind. "I appreciate you taking the time to talk to me about my future a few weeks ago. I do want to progress, and I'm willing to do what it takes. I'll put the hours in, take on the pro-bono cases, attend the functions. Just throw it all my way."

Maureen pursed her scarlet lips. "Good to talk. I'll keep that in mind."

Charlie was in fight mode. She'd encouraged Elda to follow her career path, and now she had to do the same. She had nothing else to keep her busy.

***

Charlie pushed the revolving door and scanned the humming crowd at the bar. She spotted Jude nursing a half empty glass of wine.

"Charlie, darling. How are you?" She delivered an air kiss to both cheeks.

Charlie fixed a smile. "We should meet at the office."

Jude gave a dismissive wave. "Sweetheart, I just wanted to catch up. I'm not on the clock."

"Well, I am." Charlie laughed, which took her by surprise. She hadn't thought she was capable of laughing today. It had been a long and tough one.

"You're always bloody working, lady. You look tired. Have a night off; it'll do you good. I ordered your fave." Jude poked her in the ribs.

Charlie's phone buzzed. Her heart skipped at Elda's name, but her brain caught up and she frowned.

Hey. Fancy a drink tonight? It's my shift at the gallery but I'll be done by 7pm. E

"Sorry, Jude. Let me just reply to this message." Torn between the thrill of seeing Elda and the dread of it being one of their last times together, she kept her reply short.

Can't, sorry. I have a work thing.

"Tell me, what have I missed?" Charlie turned back to Jude and gestured to the waiter for another glass.

Jude rested her chin on her hand. "Not much. Judge Bingham is retiring."

"Judges don't retire. They die."

"Well, either way, Sandra says he's on his way out. Which is rubbish for us. He was one of the good guys."

"Depends which side you're on." Charlie squinted up at the bar's twinkling lights, remembering the cases that had gone her way. "Yeah. He was a fair judge." She stared at her phone, willing the screen to illuminate. She couldn't settle knowing that Elda wanted to see her, and she'd said no. She looked around the bar to distract herself. Glasses clinked and people talked over each other.

"You okay?" Jude frowned.

Charlie stared at her wine glass as condensation dripped around its curve. She let it hang for a few moments before rubbing it away with her thumb. A resigned sadness washed over her. She'd let Elda walk out of her life, and she hadn't given them a chance to get started.

She looked at Jude and remembered the last time they'd been together. They were familiar. They knew each other's bodies, what worked and what didn't. But nothing more than that. Charlie straightened her back, ready to confront her behaviour. "I haven't been good to you. In fact, I've been a bit of a shit." She took Jude's hands in her own and noticed their fragile size for the first time. Perhaps Jude had feelings that she'd played with and ignored. The guilt hung heavy across her shoulders.

"What are you talking about?" Jude recoiled and her cheeks coloured.

"I mean it. I've slept with you and then treated you terribly. I'm sorry."

Jude leaned closer and pushed Charlie's short hair away from her ear. "Charlie, darling. I'm not in love with you. Our arrangement was entirely mutual and a complete pleasure." She giggled into her glass. "Why the sudden guilt trip?"

"Jesus." Charlie ran her hand through her hair and took a sharp breath. "I don't know. I just feel a bit weird."

"Have you fallen in love, sweetheart? Have you discovered unknown depths to your feelings? Been there, darling. It hurts. And you realise everything before was just performance, really."

Charlie sat still for a moment and digested Jude's analysis. She was spot on. Charlie *had* fallen in love. "Why would you say that?"

"You don't let anyone in, do you?" Jude looked smug, like she'd discovered something Charlie was trying to keep hidden. "You've spent all these years with your guard up, and now you've fallen for someone. Admit it."

Charlie wriggled under the interrogation, conscious of how exposed she was. "Maybe. It can't go anywhere though."

"Why not?"

"Well, she's moving to bloody Paris. With a guy."

"You're not the first to fall for a straight, attached woman, Charlie, and you won't be the last. Don't tell me, he's gorgeous too. They always are." Jude took a sip of wine.

"No. They're not together. He offered her a job. It was a good career move. I encouraged her." Charlie covered her ears with her hands. Trying to explain this was painful, and she wasn't sure she could stand her own ramblings.

"So, she's not straight or with the guy, and you told her to move to Paris?" Jude raised a single, preened eyebrow.

"The job was perfect for her. And yes, I told her to go. I couldn't ask her to put her dreams on hold for something so intangible. I don't even know if she likes me."

"Oh, bugger that. You're irresistible. Go and bloody fight for her." Jude picked up Charlie's wine glass by the stem and handed it to her. Her face glowed, and her eyes crinkled at the corners.

Charlie had thought she didn't have anyone to talk to about her feelings for Elda. If she'd confided in Jude earlier, maybe it wouldn't have unravelled so easily. She might have recognised the power of her feelings before Elda was swept along on Francis's ride.

It was pointless to go over the chronology of it all now. They'd only known each other a few weeks. Charlie couldn't have understood and acted on her emotions in that time. She kicked herself. Coasting through life like she was untouchable was one way to protect her heart. But losing the only person she'd connected with in almost two decades was a tragic waste.

CHAPTER THIRTEEN

ELDA RESTED AGAINST THE bench and lifted her head. The sunlight made orange patterns behind her closed eyelids, and when she opened them, she was blinded for a few seconds.

She was fresh off the Eurostar, grateful for the cool air under the Paris sky and the hum of tourists. She was no fan of the tunnel itself. It made her panic to travel under the seabed. She took a deep breath and looked up at the thick grey arch above her, its criss-cross pattern stretching into the clouds. From this angle, the Eiffel Tower looked short and squat, like an iron bridge. It was a terrible cliché to start her new life here, but Francis had wanted to show Elda the sights. "So, when are we going over to the university? I want to check out the spaces and find a proper place to live."

"Soon." He stroked his chin. "I think we should walk to the river and catch a boat to the Pont Neuf. I'll take you down to the Notre Dame and then onto the hotel I booked for you."

"Okay, but I can't wait to see everything." Pent up with ambition and excitement, she wanted to get started, but Francis seemed slow to move.

"In Paris, we enjoy things. Work will come."

A few hours later, Elda was disorientated. They'd had too many little jugs of red wine, and she wasn't sure which side of the River Seine they'd ended up on. They'd spent the afternoon meandering through the Latin Quarter, stumbling across pretty squares full of cafés and conversation. Young men played chess, beautiful women chatted, and waiters carried out trays of beer and pastries to the terraces. She felt like a tourist, forgetting that this wasn't a holiday.

Francis was talking art, and his hands grabbed at the air as he described his vision for the team. His mannerisms and accent were even more foreign to her than a few weeks ago. He was more Italian, more French. He was a stranger. But he knew Paris by heart. Unlike her last trip with Rebecca, she'd been whipped away from the Gare du Nord to the most sumptuous parts of the city, skipping past the grubby backstreets. The alleys they stumbled upon were cobbled and full of charm.

They sat in a late-night bar around the corner from the Sorbonne University. It was dark and luxurious, with a velvet curtain draped across the doorway. The waiter nodded towards a corner table facing the picture window. Elda could just about see the river, edged by festoon bulbs, when she stretched her neck.

Her head pounded behind her eyes, and the undercooked steak she had forced down earlier was threatening to make a reappearance. She struggled to concentrate on Francis's latest anecdote, and she stretched into contortions on her wicker chair in an effort to get comfortable. She excused herself to find the toilets. A man polishing glasses at the bar gestured towards a single door at the back that met neither the ceiling nor the floor. Elda pushed through to find that it divided the dimly lit bar from an even darker, single hole in the floor.

Her stomach cramped, and she doubled over in pain, with no time to be horrified. The wine made her head swirl, and she worried that she was going to be sick. She dropped her jeans and scooped them towards her chest, then said a silent prayer that she could stand up without falling into the hole and breaking her ankle. *Christ, that would be awkward.*

When she stood, she examined her face in a single reflective tile blackened with age spots. She splashed water on her cheeks and reapplied her lipstick, trying to rearrange her face to neutral. She wished Charlie was here. She would've found the whole situation hilarious. But the humiliating thought of Francis seeing her like this made her stomach groan again.

She returned to the table, trying not to sway into any chairs or give away her inner drunk.

Francis cradled the remnants of a cognac and was talking to a stranger at the next table. "Elda, we have a party to go to. My friends from work are gathering at their place. It's just across the road."

"Oh, please, I just want to head to the hotel." She fiddled with strands of her hair. The absolute last thing on Elda's mind was going anywhere else where she would have to talk French to people she didn't know. But he took her hand, settled their bill, and led her into the darkness. She had no choice but to follow him since she didn't know where she was staying, and her bags were at his apartment.

Less than thirty minutes later, they'd reached their next destination.

"I present to you Armelle et Marie." Francis rolled a long *r* with his tongue, which made his French neighbours giggle.

Elda smiled and received two kisses on each cheek from her new friends. She held in her cramping stomach and shook her head at the passing tray of champagne flutes. She couldn't make out the full extent of the apartment. Elegant people gathered along the sweeping staircase. The rooms blended into one another and never ended. It was overwhelming, and Elda craved the four solid walls of her room back home.

In the middle, a woman played music from a laptop. It was noisy and distorted, but everyone else in its reach seemed to resonate with the rhythm. There were deep window seats where others gathered to smoke cigarettes. Tall panes of glass stretched up to the ceilings behind them, flanked by shutters pinned back to the wall.

Elda lost sight of Francis and walked through the hallway to find him. She made herself smaller, disappeared into doorways and ducked past groups of people in animated conversation. She saw Armelle and Marie standing against a wall by the bedroom. They were frozen in conversation, transfixed by each other. Marie kissed Armelle, wrapped her arm around her back and drew her closer until there was no space between them, and their bodies had merged.

Elda was stuck to the spot, staring at the couple, wondering what they tasted like. Her insides lurched, and she was transported home to Charlie. She wanted so much to feel Charlie's lips against hers. Elda closed her eyes and turned ninety degrees. She was here to work, and there was no point in tormenting herself with fantasies of Charlie.

In another room, Francis leaned against the balcony, enveloped in cigarette smoke.

"Elda, where were you?"

He had a wild expression, and she stepped back. He was drunk, and his friends gathered around him in a small circle. He was incapable, for now, of catching her up in English. She turned away and rubbed the chill of the early hours from her arms. Finding space on a sofa, she kicked off her shoes, folded her legs, and rested on the bulky arm. As she closed her eyes, the chatter and melodies melted away.

When Elda awoke, she was under a warm blanket. Armelle sat at her feet, and Marie was draped across her lap. They looked peaceful together.

Francis stood over her with his jacket hanging by one finger over his shoulder. "Come, my dear," he said. "It's time to go home."

He led her by the hand, and they climbed over the sea of sleeping bodies strewn over couches and floors like discarded coats. Rubbing her eyes, Elda followed Francis down the wide staircase and out onto the street.

Dawn streamed through half open shutters. The metal grates of bakeries screeched as they were lifted open, and tiny bin carts moved like aliens from corner to corner. Elda could barely stomach the smell of Paris in the morning. Stale cigarettes, blocked drains, and the hangover of the night before formed a cloud around her, and she covered her nose and mouth.

It hadn't been the greatest start to her life in Paris. But today,

Francis would show her around the university, and she'd start her search for an apartment. She yawned and reset her body. Yesterday was the journey. Today was day one of the rest of her life. She ignored the nagging feeling that she'd left something, or someone, important behind.

CHAPTER FOURTEEN

WARM WATER POOLED AT Charlie's feet. She leaned further in, allowing the rainwater shower to tumble down her back. Staring ahead, she traced a pattern on the tile. Her world had grown quieter since Elda had left for Paris. The buzz of Elda's text messages were fewer and farther between. She craved her company on a spontaneous night out. She missed cradling a hot coffee in the studio.

Charlie's caseload filled the void in her head, but it wasn't enough to comfort her heart, and she grew more and more miserable with each passing day.

"Are you nearly done, love? I'm heading into the jungle steam when you're ready. I just need to find somewhere to put my glasses," her mum said over the frosted cubicle.

"I'm coming." She rubbed her eyes and flicked wet hair from her forehead. Towelling off, she fixed her expression, not wanting to worry her mum on their only day together in months. The shower door creaked open, and she came to face-to-face with a vision of her future self. The resemblance between her and her mother was often commented on when they were together but recently, Charlie had noticed it more herself. She smiled. Without a layer of make-up, her mum's skin was lived-in, creased with age, weathered by the sun. But she looked kind and graceful. *Could be worse.*

"I love it here, don't you? It's one of the things I miss most about the city."

"I do love it here. Happy birthday, Mum." Charlie pulled a sumptuous robe around her shoulders and tied it at the waist.

"Thank you, my darling. I'm truly blessed." She led the way to the steam room, her sliders flapping against the terracotta tiles.

Charlie opened the door to a fog of steam. Inside, the scorching cloud gathered around them, and she patted the walls to find the tiled bench. She stubbed her big toe against the hard surface and screeched as the pain shot through her foot.

"Careful. You can't see a thing in here," a man said.

No shit, Sherlock.

"It's terrible, isn't it?" her mum said.

"It's a steam room, Mum. What did you expect?" Charlie failed to temper her frustration. She sensed a movement, and the man opened the door to leave. Steam escaped at his exit, giving them a brief break in the cloud.

"What's wrong, Charlie? You're not yourself today. Have you been *out* out again?"

"What do you mean?" Charlie bit her cheek. She hadn't meant to snap.

"Have you got a hangover? Do you need something sugary?"

Charlie laughed, knowing how many times she'd bounced back with a carb load and a big hug. "No, Mum, I'm not hungover. Sorry. It's a bit full-on at work, and I'm just tired."

"It's not that. Something's eating at you, Charlotte. I can tell. You can spill the beans now, or you can wait until we've had a glass of wine at lunch. Either way, I'll get it out of you."

Charlie hadn't realised that she'd been so transparent. Weighing up her mum's challenge, she decided it would be much easier to talk without being able to see her face. "There's a girl." The heat grew even more intense and sweat poured from her forehead.

"How wonderful. Tell me about her."

"Don't get too excited. It's actually a bit rubbish."

"Oh, I knew something was up." Her mum shuffled on the bench. "Wait. I can't stand the heat anymore, love. Can we get out of here?"

Charlie sighed and followed her mum out to the plunge pool. Setting foot in the ice-cold water shot every nerve in her body into action. She sank below the surface and experienced a momentary breathlessness. The air in her lungs froze in panic. She bobbed back up and gasped, inhaling life back into her body and embracing the adrenaline rush.

In the neighbouring pool, her mum screamed with a blend of fright and pleasure. They clocked each other and giggled.

Charlie put her robe back on and followed her mum to a pair of pool loungers. She laid down, and every muscle relaxed against the foam. A waiter approached.

"A latte for me, please. Charlie?"

"Cucumber water, please."

"Right then. Catch me up with all this." Her mum sat up straight, clearly expecting a full debrief.

Charlie took a deep breath. It wasn't the first time she'd talked to her mum about girls. But usually, she'd throw around a name and gloss over the details. Apart from when they'd talked about Theresa, there had never been any reason to delve too far into her feelings. So she'd always managed to maintain a shield around her most vulnerable parts. But she trusted her mum more than anyone, and there was no reason to hide how she felt. "Her name is Elda. I met her on the way back from your house last time I visited."

"Really? What a coincidence. Does she live near us?"

"No. I nearly ran her over." Charlie waved her hand at her mum's gaping mouth reaction. "That bit isn't important."

"But was she hurt?"

"Bless you, Mum. No, she wasn't hurt that badly, but she did break her arm—or rather, I broke her arm, I suppose." Charlie adjusted her position on the lounger to get comfortable. "I went to see her to check she was okay. She's an artist at one of those old mill buildings by the office."

"How lovely. I would've loved to have been an artist. Or married an artist."

Charlie smiled at the tangent.

"Then what?" Her mum gripped her arm.

"I liked her. I wanted to spend time with her, which has never really happened before. Then she got offered a big job in Paris, and she's there now."

"She left you?"

"God, no. We weren't together. But we could've been, I think. It's a bit of a waste really."

A pause settled between them. Her mum held the space for Charlie to sink a bit deeper into the loss she felt.

"Oh, Charlie, I haven't seen you this sad about anyone for a long time. She must be quite special."

"She is. Who knows, maybe our paths will cross again? It just wasn't the right time for us."

"I hope so, love. Sometimes you have to fight for these things though. Have I ever told you about the time your dad travelled all the way to Edinburgh to ask me to a dance?"

"What do you mean?"

The waiter returned, and her mum held her response until he'd put their drinks on the table and left.

"I was visiting a friend for the summer holidays. We were all in our last year of university. I had my eye on your dad, but I didn't think he was interested. He played it very cool."

Charlie raised her eyebrows, surprised that her dad could ever have played it cool. He adored her mum.

"Then, I was at Joyce's for the summer and one afternoon, her mum shouted upstairs to us: 'Someone called Harry Mason is at the door for you girls.' I almost died of embarrassment. He'd travelled for hours on the train. He took me out, down the Royal Mile, and asked me if I'd go to the freshers' ball with him as a supervisor."

"That doesn't sound like much of a romantic first date. Supervising a load of freshers." Charlie's laughter rang out across the pool house.

"Well, it was a very practical first date, I'll give you that. But it was the first date of the rest of our lives." Her mum's eyes glazed over, lost in memories. "And all I'm saying is that every so often, it will take a bit of effort to find the right one. Perhaps even a journey or two to get their attention." Her mum looked pleased with herself for dishing out that piece of advice.

Charlie chugged her water. "When's lunch? Is there time for Pilates?"

"Not 'til one. We can head up to a class after my coffee if you'd like?"

Charlie laid back to inspect the wood-panelled ceiling, relieved to have shared her messy feelings about Elda with her mum. She wasn't sure she'd gained any clarity. If anything, today had so far reminded her that she had her mum's face and her dad's facade. But did she have her dad's courage to run after Elda like he had with her mum?

She shook her head at the wild thought. That sounded like a story which had grown more romantic with the passing of time. Jumping on a train to Paris and turning up at Elda's door was the last thing she'd do. She had never walked, let alone run, after anyone. Not since Theresa.

CHAPTER FIFTEEN

ELDA CONTEMPLATED A PLASTIC bag flapping in the wind like a pigeon. It reminded her of London. The air whipped at her food wrapper as she sat on the café terrace. "People think Paris is all about the high-end food. But there are more burger places here than I've ever seen," she said between mouthfuls of fries.

Sylvie, her newest friend, sat beside her and grunted in Parisian, offering no clue as to whether she agreed or not. "Beats English food though, non?"

Elda wasn't sure. Two weeks into her new job in Paris, and she was already missing beans on toast. "I guess."

"You want to go out tonight?" Sylvie pushed a wayward curl behind her ear and wiped mayonnaise from her lips.

"No, I'm going to the museum."

"D'Orsay? Again? There are a thousand art galleries in Paris, and you head for that tourist trap. What is it with you and that place?" Sylvie chuckled into her espresso.

"I like it there. It's grounding. When the sun goes down, it feels like you've got the place to yourself."

"Seriously, Elda, you've been three or four times. You must've seen every work of art on show."

"Don't knock it. I like being among the masters and their masterpieces; it's intimate. And overwhelming. It reminds me that we're all just artists in training, with our works in progress. Everyone's sketches are just that—first drafts. And I like the routine. It beats spending the evening tiptoeing around Francis's apartment." She looked across the pavement towards a woman cutting through the crowd with a folder in her arms, dressed in a classic calf-length coat. For a moment, she wanted to be that woman, striding through the capital. She rolled her eyes, realising the stranger reminded her of Charlie, and a pang of misery hit her in the ribs. "Actually, yeah. Let's go out somewhere tonight. What are you thinking?"

"To the café at the university. There is a poetry reading and my friend Alex will be there. You'll like her."

"Done." A break in her routine might be just what she needed to shake off the melancholy. Elda filled her diary to mask her loneliness. She had started teaching classes in Francis's new department, but she was spread across the faculty, and the timetable was a jumble of fine art, English and American film. Clueless, she followed the curriculum and made the students do most of the talking.

"What is it?" Sylvie looked over her sunglasses.

"I'm fretting."

"About classes? Don't take it so seriously." Sylvie huffed again and waved away Elda's worries.

"No one in Paris wants to be taught by an English teacher, Sylvie. Some of them don't care if I teach them English, even film, but art? It's like I'm a fake."

"Until they realise that you're not. That you know what you're talking about." Sylvie bit into a long, skinny French fry.

"Yeah, maybe halfway through the second term. But I'm only a fortnight in. It's painful." She slurped at her diet Coke and made Sylvie giggle in disgust.

"I bluff my way through all my seminars. Just keep going. No one cares about you."

Elda loved Sylvie's honesty. She was a brash and brutal friend, and she was authentic. Everyone else she'd met here had been presenting a palatable version of themselves. There was fashion, art, and music, but it was all a scene that Elda couldn't keep up with.

"You homesick?" Her friend prodded at her again.

"Of course. I miss everything and everyone. But I'm here now. I've made my choices."

"Life isn't binary, Elda. You don't have to abandon one thing to be another." Sylvie fiddled with a packet of Gauloises cigarettes, signalling their departure. "Why is your face screwed up?"

"I'm thinking." Elda twisted the hair at the base of her neck.

"You think too much, ma chérie." Sylvie tutted and bit down on her unlit cigarette.

The next day, Elda covered a single wall of the one-bed apartment she shared with Francis with notes and planned her lessons for the next week. She looked up at Francis, installed at his mahogany desk. His brow was furrowed, but his body was relaxed. He was drawing up proposals for a new workshop space at the university.

Elda wiped at sweat on her forehead and whispered the lecture timetable to herself, searing it to her memory. She'd been bunking on his sofa since she'd outstayed her budget at the hotel. She had struggled to find anywhere to rent with no cash up front and couldn't fathom the French guarantor system to get a place of her own yet. She'd only packed up a few clothes, her sketch pads, and painting tools. Jack was due to ship the rest over when she had somewhere more permanent.

She wished he was here with her. He'd fill her up with stories and love. But she was alone, learning to live in Francis's orbit without making too much of a mess. Elda's world had got a little bit quieter. She missed the natural pattern of a conversation with a stranger in a shop. She couldn't just switch on the TV for company anymore. She was bombarded with words she couldn't quite make out and sentences she was struggling to pull apart and put back together.

At every opportunity she played familiar songs in the flat. She tried hard to learn French, but until she was near perfect, no one in Paris would entertain her attempts. So the chances of practicing were limited to her small evening class and Sylvie, if she was in a patient mood.

Francis moved from his desk to rearrange a bookcase. "Elda,

are you nearly finished with all these stickers on the wall?" His smooth voice had an edge of impatience.

"Sorry, there's too much to do, and I just need to get my head around the lectures." Her hands swept across the landscape of little square notes. If she dipped her eyelids, they could be the pixels of an abstract painting. She ignored a growing bitterness in her mouth. A little piece of her spirit had been left in her studio back at the mill. Her creative confidence was being slowly crushed in this city, and she was questioning whether she could even paint anymore. Whether she had the right to create something here, in the same air in which great masterpieces hung on walls. She was being dramatic, and her self-talk was unkind.

But she also burned with resentment. Their lives were bobbing along to Francis's rhythm. He had become the author, editor, and publisher of their story, which had somehow become intertwined, and she was frozen with inertia. She was trapped in a job he had found for her, living in an apartment in his name.

Back home in the warehouse, when he'd described his vision for her, it had made her heart race. Now, she begrudged such power.

"Elda, we have dinner plans. What are you going to wear?"

She bit her lip. "Do we? Who with?" She placed her palm across her forehead as the notes peeled off the wall. This was the next in a line of social engagements that made her feel that she was coasting along in the sidecar of her own life.

"I told you. Monsieur Michel from the university. It's important. Please try to look nice and get yourself together."

His words were soft, but every one of them was pronounced. Elda knew by now that Francis's English was blunt, especially when he rushed. But this time, she knew he meant it. She looked across at him, at the crisp white shirt collar framing his stubbly chin. "I will." Her lip turned up in disgust, and she left an echo of footsteps behind her.

***

A week later, Elda perched on the edge of her desk at the front of the classroom, looking over the bowed heads of her students. She had led the group through their exploration of female desire in sculpture. It had been two hours of slideshows, debate, and insight which had left her exhausted and empty.

She knew the aching need she had was for Charlie. She'd been working later and later at the faculty. She'd creep back into the apartment and crawl onto the futon fully clothed, not wanting to disturb Francis and face his questions. She'd been sinking deeper into listlessness, missing Charlie's voice, her movement, the crease of her smile. She slept poorly through the night, awoken by vivid dreams. Few things brought joy. In class, her voice would shake when she delivered lessons. She was a fading copy of herself.

After dismissing the class and tidying her folders, she stepped out into the December night. Trees along the main boulevards glistened with strings of lights. She made the metro with seconds to spare and found a window seat.

Shops brimmed with treats and red ribbons hung like bunting between buildings. Rather than kindle a festive fire in her heart, it made Elda feel the void there. She yearned to be home for pub crawls with Jack, cocktails with Charlie, and Christmas dinner with her nan.

When she reached Francis's apartment building, he was standing on the front step, dressed in a dinner suit, all set to attend the gala organised for funders of the new hall. It had been etched in black permanent pen on the calendar since she'd arrived.

"Have you forgotten?" Francis asked.

"I can't make it tonight. I'm not well." Drained of energy, she couldn't face another social engagement.

"We'll be late." Francis stared at her, looking agitated.

"Go on without me." Elda's feet rooted to the spot. She wouldn't move at his command.

"I want to arrive with you," he said. "Get on with it. I won't be embarrassed by you."

His words stung. She had been vaguely playing the part of his assistant and ambiguous plus-one since she'd arrived. A part of herself had been lost in Paris, and a voice inside her head screamed at her to stop bending to his wishes. "No, Francis. Go without me. I won't be your mannequin. I will not prop up your ambition and sacrifice my own life. And I resign as your mute English assistant or whatever-the-fuck I am." Fury surged through her. "I'm going home for Christmas, where I will be bloody welcome." She needed to be home, whatever the consequence for her career.

His eyes blazed. If he tried to, he could sweep her up, dress her, and carry her to the dinner. She was exhausted and despite her momentary protest, she was a puppet, and he was more than able to pull her strings if he'd wanted to.

But he hurried down the stairs and strutted along the street towards the bright lights.

Her hands shaking, Elda checked her phone for the train times before calling Sylvie.

"Allo?"

"Can you meet me at Gare du Nord and lend me some money?" *What a loser.* But it was worth begging a few euros to get herself home and try to fix her life. Could it all unravel that easily? Saying no to Francis and walking away from the best opportunity she'd had in her whole life? She didn't want the time to overthink it. She pulled the contents of her wardrobe into a wheelie case and made her way to the Gare du Nord with her coat buttoned up, holding in her scarf and her tears. There was only one person she wanted to see. She needed the arms of someone who cared about her, just for who she was, not for dressing up and acting like someone else.

CHAPTER SIXTEEN

"THE CITY OF LOVE. It's a bit of a death knell, isn't it, Elderflower?" Jack held her gloved hand and dodged another frankfurter held aloft in the crowded Christmas market.

They were reunited, and Elda was living in Jack's spare room, trying not to think about the career-ending move she'd just made. There, she could wallow. There was no expectation other than to be with him, listen to his stories, laugh at his jokes, and make the tea when the adverts came on between episodes of a TV program.

"Have you called your mum yet?"

"Don't remind me. I'm dreading it. I can already hear the disappointment in her voice." Elda nudged him toward the mulled wine cabin. "You owe me a drink."

He didn't owe her anything, but she needed to change the subject and had no real money of her own.

As they settled into a pine booth, Jack's lips turned down and his expression grew serious. "Have you spoken to Charlie?"

Elda tipped the festive mug to her lips and scorched her tongue. "What is this? A rundown of my phone book? No, I haven't called Charlie. Not yet." Elda rubbed the rim of her mug. "Anyway, I'm not ready to see her. Maybe after Christmas, when I'm more settled. I'm a bit of a mess, aren't I?"

"She'd be the first to straighten you out, so to speak." Jack softened his smile and cupped Elda's chin. He made a fake pout, and she laughed.

"I'd rather just get through Christmas without any more drama," she said.

Jack leaned in, and his serious face returned. "I fancy a sausage.

You want one?" And he was off with a tenner in his hand.

The next day, Elda was in Jack's kitchen, covering it in flour and mincemeat.

"Why don't we have one of those cutter things?" said Jack.

"Because we're not grown-ups yet." Elda sipped a sweet drink and let the warm alcohol sting the back of her tongue. She perched on a kitchen chair, enjoying the last days of freedom and obscurity before facing life. She'd avoided her mum's calls and texted a promise to go home for Christmas Eve.

"So, are we going to talk about the C-word?"

"Carols?"

"Charlie."

"What about her?" Her nerves fluttered, but she kept her eyes on the pastry.

"The chemistry between you two." Jack smirked and flicked flour across the worktop. "I've seen you scrolling through your phone every night. When are you going to get your shit together and call her?"

"What the fuck, Jack? I'm still reeling from my career-ending flounce out of Paris. The last thing I need is more complications. And Charlie isn't into me." Elda was being dramatic. Part of her was thinking about her and Charlie together. It was the part that helped her drift off to sleep every night.

"Keep kidding yourself. You live for complication, and Charlie would love to see you. You just can't swallow your pride and make the first move."

"Really? You think so?"

"I know you. And I can see through Charlie's tough exterior. She's gagging for it."

"Jack!" Elda threw a pastry star in his direction, and they both laughed.

Re-runs of *Victoria Wood: As Seen on TV* nattered in the background, and when the time came, they were in two minds about leaving the house for the frosty walk to the carol service. Full of pastry and warmed through with brandy, they jogged across the main road arm-in-arm, said a cheerful Merry Christmas to someone on the door, and crossed the threshold of the imposing brick building.

Apart from as a tourist, Elda hadn't been to church for years, but she and Jack still knew the words by heart from school. It was like muscle memory springing back as they opened their mouths and responded in the gaps that Father John left for the congregation.

Elda scanned the room. It was a modern building by church standards. Its rows of wooden pews were packed. There was a functional ugliness about the whole place, but in the flickering glow of candlelight, it was charming. A giant crucifix was suspended above them. Elda was impressed. Rigging like that wasn't cheap.

Coming to church reminded her of home and family. It stirred memories deep inside of being with her grandmother. It was joyful to remember being so cared for, and she began to regret staying away from home for so long. It also made her think of what could have been if her family had stayed intact. If her father had been with them, would her mum have become so unhappy?

As the chords of the organ started up and voices lifted to the tune, tears filled her eyes. She could feel those who had loved her and their loss. She grieved the future that she feared she might never have. Jack took her hand. There was silence between them, but she knew he felt her pain. He carefully wrapped his scarf around both of their wrists, and with a single body part cocooned in warmth, softness, and the touch of her best friend, she felt better already.

***

Elda lifted her hot tea and blew ripples across the scorching surface, while scanning the paper for job listings. She doodled at the edges of the adverts, creating shapes that might become future paintings. It was a dead time for job hunting, and she was dipping further into her overdraft. She'd never been flush with cash. Her mum had raised her with nothing to spare. As part-time artist and full-time office worker, she'd scraped by. But now, she was living off prayers and generosity.

"Anything?" Jack asked as he came in the front door.

"Not really."

He bumped through the hallway balancing a twenty-four pack of beer and two bottles of white wine.

"I'd do anything just to get my foot in the door."

"Well, I've got just the thing to take your mind off it all. It's office party time. We've decked out the boardroom and a few of us are chipping in for pizzas. There's some of the old crowd there and neighbours too. Get your glad rags on, girl. It's a cheap night out."

"I don't know. I've had enough of being paraded around parties feeling like a spare part."

"Hey, I'm no Francis." He put his hands on his hips and arched his eyebrow before he smiled gently. "There's no pressure here, my love, other than to be yourself, drink some wine, and relax."

Jack bounced with excitement, and she raised her eyebrows, matching his grin. She couldn't resist him. Within twenty minutes, she'd tried on every outfit combination from her suitcase and was red-faced from the effort. Finally, in a half-arsed attempt to look snowy, she pulled on a white jumper over a pair of jeans. "How's this?" She ventured onto the landing, and Jack looked up to her with a fondness that made her feel loved.

"Casual, wintry chic. Perfect. Just don't drop pizza on that top; it'll be a bugger to clean."

She descended the stairs and Jack draped her winter coat around her shoulders.

"You're a true gentleman." She laughed over her shoulder, already feeling more relaxed about seeing new people.

At the bus stop around the corner, Elda dug into her pocket and produced a dry old lipstick. Peering into the plastic glazing, she tried to apply it.

Jack rubbed her cheek. "You look the part."

She was glad to be back and grateful to be welcomed home by her best friend. But there was an emptiness growing, and she was terrified of not knowing what to do next. She'd upended life to work with Francis and then bolted back to where there was virtually nothing left of her old self. Now she had to pull herself and her life back together. Jack was right; she needed to call Charlie. She was the reason she'd come home, after all. The thought of explaining herself made her feel sick. Elda didn't know where to start, but she knew one thing: Charlie had been the cause of every sleepless night she'd had since leaving for Paris.

CHAPTER SEVENTEEN

CHARLIE LOOSENED HER GRIP on Joshua's shoulder and the fizz bubbled through her. She grabbed another glass from a passing tray and tried to focus on the suit in front of her.

"And then, we struck gold," the man said.

Charlie shrugged and turned to face the crowded room. She squinted, turning glittering dresses into disco balls, and ran her hand through her hair. *How can I get out of this?*

"All right, miss?" Joshua asked as he guided her away from the corporate lawyers she'd been stuck with. "There's an after-party upstairs if you want to escape. Someone Nia knows in the offices."

"Will there be booze?"

"I expect so. Pizza and beers, or something like that."

"Yes. A million times, yes. If I have to listen to another old white man talking about money, I'm going to be sick."

Joshua chuckled and grabbed their coats from the cloakroom.

"Are we overdressed?" Charlie looked down at her tailored trousers and silk shirt. She fingered the knot around her neck and scanned the sea of cocktail dresses.

"Do we care, boss?" Joshua hooked his thick arm through hers and led her through the revolving doors to a three-storey atrium.

They got into an elevator, and Charlie breathed on the glass walls and drew a Christmas tree with her finger. "And relax," she said, closing her eyes against the fluorescent lamps above their heads. She couldn't wait to kick off her boots and down a cold beer.

When they reached the third floor, a dance soundtrack pumped out of the offices, and she smiled at the rowdy voices and unbuckled laughter. They tumbled, arm-in-arm into a steel and concrete foyer. Joshua took her coat and left her for a moment, and she walked towards a glass wall. There were three or four rooms, usually the scene of serious business. Tonight, the office chairs were strewn with half-naked upper limbs, and tabletops were covered with redundant beer bongs and greasy pizza boxes.

Charlie wandered through a corridor, observing the scene like an urban still life. Her edges were fuzzy from no food and plenty of champagne. Her head throbbed, and she forced another breath from deep in her lungs, feeling her shoulders relax as she shook off the binds of corporate entertaining.

Charlie caught sight of a familiar figure nestled on a sofa at the edge of the main conference room, her head tipped back, laughing. Charlie remained motionless as delight surged through her and heat crept across her neck.

She met Elda's eyes, marched across the carpet, and pulled her into her arms. It was like a second hadn't passed between them. "Wow, look at you," Charlie said with uncensored volume. "When did you get here? Are you back for Christmas?"

"I'm back," Elda said, "forever."

They locked eyes as Charlie tried to understand what was happening, and Elda looked like she was trying to explain everything without speaking. They burst into laughter, and Charlie's cheeks stretched in a smile that mirrored Elda's. "What now?" Charlie hadn't planned any further than midnight, but she saw a whole new path stretch out before her.

"Drink?" Elda held out her hand, and Charlie followed her to the makeshift bar in the corner.

Hours passed, and Joshua had long since escaped. Jack scraped plastic cups and cold crusts into a black bag. The turntables had been taken over by two apprentices, and they were entertaining dwindling numbers on a dance floor that had no distinguishing features from the rest of the carpet tiles.

A pile of coats, thrown over a couple of office chairs, was fast diminishing, and mismatched folk were snaking away, arm-in-arm, their loud singing voices fading.

Elda had draped her legs over Charlie on the blue oversized sofa in reception. They'd fashioned a couple of cushions earlier with some jackets and had sunk down together.

"Didn't Francis try to stop you?" Charlie screwed her eyes up as thoughts darted around her head. It had taken a couple of hours to dissect the last couple of weeks, but Charlie kept asking the same question in different ways.

"No. I think he knew that we weren't really there for the same reasons, and I was beginning to feel like a spare part."

Elda pulled at the soft hairs at the back of her neck and Charlie had to sit on her hands, so she didn't reach out and join her.

"I was an accessory in his very busy schedule. I'd uprooted my life to chase a fantasy. It was all a bit pointless." Elda rubbed her arms as if she was giving herself a hug. "I'm sorry I didn't call you sooner."

"Why didn't you? I'd have come straight round." Charlie sipped at her beer, wanting to know why Elda hadn't come running back to her. But she was paralysed with fear. She didn't want to know that Elda hadn't thought of Charlie as regularly as she had.

"I wanted to get myself together before I saw you." Her cheeks reddened. "I didn't want you to see me like this."

"Like what?" Charlie screwed up her nose.

"I just don't want to come across as a bit of a loser. You have your shit together, and I clearly don't." She shook her head, and a shadow of regret passed across her face. "I just want to find a job and get back on track. I feel like the last few weeks have been a complete waste of time and money."

"You haven't failed at anything." She tried to cut through Elda's self-doubt. "This isn't a project that you had to keep on track at all costs. This is just life throwing things at you. You don't have to be perfect at everything." Charlie held the warmth of Elda's knees on her lap and rubbed her legs through the denim. "I'm glad you're back."

Elda looked up and sighed. Charlie thought she'd made it up, but there it was, the connection between them. She willed herself not to look away first but didn't trust her body not to melt into Elda's arms. She turned her head just as Elda's intense gaze became too much to bear.

***

By Monday, the hangover was wearing off. Charlie leaned into her swivel chair and took her feet off the ground. She shivered. It was an old building, with heat escaping from every crevice and crack. Nothing about it flowed, and the rooms were all shapes and sizes. Her office was at the end of a corridor, with a tall window looking out towards the city. Elda's old mill building was in her eye line every time she scanned the horizon. It was a constant reminder of the gaping hole she was trying to fill with work.

Charlie surveyed her office. She had stepped into the shoes of a retired old guy, but she'd been busy filling those shoes. She stroked the curves of her oak desk. Her closed laptop sat on top, dwarfed by a tower of loose papers. Against her desk leaned a dusty yoga mat and a skinny roll of Christmas paper. Both were frayed at the edges. She'd been distracted by Elda these past few months and let her routine suffer.

She reached for the photo of her with Theresa in her arms and smiled at the memory. That had been a day of discovering new places and new feelings. She stroked the flat image of Theresa and remembered the sun on her hair and face, catching on her eyebrow piercing. Charlie's heart still ached with loss when she thought about how much she loved her, even now, seventeen years later.

Charlie's gaze rested on the black suit hanging on her office door, and she pushed away the memory. She had to get on with what was right in front of her. She shuffled beneath her desk to find a pair of heels for court. After slipping them on, she stood and checked herself.

She forced her top drawer open and reached for her diary. Pages were folded over and scribbled on. She was ordered and disciplined with her schedule, but along the margins she wrote things to remember from her day, ambiguous case notes, and reminders. On several pages she'd underlined the words "CALL ELDA."

There was a knock, and Joshua came in.

"Miss. You ready for court? Should be a quick one."

"Done in time for turkey?" Charlie asked.

"Not that quick, miss." Joshua retreated, leaving her with her own thoughts again.

Charlie slowed down and took a moment. She closed her eyes and basked in the memories of Friday night with Elda. She'd been given the chance to tell Elda how she really felt. But it was all too much of a risk. Their unexpected time together at the Christmas party had reminded her just how much of a wonderful friend Elda was, and she was desperate for her to stick around this time. If that meant putting aside her aching need for more, then that's what she'd do. She was used to putting up barriers and blocking emotions. She'd just have to channel her inner barrister. She picked up the phone and dialled Elda's number.

"Hey you," Elda said.

Charlie's insides melted. It was going to be tough not letting her feelings get the better of her. "Hi. Listen, I haven't got long, but I just wanted to ask you..." Charlie struggled to find the right words. "I'm house-sitting for a friend the weekend after New Year. Well, I'm looking after her cats while she's away. She's got a house in the countryside. It's a lovely spot up north. Do you fancy keeping me company?"

The silence was brief but enough for Charlie to doubt herself three times over.

"Will there be a roaring fire and leftover mince pies?"

"I can arrange that, if you wish."

"Sold. I'd love to spend the weekend house-sitting, stroking cats, and keeping you company."

"Great. Good. I'm off to court. I'll text you the details and pick you up next Friday afternoon. You'll need—"

"A toothbrush and pyjamas?" Elda giggled.

"A proper coat and boots." Charlie smirked. "Have a great Christmas, Elda."

"You too. See you very soon."

With the air cooling around her, she promised herself one thing. She wasn't going to spoil everything and scare Elda off. She was back, and that's all that mattered. If that meant they stayed in the friend zone, then that was fine. Charlie could definitely use a good friend.

CHAPTER EIGHTEEN

On Christmas Eve, Elda borrowed Jack's Mini and headed south towards her rural hometown. It wasn't far, but Elda, as usual, dreaded turning the key to her childhood home.

She took a left into a horseshoe-shaped crescent of identical houses and parked in the short drive which had been carved from her tiny garden. There were fairy lights thrown around the blue door and a little sign imploring Santa to stop. She smiled to herself. Santa hadn't stopped there for a while.

She knocked, crossed the threshold, and gathered her nerves.

"Elda, is that you? Come in, I've got your nan in my arms," her mum shouted from the living room.

Elda set down her bags and slipped off her shoes and coat. By the time she entered the living room, her mum had settled her nan in the armchair. Her mum was shorter than Elda and slim from not eating and smoking too much. She had cut her brown hair short when Elda was a teenager, and it looked greasy from at least a week between washes. Her baby-blue jumper was from the Boxing Day sales more than a decade ago. Everything was a bit tired; tempers weren't the only things fraying.

"You look tiny. What have you been eating? Nothing by the looks of it." Her mum turned her nose up at Elda's waist.

"Mum, I'm exactly the same."

"Yeah, well, you don't look it to me. Does she?" She shot a look towards Elda's grandmother. Her brow was furrowed as if she was trying to work something out.

Her nan swallowed back tears. Elda kissed her cheek and squeezed her bony shoulders. She was shrinking. "I'm sorry I've left it so long to come home."

"Don't you apologise, lady. You live your life." She patted Elda's hand.

Her hair stood on end, with whispering white strands just a couple of inches long. Her face was wrinkled in all the right places, and beneath its age was an unforgotten beauty and grace. She looked like she'd been smiling at people her whole life.

Elda walked into the kitchen and flicked on the kettle. Her eyes scanned the ceiling and saw the bottles forgotten on top of the cupboards. Coming home was hard. There was hope, but it soon faded with impatience. There were endless questions to answer and expectations to set straight.

As she sat with her family to enjoy cold meats, pork pie, and oven-warmed rolls, Elda skimmed through the chronology of the last few months and tried to sound as buoyant as she could about her current situation.

"Life isn't always as you expect it to be, Elda. There's nothing to be ashamed of in that." The lines on her grandmother's cheeks scrunched together as she smiled.

"You need to sort yourself out." Her mother's face was screwed up, like her onion was too pickled. "Whether that's a decent job or a decent bloke. Or woman, I don't care. I'm not saying settle down and get married. I'm as feminist as the next woman in the queue. But you've got to have one or the other, don't you? Otherwise, you can't take care of yourself."

Elda looked down at the roll of ham on her plate, her mum's words gnawing at her.

Her mum chugged a can of beer. "What gets me this time, Elda, is that you had a nice flat and a good job, and you left it all for a couple of weeks pissing about in Paris."

Bang. Elda had been waiting for her mother's killer blow since she arrived. She knew how to take a tiny flaw and blow it up to the size of a gaping hole. "Is that what you think I was doing? I was trying to build a career. I was trying to be an artist and an academic, stringing conversations together in French at fancy parties. I was trying to be as beautiful and creative as everyone else. And become a bloody bilingual art teacher." Her hands shook. Her mum had poked a sharp stick at every single vulnerability that Elda had packed in her mind when she'd jumped back on the Eurostar.

"Girls, don't do this." Her grandmother slapped her hand on the table. "Every time, there's something. Now, just sit and enjoy your food together like a nice, normal family."

Elda obeyed with a raised eyebrow. Even her grandmother couldn't temper the fury that her mum unleashed when the mood took her.

"This is what families do. They tell hard truths about what's going wrong in their lives. Elda has had it all on a plate and is throwing it away again," her mum said, barely taking a breath. "Some of us have had to go through life on our own, without decent fellas falling at our feet. Think yourself bloody lucky, girl."

Elda had no intention of rising to her mother's bait. She'd seen this pattern of self-loathing play out before. Her mum had to do it on her own. Elda had spoiled it all. She took a deep breath and summoned her self-control, flexing each muscle from her calves to her shoulders to remind herself that she was in control of her mind and her body. "I'm sorry, Mum. I'm gutted too. Life isn't exactly going as I had it in my head, but I just need a breath to sort myself out. I'm staying with Jack, and I've got some job applications lined up. Give me a few weeks, and we'll all be laughing."

"You know your cousin Clare is getting married next year? Ben proposed on Christmas Eve down the pub. Your Aunty Sheila said it was marvellous. They all had a meal afterwards, and Ben's parents paid for the whole lot." Her mum cut through a pork pie and pasted it with brown sauce. "Clare knew about it before, mind. They'd talked about it and planned a nice engagement."

Elda's teeth clamped down on the processed meat in her mouth. She mumbled in the right places until the meal was over, then she rose to scrape away the waste and wrap up the leftovers.

She hoped that the battle was over for now, and that she could sit in peace in front of the TV for a couple of hours.

While her hands were busy, her mind drifted to Charlie. She imagined waking up on Christmas Day together, lying on the sofa, legs intertwined, feeding her After Eight mints. She remembered the feel of Charlie's body beneath her legs at the office party, and how she'd had to fight the instinct to lean into her. She had missed every part of her while she was in Paris.

Elda walked back into the living room, drying her hands with a tea towel. Her nan looked across from her upright chair as the front door slammed.

"Where's Mum gone?"

"She'll be off to the club. Her friends will be having a Christmas drink, no doubt. She can't stay in the house for very long, Elda. She gets too twitchy with everything."

"Is she still knocking about with that guy?"

"Rob? I think so, but she doesn't say. She's got worse over the last few months. Very up and down. She spends a lot of time down the club or in her room."

"It must be like living with a teenager." Elda sighed. She wished for more.

"Well, you weren't like it, my lovely."

Her nan smiled, but Elda saw through it. Her mum was draining to be around.

"She's always struggled. You know how she is. I'm lucky to have her close, where I can keep my eye on her."

Elda saw a version of her life without her grandmother in it, and she shook the thought away. "She's fifty now, Nan. She's old enough to act like a grown-up around both of us."

"She gets overwhelmed, though. It's always been the same. Life is too much for her sometimes. Like her father. Let's be thankful she's with us."

Elda's grandfather had bolted from the family home when her mum was a toddler. Her nan never knew where he'd gone, or if he was still alive. She just got on with raising her daughter and then her granddaughter.

"Why does she always have to bugger off down the club though, Nan? She'll come back steaming, and we'll have to pick up the pieces." Elda had never been enough to keep her mum sober and at home.

"It's not all bad, love." Her nan inspected the carpet. The guilt she bore on behalf of Elda's mum wasn't fair. "Tell me, how're you feeling?" She touched Elda's hand.

"I'm tired. I feel like a failure. I want everything to stop for a bit, so I can work out what I'm doing with my life." Elda's words caught in her throat, and she put her hand to her chest. "I'll be okay. I just need a bit of time out." She wanted to spare her grandmother from the worry.

"Elda, I need to tell you something." Her voice was low. "I'm not feeling well. It's been coming on for a while, and the doctors aren't sure what's going on."

Elda sat still for a few seconds. There was a knocking in her ear, and she clenched her teeth. No. She couldn't handle anything happening to her nan. "What have they said? Is this the GP?"

"Well, I've seen the doctor. He's been helpful, and I've had a few tests at the hospital. I just wanted you to know. Your mum won't tell you because she's frightened and not sure what to do. She'll need you if I'm poorly."

"I can't handle Mum like you can." Elda rose and paced around the room. The thought of managing her mum's erratic behaviour on her own filled her with panic.

"You can. She'll calm down, anyway. When there isn't an audience for it all, she's much calmer, and she drinks less."

Elda knelt at her grandmother's feet and put her head on her lap. Inside, she shrunk to her eleven-year-old self.

"I don't want you to worry, love." She stroked Elda's hair. "You'll be okay. I'm not going anywhere for a while anyway."

The words kicked Elda right in the ribs. People she loved

wouldn't live forever. But she was terrified of this change and what it would bring for her and her family. Her nan was their leader. She was Elda's protector. She was the glue that held everything together. Without her, the future was unthinkable.

Elda wished she hadn't come home. She should've stayed at Jack's where no one could tell her that her nan was poorly, and where she could've been spared the annual reminder that her mum was a selfish drunk. She wished she could climb under the pile of coats at Jack's office party and curl up with Charlie. Together, they could block out the rest of the world.

CHAPTER NINETEEN

CHARLIE CRUNCHED HER BOOTS against the leaves. A veil of frost covered the hard ground. Despite the orange glow of the winter sun breaking through the blue sky, her breath clouds gathered in the air. The walk was familiar. She had looked after her colleague's cats for the past three years. She loved to escape after the busyness of Christmas week to their country house. She could decompress and plan for the year ahead.

This year, there was no such clarity. Charlie glanced towards Elda, her cheeks peeking out from her scarf as they stomped through a sloping field to pick up a footpath. "You made any resolutions this year?"

Elda pulled her scarf up towards her ears. "Maybe start with a decent job." Her face flushed.

"You have a job. When do you start?" Charlie pulled Elda closer to avoid a foot-sized hole.

"It's only a temp job. I start on Tuesday. I'm not looking forward to it, but I need the money, and I've got to get out of the house. I'm doing Jack's head in."

"It'll be great. The teaching will be loads easier than back in France, and they might even give you a classroom or somewhere to paint."

"Maybe, but I'm not holding my breath."

"Once you're in, you'll wow them, and they won't want to let you go." Charlie gritted her teeth. *Too much. Chill out.*

Elda and Charlie had been talking on the phone most nights since the Christmas party. It hadn't taken long to fall in sync, speaking in half sentences and filling the gaps. She'd invited Elda for the weekend away in a moment of impulse but hadn't thought through how nervous she'd be with her in touching distance again.

"Thanks for bringing me out here. A break from the city is just what I needed," said Elda.

"You're doing me a favour. The cats are great company, but I don't want to house sit alone. It's a bit spooky out here on your own."

"Big, strong Charlie, scared of the dark? I find that hard to believe." Elda gave Charlie's bicep a quick squeeze through her jacket. "It's perfect, and it's a chance for us to catch up properly." Elda took a deep breath. "God, it's so peaceful out here. Look at us." She scooped up Charlie's arm and pulled her close.

Blood rushed to Charlie's cheeks, and she drew her arm away. She couldn't handle more physical contact than was absolutely necessary. They walked and talked for another mile before Charlie pointed to a stile in the woods, and they went to climb it. Charlie held Elda's gloved hand, taking her weight as she leaned in. She licked her lips, the ice-cold air stinging her skin.

She dusted off and steadied her breath, then they marched on a few hundred yards down a gravel track to a country pub.

"Is it closed?" Elda stood back from the faded sign, rubbing her hands together.

"There's smoke coming from the chimney." Charlie tried the door, and it creaked open.

They shuffled inside, and Charlie stripped off her layers of coat and jumper to bathe in the heat of the roaring fire. The smell of burning wood and stale beer filled the small room.

The bar stood at the back, nothing more than a wide shelf and two brass pumps. Half a dozen or so tables were dotted around. It was a homely place, empty except for a couple of old guys chatting over their tankards.

Charlie ordered while Elda chose a fireside table. Settled with two amber-coloured beers, Charlie rubbed at her stinging cheeks, and she wriggled her fingers to draw the blood back to the tips.

"How have you been feeling this week?" Charlie bounced her knee with nerves.

"I've blocked out my mum's Christmas meltdown, so I'm not too bad, all things considered." Elda's face softened, and she smiled and tilted her head. "I'm better now, here with you."

Charlie's back stiffened, and her stomach flipped. She remembered this feeling from before and tried to think of something else. "I'm glad. Nice beer too." She forced a smile. "Your mum must be worried about you. My mum frets about me too. It just comes out in a weird way."

"I don't know. It doesn't feel like worry. More like disappointment. She has a view of me that I'm not quite living up to." Elda closed her eyes.

Charlie stayed silent. Half of her wanted Elda to open up in the space she left, while the other half wrestled with what to say.

"She's always acted as though she has something to prove, you know? She raised me on her own, and if I'm successful, she's validated. It's not even about me being happy, just her being able to feel better about being a bit of a crap mum."

Charlie scratched her palm. It had been a long time since she cared about how anyone was really feeling. She wanted to say the right thing but couldn't find the words.

"She didn't even raise me anyway. It was all my nan after my dad left," Elda said.

"Your mum sounds angry with the world. I'm sorry you're having to deal with it." Charlie reached for Elda's hand but stopped herself. *The last thing she needs is more complications. She just needs a friend.*

Charlie steered the conversation away from family drama and they swapped stories, chatting easily over their cold beer and warm pies. Elda shared her hopes and fears for the next few months. Charlie drank in her passion and trepidation.

Time flew by, and she didn't notice the sun setting behind them until they stood to make their way to their home for the weekend.

The country house sat on a sharp bend along a single-track road. The corner bricks were painted bright white as a warning to oncoming drivers on the blind corner. At the back, it extended into the countryside, with rolling fields on both sides and views towards the hills. In the dark, Charlie could only see the twinkling of the neighbours' lights in the distant village. She pinched herself. This place was pretty good most years but with Elda's company, it would be near perfect.

They stripped off their coats and jumpers in the stone porch, with Elda hopping on one leg while Charlie helped pull her boots. Two cats squawked their greetings.

"I know, I know. You haven't eaten for hours." Charlie put the kettle on and set about feeding her furry friends.

"Shit, my feet are killing me," Elda said.

"Bathroom's at the top of the stairs. Help yourself. I'll get the kettle on."

Elda headed upstairs, and Charlie heard the bathroom door shut before the low growl of the boiler kicked in. She opened drawers and rustled through cupboards to see if she could conjure up a meal later. She had to keep herself busy. It was a bit much knowing Elda was undressing with just a ceiling between them.

She smiled as a cloud of steam emerged from the kettle. There was a familiarity about this scene from her daydreams. She blinked away the feeling and poured the hot water into the heavy-bottomed mugs to make tea. She climbed the stairs and hesitated outside the bathroom. "Your tea is ready when you are. I'll pop it in the guest room," Charlie said, shuffling from one foot to another on the soft carpet.

"Bring it in for me, Charlie. It'll be cold by the time I'm out."

Charlie looked up at the ceiling and clamped her jaw tight. She thought about the boundaries she had set herself. *I'm in control.* She opened the door, set the tea on the edge of the bath, and turned to make a swift exit.

"Sit and talk to me," Elda said, as if nothing was amiss.

Charlie forced herself into the chair in the corner. Elda was covered in bubbles and just her head and knees were visible above the surface of the water. Her hair was dripping wet and scraped back from her forehead, and her skin glistened with water and heat.

Charlie tried to ease her back into the chair, but nothing about this situation was relaxing. "I was thinking about going to Denmark this summer. A cabin on the beach, maybe." Her skin was crawling, and she didn't know where to rest her eyes. There were mirrors and reflective glass everywhere. "Someone at work mentioned it. They go every year with their family." Charlie was spiralling, and she had no idea what to say next. She stared at the bath. It stood on elaborate legs in the middle of the room, deep purple on the outside. It was luxury that neither of them were used to.

"That would be cool. Just you and me on the beach. You could read, and I could paint."

Charlie's stomach lurched at the assumption Elda would join her. A secluded cabin for two in the Danish rushes would be heaven. "What are you working on?" Charlie had been waiting for a moment to probe Elda about her art.

"I'm not. Not since before Paris. There hasn't been the space." Elda closed her eyes, and her tone flattened. "I haven't had anything in me."

"Sorry. I shouldn't have brought it up." Charlie's gaze fell onto Elda's arms and moved up to her face. Her breath came faster, and she blushed as her heart raced.

"No, it's not you. It's just everything. But this has been a lovely day. Thank you."

Elda drew her knees out of the water and dipped her head under. Her movement revealed the outline of her breasts. It was too much. Charlie stood up and busied herself smoothing out the thick bath sheet. "Don't let your tea go cold. I'll go and start the fire." She pulled the door behind her and screwed her eyes shut. Her hands rose to her temples in an attempt to rub away the last few seconds. She gripped the rail on the way down the stone staircase, desperate to regain some control.

The heavy door to the living room was ajar, and she flicked the two light switches. The room was bathed in a warm light and for a moment, Charlie wanted to disappear into one of the giant sofas. Her head swam. She had played many versions of this evening through her mind, but she had pushed all hope of anything more than friendship with Elda from her mind when she left for Paris. When Elda chose Francis and her new job, Charlie had shut her feelings down. She'd got on with work and focussed on her career, even if it made her world a bit empty. But now Elda was back, everything had changed. Feelings had stirred in Charlie, and she was terrified of her own instincts.

Her breath was ragged, and she blew out a thin stream, trying to slow her heart rate. She began to dust the remains of last night's embers. She tied newspaper into loose knots and stacked a pyramid of kindling and logs. It took three strikes to make a flame, and her shaking hand moved towards the firelighters she had buried.

The flames burst to life, and she was hypnotised by its power. There was nothing, and then there was everything. She closed her eyes, overwhelmed by unresolved feelings. She had buried them all so deep, she'd hoped they were gone.

Elda's shadow filled the doorway. She'd changed into a pair of pyjamas and Charlie's dressing gown. The ease with which Elda moved in Charlie's space made it even harder for Charlie to keep her distance. "Elda, I need to talk to you. There's something going on here that I can't really explain. Since you came back, I've been a bit all over the place, and I've got to the point where it's all or nothing." She froze. She wasn't sure whether she could be this honest.

Charlie tried to work through all the possible ways this evening could end. She had visions of Elda storming back upstairs and gathering her things. Charlie would cry, and then she'd go back to work on Monday and get over it. Or Elda would understand how she was feeling. Maybe they could talk about it. Perhaps being honest would strengthen their friendship.

Charlie held her breath, and the pulse in her temple grew thunderous. Paralysed with fear, she could no longer bury her feelings. She wanted to hold Elda, strip away all her insecurities. Charlie wanted to kiss her and touch her skin. To touch every part of her. Elda had woken a hunger for connection that Charlie had long since put to bed.

"Hey, take a breath." Elda touched her hand.

Charlie took a lungful of air and pushed out her chest. When she exhaled, her words tumbled out. "I feel sick when I'm not with you. I walk around, thinking about you. I don't know when it started, but I've been like this for a long time. And I've tried to be friends. I even let you go to another country without saying anything. But I can't do it anymore."

Elda took Charlie's hands and looked up into her face. Her eyes were soft. "Don't." She put two fingers to Charlie's lips.

Charlie's shoulders sank. She'd said too much and ruined their friendship.

"Charlie, I've wanted you since that first day you came to my studio. I tried hard not to, and for a little while, I abandoned you for work. But I want you too." Elda wrapped her hand around Charlie's neck and their lips met.

It was gentle, barely there. Charlie drew back. She cradled Elda's cheeks with her palms. They stood still for a few moments, their breaths shallow and rapid. "Really?"

"Really." Elda's voice was low and certain.

She drew Charlie back into the kiss. It lingered and their breasts came together. It was harder this time, desire rising through Charlie's pelvis. She steadied herself, pushed away the dressing gown from Elda's shoulders and exhaled at the beauty of her bare neck.

Usually, Charlie would be half-naked by now and calling the

shots. But this was different; she wanted to take in every moment of Elda. She took a half-step back and traced the fabric of Elda's pyjamas. She pulled at the thin layer of cotton separating her from the body she was so hungry for.

Elda came closer and kissed behind Charlie's ear. It was like a nerve had been switched on between her neck and her groin. Everything was alive. Charlie slipped her hand beneath the fabric and drew their lips together. Elda unbuttoned her pyjama top. Charlie kept kissing her, breaking away to sigh at Elda's body in the firelight. She cupped Elda's breasts then took a nipple in her mouth.

Elda gasped and tipped her head back, and Charlie's thighs quivered. She was so wet and aching, it was almost painful.

She pushed Elda's pyjamas down to the floor and guided them both to the sofa. After laying Elda down, she stepped out of her own jeans and pulled off her T-shirt. When their bodies reconnected, Charlie straddled Elda, and her skin was on fire. Every touch sent waves of pleasure through her muscles. This was like nothing she'd ever experienced with anyone.

"You still have too many clothes on," Elda said, kissing behind Charlie's ear and pulling her bra over her head.

Charlie's naked breasts touched Elda's, and she thought she might come just like that. But Elda's fingers were at the back of her thigh, reaching under the edge of her underwear, discovering how wet and ready she was.

"You feel amazing," Elda said, as she drew her finger over Charlie's centre.

"I want you inside me." Charlie craved Elda's body. Every nerve stood on end, expectant.

Elda pushed away Charlie's boxers and filled her with two fingers. She rose and fell slowly, first kissing Elda and then stretching up to nudge her nipple between Elda's welcoming lips.

Elda used her thumb to reach Charlie's clit and brushed it lightly and then more firmly.

It was too much. Charlie pushed her hips against Elda's hands, weak and unable to control her impulses. She dipped her head and took Elda's lips in her mouth, desperate to kiss her. Their eyes met, and Elda smiled and quickened the pace of her touch.

Charlie grabbed the back of the sofa and rode through her climax. She came with Elda clamping her breast, her fingers curling inside her, and her thumb at her centre. It was everything. Elda slowed down, took Charlie's face in her hands, and eased her fingers through her tangled hair.

Exhausted, Charlie moved back to study Elda's face. "Here you are." Charlie smiled and touched Elda's earlobe.

"Here I am," Elda whispered.

The ecstasy and fear took a sudden hold and threatened her. She knew how losing her person could leave her hollow and broken. Now she'd found Elda and opened herself up, she was shaken by how much more she could lose.

CHAPTER TWENTY

ELDA WOKE UP WITH the warmth of Charlie's body against her. She replayed last night, and a heat rose up through her legs to her cheeks. She had imagined touching Charlie for weeks. She leaned back into the bed and took in what was in front of her. Her fantasy was beneath her hands as she stroked Charlie's spine and lower back. She swallowed, wrapping her mind around what had happened. She'd lost all control in Charlie's arms.

Her breath was shallow as she kissed Charlie's hairline. There would be time to rationalise all of this, but for now, her body was in charge. Elda already knew her way across Charlie's skin. She traced the contours of her ribs and breasts and pulled her into a close embrace.

Charlie stirred under her fingertips. She sighed and turned to face Elda. In the winter dawn, they looked at each other without speaking, knowing so deeply that no words were needed. Elda gave in. Her body had been holding back so much. Every time she had given herself to someone else, she hadn't even known that she was only half there.

Here, she let her whole self be seen and touched. She opened her eyes as Charlie kissed her neck and pressed her lips over her chest and stomach. Heat rose inside her, almost too much to bear.

She rested. Safe in Charlie's arms, allowing her thoughts to drift.

"Are you okay?" Charlie asked.

Elda raised her sleepy eyelids and smiled her affirmation. "I'm more than okay."

Their bodies merged into each other, and Elda closed her eyes and followed the rise and fall of Charlie's breathing.

Everything was still. Elda had slept through the afternoon, and dusk was leeching into the house. She rubbed her eyes and parted her lips to speak.

"I'm sorry, did I wake you?" Charlie asked. She sat, fully clothed, at the end of the bed.

"Are you just sitting there, watching me sleep?"

"Maybe." She crawled across the bed, cupped Elda's cheeks with both hands, and caressed her lips with her thumb.

Elda's heart stretched, and she held on tight.

"I'm so glad you're here," Charlie said.

"I came back for *you*. I should never have gone to Paris."

"Don't." Charlie brought her hand to Elda's lips. "I pushed you. We both thought it was the right thing to do."

Elda pulled Charlie towards her, kissing her softly at first, then harder, as she caressed her neck.

"Come with me." Charlie pulled her to her feet. "You'll need this." She handed her a dressing gown.

Confused, Elda reached the back door and stepped into the cool evening. She wrapped the fleece around her for protection against the elements. "Where are we going? It's freezing out here."

Charlie led her around the back of the house towards a cabin. It was hidden from the main road, with its own uninterrupted view of the villages below. Underneath the cabin's outdoor canopy sat a steaming hot tub, spitting foamy bubbles into the night.

"Nice touch. Very romantic." Elda shivered through her grin. It was idyllic. She'd never felt so special.

Charlie placed a glass of champagne in her hand. "Get in before you get too cold. I've had the log burner on for a few hours, so it should be toasty."

Elda shrugged off her robe, and the icy breeze made her breath stutter. As she stepped into the water, its contrast ignited her skin. She sunk beneath the surface, and the water warmed her. As Charlie stripped and climbed in opposite, moonlight caught the contours of her face. Her grace brought tears to Elda's eyes, and she had to look away.

The night was all theirs. Nothing moved around them except for the water holding their naked bodies. "This is beautiful." Elda breathed in the scent of winter, trying to commit it all to memory. "Thank you."

Elda crossed the jacuzzi and straddled Charlie's naked lap, relishing the contact of her skin in the scorching water. "I've dreamed of being this close to you," she said, nudging at the soft skin behind Charlie's ear.

"Me too. It's something I've had to get my head around."

"Why?" Elda laid back in the water, and her breasts rose above the surface to meet the icy air.

"Because I don't do relationships, or feelings. You know this." Charlie laughed, but it didn't conceal her unease.

"Is that what we're doing? Feelings? Relationships?" Elda held her gaze, begging Charlie to yield to her infatuation.

"We're definitely doing something, and I'd like to do it repeatedly for the rest of the weekend." Charlie put her hands at Elda's back and drew her back to her chest, and their lips met for a greedy kiss. "At least."

***

They played house for three more days, taking turns to cook and tidy. Being together in their borrowed bubble made sense. Elda laid back in Charlie's lap, suspending reality until the very last moment. "What happens when we get home?" Elda sat up, trying to keep her voice airy. She was terrified that this would burst around her.

"This happens. I want to be with you. I want to feel like this all the time." Charlie took Elda's face in her hands and kissed her hard.

She sighed, and the burn of desire rushed through her again. Elda pushed Charlie's shoulder gently. "What is this though? I just want to understand what's happening to us."

"I don't know." Charlie picked off a piece of wool bobbling on her jumper. "But it feels good, doesn't it? And I don't want it to go away."

Elda needed more. She didn't want this to be another false start at a relationship. She wanted Charlie more than anyone, ever. She was so exposed.

"Has this all happened a bit too quickly for you, El?" Charlie asked.

Elda wanted to feel safe enough to stay and not destroy this before it had a chance to succeed. She drew her arms around her body, and Charlie mirrored her, as if they both needed to be held.

Charlie laid her hands on Elda's shoulders. "You don't need to be afraid of this. I'm exactly where I should be, I know it." She tipped Elda's chin to meet her gaze. "I know we're in a strange place right now, and this all feels a bit weird."

Elda considered what Charlie was saying.

"We'll take it slowly. You only came back from France three weeks ago, and now you're all hot and naked in my bed."

"Well, Angela's guest bed." Elda grinned. "It's just a bit bonkers. I'm worried that after we pack up, I'll kiss your face off, and it'll be over." She caught Charlie's eye and fell back on the sofa, laughing. Elda put her head on Charlie's shoulder and relaxed.

"I don't think so. It'll take more than that to get rid of me." Charlie wrapped her arms around Elda and kissed the top of her head. "And I'm not going to let you get away so easily next time."

An hour later, Elda stepped a foot out of Charlie's car and leaned back in for a final kiss. She opened the back door and grabbed her bag and boots. As she walked towards the house, she felt Charlie's eyes on her but resisted the urge to turn around and get back in the car. Trembling with adrenaline, she reached deep into her pocket for the keys to the front door. The light was on, and she took a deep breath.

Jack looked up from the kitchen worktop. He was chopping carrots and watching TV. "Hello, stranger. How was your fancy weekend in the country?"

"Hey, Jack." Elda's voice strained at the edges. Part of her wanted to burst, and another part wanted to keep the delicious memories of Charlie to herself for a bit longer. She hugged him from behind. "It was splendid. How was yours?"

"I had Christian over, delightful as ever. He cooked." Jack turned around and stopped, the knife suspended upwards.

Elda didn't meet his eyes.

"Wait. There's something. What's happened?" Jack asked. His eyes were screwed up, inspecting Elda's face. They grew wide, and he opened his mouth. "You've been kissing Charlie."

Her laugh erupted. "I'm still trying to wrap my own head around this, so please don't come at me with your sixth sense intuition or whatever you've got going on here." Elda waved her hands in a circle.

"You did it, didn't you?"

He placed the knife down and scooped Elda into his slim frame. She could do nothing but submit to his joy. "Yes. I did," she said. "No more fuss though; I'm a bit overwhelmed tonight. I need to get ready for this new job tomorrow. I don't know what to wear, and I've done nothing to prepare. I'm all over the place."

"Sit down, Elderflower. Let's have a tea, and you can tell me what the hell happened out in who-knows-where. I thought you were going for a nice walk, you filthy bitch." Jack flicked on the kettle and tossed the carrots into a pan of water. He pulled two chairs across and pushed Elda's shoulders down to sit. "You're really doing this then? I thought you two were stuck in the friend zone."

Jack's questions had been rolling around Elda's head for days. "I think so." She still couldn't look at him. "I don't understand it. But being with Charlie makes me feel like I belong somewhere."

Jack pushed her hair away from her cheek.

"Charlie..." She wasn't sure she was capable yet of describing Charlie in her own words.

"I know. She's special." Jack stroked her palm, easing her

breathing. "I think it was obvious it was going to happen between you, eventually. Charlie is obsessed. You just need to be sure about how you feel."

"She's special. I just had to figure it out in my own time." Elda's stomach grumbled. "I'm tired and so hungry." She'd put her basic needs on hold for a while.

"Well, I've got the makings of a chicken casserole going on here, but it won't be cooked for an hour. Get yourself in the bath and don't fall asleep! I'll give you a shout." He kissed her forehead and put an open packet of chocolate digestives in front of her.

The bliss of the last few days echoed around her head. She wanted to keep reliving the pleasures Charlie had given her. Elda shoved a biscuit in her mouth, letting the chocolate melt against her tongue. She didn't want to question what would happen next. Between them, their track records were dismal, but this could be different, if they both allowed it to happen.

CHAPTER TWENTY-ONE

ELDA FLINCHED AT THE pain across her toes and vowed to wear her trainers for the rest of the week. "It's nearly the end of class, so please stay focused. Tomorrow, we're going to be working on your text..." She fumbled for a moment. "*The Tempest*. Bring your books, please. Now, let's get packed up."

The sea of black and white uniforms looked like a school of orcas. For a brief second, she saw Charlie's naked leg wrapped in a white sheet. Elda shook the vision from her head and picked up the worksheets. Her aching feet were a welcome distraction from the flashbacks of her weekend with Charlie. The thought of Charlie's tongue over her body made her heart race, and she crossed her legs to halt the sensation between her thighs.

She had a good feeling about the school. She'd begged the agency for the job and told a white lie about how much she'd taught in England. Her footsteps clicked along the laminate tiles. Overhead, the strip lights cast a blue shadow, catching on the metal lockers. Elda hadn't stopped smiling all day, even though her head was swimming from teaching Shakespeare to excitable eleven-year-olds.

Outside, she pulled her wool coat around her waist and hunched over. The wind howled through the playground, but nothing could deter the trot she broke into when she spied the Capri beyond the gates.

"Hello, Miss Brown." Charlie laughed as Elda climbed in and kicked off her shoes.

She pulled her into a welcome, deep kiss. It had been too long since they'd touched. Elda stifled a groan and broke away before any of the school staff walked by. Charlie put the car into gear and drove.

Charlie lived in a large semi on the west side of the city. There were three rows of identical houses surrounding a small green, edged with tidy black railings and clipped hedges.

She parked and the engine fell silent, the cold air creeping into the car. They turned and kissed again. Charlie broke away and she led Elda inside. They spilled into the living room, their bodies pressed together, kissing with fury. They fumbled at buttons and zips to remove their coats.

Charlie flicked on a table lamp, which cast a warm glow throughout the room. Elda took in the familiar, mid-century furniture and smiled at how perfectly Charlotte Mason the place was. A pain shot through her shin as she bumped into a low table. It was littered with coffee mugs and red wine glasses. She stretched Charlie's jumper above her head, exposing her toned limbs.

They moved to the oversized, white sofa, and Elda pulled Charlie down on top of her.

"So, how was your day?" Charlie caught her breath, and they collapsed laughing.

Elda realised how ridiculous her adolescent longing was. But it didn't stop her body from yearning, her lips finding parts to kiss, or her hands pulling through Charlie's hair.

"We have to eat, Elda, or we'll waste away," Charlie said.

"Are you being a grown-up?" Elda laughed.

"Well, we can't survive on red wine and chocolate."

"We could try though." They slid down the sofa, and Elda knelt on the floor. She pulled down Charlie's trousers and discarded her boxers. Charlie arched her back into the cushions and gave in, offering Elda access.

Elda closed her mouth around her, softly at first. She breathed in Charlie's scent and tasted her. She was wet with her own need. She moved into Charlie and pressed her own legs together.

Charlie guided Elda to the right place, and her hips rose to meet Elda's tongue, which was expertly pushing and releasing her to a building orgasm. Elda leaned in, craving the power over Charlie's body that she had relinquished. She kissed and sucked at her clit, feeling the ebb and flow beneath her hands. She tipped her head back briefly and opened her eyes to take in the beauty above her.

Charlie's head relaxed in submission against the sofa. The image of her, naked from the waist down, and the taste of her desire was almost enough to bring Elda to her own climax. She increased the pace of her tongue.

"Touch me." Charlie groaned.

Sensing Charlie's need, Elda inserted one and then two fingers inside. It was too much. The rhythm and intensity built to a crescendo, and Charlie came in Elda's mouth, calling out.

Elda leaned against her thigh, smiling. Leaving a trail of kisses on Charlie's stomach, she made her way up to taste her lips. She ground herself against Charlie, needing her touch.

Charlie knew it. She flipped Elda onto her back.

"Fuck me." Elda's breath caught in her throat, and she surprised herself with her command.

Charlie didn't waste any time. She pulled Elda's pencil skirt around her waist and slipped off her pants, then pushed her knees apart and left her wide open. Charlie brought her fingertips to Elda's lips, dripping with anticipation. She tipped her pelvis towards the ceiling while Charlie entered with one, two, then three fingers.

Elda groaned, and she bucked into Charlie's hand, losing all control. She opened her eyes, wanting every moment of this. Charlie sat back as Elda squirmed against her. Her body was full, but she needed more. Elda pulled off her top, uncoupled her bra, and drew Charlie's lips to her breast. She needed every part of her to be touched, devoured, wanted.

Charlie fucked her faster and harder and used her thumb to flick at Elda's clit. She clamped her mouth onto her left nipple and bit down gently. Elda felt her release coming. She focused on every stroke, anticipating each vibration that Charlie sent coursing through her veins. Elda rode the wave of one pulsating orgasm followed quickly by another. She gave herself to the moment. Elda belonged here, entrusting herself to Charlie in a way she'd never done before.

***

Elda looked up at the bright sky. She could see the tips of tall, wide trees swaying in the gentle wind. The branches were naked for winter, but some showed off their berries like jewels. She reached out to hold Charlie's hand without thinking. She loved how she'd gotten used to their casual touch.

Jack was wittering about someone at work borrowing his spoon. "And then he said he'd washed it. But he obviously just wiped it. Which is a bit out of order. So, I've sent one of those all-staff emails and put it on the noticeboard. About spoon etiquette. Don't take people's spoons." Jack walked backwards, waiting for his friends' reactions.

Charlie and Elda caught each other's eye, and the three of them bent over laughing. They wandered across to the park's café. Charlie and Jack took seats at a small metal table while Elda joined a queue for drinks. She stared at her two favourite people from across the gravel clearing. Jack smiled at Charlie and pulled off his brown beanie. His hair stood on end, and Charlie reached over to pat it down, looking so gorgeous it made Elda's ribs ache. She wanted to freeze time so that they could stay like this.

She watched Charlie from across the courtyard until her heart skipped and she had to steady herself. She looked over to the ripples of water across the lake and took in the contours of the bank and the people walking on the path.

Balancing three cups of hot liquid, she reached the silver table. The sound of a ringtone from Charlie's inside pocket disturbed them all.

"Arnold. What's happened? The case file. Transferred yesterday, by courier. Not sure, to be honest. Maybe. I'd have to check." Charlie frowned and looked at her watch. "Yeah, I could do that. No, it's fine. I'm just around the corner. Will do. Speak soon."

"Everything okay?" Elda pushed a coffee towards her.

"I need to pop to the office after we've had these." Charlie hesitated for longer than usual. "You guys can come along, if you like."

Elda sat up straighter. She'd never been invited into Charlie's office. As the three of them walked up the stone steps to the old building, Elda and Jack fell behind like two children. Charlie swiped her ID card and pushed at the heavy double doors.

"I feel like we're in a library," Jack said, tiptoeing across the tiled floor behind Charlie.

Elda giggled into her sleeve. She knew that work was important to Charlie, and if she had to come in for something on a Saturday morning, it was no joke. They walked through a maze of corridors until they reached Charlie's door. She pushed the handle.

"This door is awkward. Be careful when you come in."

The room was underwhelming, but Elda craned her neck to take in every detail. She'd imagined Charlie's office like something out of an architect's journal. But this was like an old house had been converted into cramped rooms. Either way, they'd been allowed into a private space, and she took reverent, careful steps around the modest chamber.

Elda brushed her fingertips across textbooks on a shelf, leaving a mark in the dust. She could see echoes of Charlie's living room in this space, familiar titles, identical cushions, and a matching pair of lamps.

Charlie unlocked some filing cabinets and stacked brown folders on a chair. Her eyebrows were furrowed, and she clicked her tongue.

"Who's this, Charlie? Is this you?" Jack held a photo of two young girls.

Charlie took the frame out of Jack's hands. "Yeah, it's me. It was a long time ago."

Elda caught the distance of her tone as Jack pulled a face. She recognised the girl in the picture as Theresa. She saw the resemblance to little Jacob.

"Who's the hot girl with you?"

"Stop it, Jack." Elda dragged him away, not wanting him to offend Charlie with one of his throwaway lines. "You're being rude."

"What're you on about?"

Charlie stepped out, and Elda heard the whirring of a photocopier. She stood like a statue, and a wave of unease crashed over her. She was suddenly aware of being in Charlie's space.

"Right. That's it, let's go." Charlie held two brown envelopes.

Elda wondered whether this was how Charlie was in work mode or whether Jack had upset her. They quickened their pace until they reached the fresh air of the city square, and Elda took deep breaths into her belly. There had been something stifling about the building, but now they were out, their casual equilibrium returned. Jack made a joke, and Charlie put her arm around him. Her face softened, and her eyes wrinkled at the edges again.

"Let's go back to ours and stick *Beaches* on. Who's up for crisp sandwiches?" Jack asked.

Charlie touched her head to Elda's as they laughed through their approval, and the three of them turned east and started along the canal.

"We could watch something else," Charlie said with a hint of hope. "Just for a change?"

"Charlotte Mason, do you not love *Beaches*?" Jack asked with mock incredulity.

He started to walk backwards again, facing them. He would put on a show for them all the way home. Elda swallowed the lump in her throat. Something strange had happened in Charlie's office. It might have been the way Charlie moved through the space or spoke in tighter sentences. She couldn't put her finger on it, but it was gnawing at the back of her mind. It reminded her a little of the doubt that haunted her back in Paris, when Francis had been quick to criticise her, or had left her friendless at a party. Elda tried not to dwell. But if there was one thing she could fixate on, it was feeling rejected.

CHAPTER TWENTY-TWO

CHARLIE LOOKED ON AS Jack performed his own fashion show. He walked the runway like a professional while she and Elda reclined on his sofa, a tangle of arms and legs. He drew laughs from his audience of two by flexing his muscles.

As a spare wheel for their tandem, he was getting ready to hit the town and make his own fun. Charlie loved to be around Jack—he brought out the best in Elda—but she relished the intimacy they shared when it was just the two of them.

Jack held two hangers against his solid chest and skinny pelvis. "Jeans or cords?"

He didn't wait for a response. His whole day was a performance, and he was, at the end of it, his own critic.

"Now, folks. To tan, or not to tan?"

"Not," Charlie said, without thinking.

"I love you two together." Elda was wiping tears from her face from laughing.

Jack turned his wrist around and rolled his eyes. "There isn't time to do all the buffing and polishing anyway." He swivelled his longs legs and exited.

Charlie pulled Elda off the sofa and drew her in. "Let's go back to mine tonight. Let Jack have the house to himself for a change."

Elda nodded and tidied away the cups and plates they'd collected.

"Let me just grab a couple of bits and say goodbye."

Charlie kissed Elda on the lips and watched her climb the stairs, two at a time, admiring the cut of her jeans against her thighs.

With their bags packed and coats on, they walked hand in hand to the car to drive the short route back to Charlie's house.

Inside, they took up their usual sofa spots. Charlie leaned against Elda, but she sensed a cold stiffness in her body. It was almost imperceptible, but her shoulders were rigid, and Charlie was sure she wasn't imagining the distance growing between them.

Elda's gaze moved to the sideboard and the messy zigzag of family photos. "You know that photo in your office?" Her casual tone didn't quite hide the strain behind her question.

"Yeah." Charlie sat up straighter and pulled her hand through her hair.

"It's you and Theresa, isn't it?" Elda looked at Charlie. "The girl in the photo."

Charlie closed her eyes and stopped for a few painful seconds. She hadn't kept Theresa from Elda, but nor had she shared the whole story. It just hadn't come up. Now it was a thing, and she would have to explain a part of her life that she'd kept to herself. "Yes, it's Theresa." She bit her lip and drew Elda towards her. "You know she was important to me. But she's also the main reason I studied family law. I wanted to help people like her. So, I keep her picture at the office to remind me why I spend so many hours there." She was skirting around the question, but she didn't know how to fill the gaps in Elda's knowledge without blowing it all out of proportion.

"Really? How come?"

It was a reasonable question, and Elda's tone was still light, but Charlie sensed there was more to it. "She died when I was seventeen."

Elda's pupils flicked from side to side. "I know. You told me."

"I haven't really ever talked about what happened because it's a lot. And to be honest, sometimes, I forget about her for a few weeks, and it just doesn't really come up."

"I know she meant something to you. But you don't need to tell me anything you don't want to."

"She lived across the road from me when I was growing up."

"Okay. And you were friends?"

Elda rubbed Charlie's arm, and she softened beneath her touch. Charlie leaned back and looked up at the ceiling. She had to give Elda more, but she didn't know if she'd be able to cope. "My neighbours across the road were her foster parents. Kim was very young and in a right mess when she had her. Let's just say that she wasn't around for a lot of Theresa's childhood. We met when we were fourteen, and she started at my school. We walked the same route." Charlie faltered. "I'm sorry. You deserve an explanation." Her mind was spinning. Could Elda trust her after this? She would think Charlie had something to hide. *This is why I stick to uncomplicated sex. Keep it simple, and no one gets hurt.* But it was too late. She was in deep with Elda, and she had to entrust her with her feelings and her past.

"Charlie, what is it?"

She blinked, wishing the right words would come out. "Theresa was the first person I ever loved. We fell in love, and we were together until she died."

Elda touched Charlie's arm and tilted her head. "I'm so sorry. What happened?"

Charlie smiled. "Why is that always the first question when someone dies?" For years that had irritated Charlie, but she had come to accept the morbid curiosity.

"I'm sorry." Elda broke away and rubbed at her own arms. She looked embarrassed. "I shouldn't have asked. I've just never seen you like this."

"It's fine. It was a long time ago." Charlie inhaled. "Theresa was beautiful and kind. She was intoxicating, and I fell for her. She taught me who I was, really."

Elda sat still, giving her the space to collect her thoughts.

"She struggled. Everything was hard for her. She never believed she deserved to be loved." Charlie swallowed and dipped her head. She'd never gotten used to telling Theresa's story. "I guess that it all got too much for her, and she ended it." Charlie tasted acid in the back of her throat. The memory made her feel sick.

"Jesus, Charlie. How do you even begin to process something like that?"

"You don't. No one really knew about our relationship at the time. To begin with, my mum and dad thought she was just the girl across the road that I hung around with. It was sad, but they moved on. I didn't even see Theresa's foster parents, and they moved away eventually. No one took any notice of me, except for Kim, who figured out that we'd been in a relationship." Charlie shrugged and looked across at Elda. "I had some counselling after university, which is why I can explain it all in a couple of sentences." Charlie placed her hands on her lap. "Anyway, Theresa is the reason I went into family law. I wanted to do something. Make the system a bit better. I'm not sure law was the answer, but here I am."

"Here you are."

Charlie shook her head and got up. She began picking up papers and piling books to keep her hands busy. She knew that Elda struggled to trust people and feared being left again. She hated that this baggage might make Elda doubt her.

They looked at one another for a few seconds before Elda rose, folded her arms around Charlie's waist, and pulled her head to rest on her shoulder.

"I'm sorry that happened," Elda whispered. "I wish I could take away all that pain."

Charlie relaxed. For the first time, she wasn't touching Elda with the fever of desire. Instead, she was sharing a part of herself which was usually zipped up tight. Charlie closed her eyes and allowed herself to be held.

***

A week later, she sat across the table, resting her chin on her hand. A candle flickered, throwing shade onto Elda's face as she picked up her wine glass by its thin stem. She tipped it towards her full lips, and Charlie licked her own.

Their food came and they chatted nonstop.

"Jack called me earlier, when I was leaving work." Elda placed her knife down. "My mum's been phoning the house. I need to give her a ring. Will you remind me?"

"Of course. Maybe we should go and visit soon?" Charlie was putting herself out there. She'd never actually met anyone's parents. "Your mum might be on her best behaviour if I'm there too."

"Maybe. She comes with a big health warning. She'll be drunk before we arrive, and she'll bring up all my failed relationships. I don't want you to have to deal with that."

A hint of shame crossed Elda's face. Charlie swallowed hard on her food and took a drink of water. She'd been with at least a hundred women, but she had never felt protective of any of them. "I don't mind. Whatever works. Let's have a look at dates when we get home." Home felt like the right description. She'd never shared her house with anyone, but Elda had been spending four nights out of five in Charlie's bed.

They ordered cocktails instead of desserts, and Charlie got up to sit next to Elda. "I have something for you." She closed her fists and held them out, just like the childhood game. "You choose."

Elda giggled and shifted her weight on the leather bench. "What's this?" She touched Charlie's right hand and turned it over.

Charlie unfolded her palm to reveal a silver key. She did the same with her left hand to reveal a bigger, brass key.

Elda frowned as she tried to work out what she was being given. Charlie put them both on the table and pushed the silver key closer to Elda. "This one is for my house, so you can come and go whenever you want." She tried to keep her tone casual as it dawned on her that this was a pretty big deal. She wavered for a second, wondering if she was doing the right thing. Was it too much? Would Elda bolt?

Elda looked up, and Charlie saw a wave of joy ripple across her face. She was so beautiful, Charlie could barely look at her. "And this one is for a studio in block B of the mill. It's smaller than your last one. And the lease is just for six months to see if you like it."

Elda swallowed, and tears fell down her cheeks. Her mouth opened but nothing came out.

"You don't need to say anything."

"Thank you," she whispered.

"I don't want to push you. You can use the space or not. It's a gift." Charlie stroked Elda's hair and kissed her. She couldn't help but raise her eyebrow. Here she was, the ultimate control freak, dishing out keys to her front door and a six-month lease. Pretty sizeable gesture for a commitment-phobe.

It had all come from nowhere, and this was uncharted territory.

"What made you think of a new studio?" Elda asked.

"I just wanted to show you how much I care about you." In all honesty, she'd been battling the guilt over the photo of Theresa and kicking herself for her clumsy explanation. She hoped this would go some way to make up for it. "I wanted you to see I'm living for now and that I'm not stuck in the past."

If Charlie admitted it to herself, she might even be starting to think about their future.

CHAPTER TWENTY-THREE

THE NEXT MORNING, ELDA took an early walk to the mill. She hadn't been since she'd given notice on her studio and left for Paris. The café across the canal was overflowing, with people spilling outside to perch on the stone steps. She recalled the view from the corner table and fiddled with the key in her pocket. Her stomach jumped with excitement. She hadn't banked on having the spare cash to pay a deposit on a new place to paint for a long time. Charlie's gift meant the world to her.

The room was miniature compared to her old studio, but it was hers. She stepped into the vacant space and peered into the high corners of the ceilings. The walls were smudged with the efforts of its previous tenants. The concrete floor was dusty, and rubbish had collected at the edges. She inhaled chemicals and stale air.

Elda dragged two plastic chairs across the room and sat for a moment with her eyes closed. In the black canvas behind her eyelids, she imagined clean, whitewashed walls and wooden benches. Her rug was back in the centre of the room, and Charlie was draped on a sheepskin cushion. She opened her eyes and grinned.

For the first time in ages, she reached into her rucksack and pulled out a new sketch pad. Her tin of pencils rattled in a side pocket. She turned a fresh page and began to create grey lines, reimagining the space in front of her.

At first, she was deliberate, but her thoughts drifted into a fog, and when she emerged an hour later, she'd sketched Charlie. Her drawing had stitched itself together from a patchwork of memories. Charlie was laid back, her forearms behind her head. Her short hair was messy, like she'd spent the morning in bed. She was full of confidence and vulnerability, her delicate lips parted, and her eyes burning off the page. Her breasts were visible, but her hips were left to the imagination. Elda had captured Charlie's raw beauty and recalled every crease in her skin.

A sharp pain stabbed her back. She hadn't moved for some time. She unfolded herself and stood, rubbing her numb hands together. Her cheeks ached from smiling, and she basked in the happiness that Charlie had gifted her.

The sound of her mobile phone jolted her from her thoughts, and she saw her mum's number flashing. Elda picked up.

"I've had a heart attack. It was all too much with your nan, and I'm in the hospital."

"What?" She focused on the concrete wall in front of her and picked at the peeling paint while her mother croaked on.

"It was the middle of the night when they brought me in. I've just woken up with wires coming out my nightie."

A nauseating dread leeched through Elda's body. She ran her hands across her dry lips, imagining the worst waiting for her back home. She made her way back to Charlie's house on autopilot and threw the contents of her top drawer into a rucksack.

Two hours later, she drove Jack's mini towards a red and white barrier at the hospital and screeched into the first parking space she spotted.

She grabbed her bag and marched towards a set of revolving doors. There were figures hovering outside, pushing wheelie drips and flicking cigarette ash. She shuddered, grateful for her own vitality.

Elda braced herself. Her mum's cardiac episode, as the doctor had described it, had been serious enough for a hospital bed. But her mother's tone on the phone had been entitled. Elda pictured her laying in a bed, barking at the poor staff.

She stopped at the shop for chocolates and a magazine, putting off the climb up to the ward. As she emerged into a vast atrium, she stood, still and insignificant, as trolleys bustled past, and families held each other's hands. Everything, and everyone, towered above her.

A robotic voice announced the ground floor and a pair of lift doors opened. An elegant stranger entered, and they both reached to press floor six at the same time.

At the cardiac ward, Elda approached the front desk and was shown to her mother's cubicle. A pale blue curtain shielded her from the other patients.

The room was stifling, a stench of cooked dinners and bleach hanging in the dead air. Elda became conscious of the sound of her footsteps, and the weight of her coat.

Her mum was awake. "Hello, love." She looked almost grateful, underneath her grey hue.

"Fill up the water, love. You can help me to the loo in a bit?"

"Of course. How're you feeling?"

She was jittery. "Will you fetch some milk for my tea. The old biddy didn't leave me any. And they've left my clothes all over. Can you fold them?"

Elda couldn't bear it. "Mum, I can't stay long. I need to go and check on Nan."

"She'll have been okay, because Aunty Cath was coming in this morning, and she'll have got her breakfast and a bit of lunch."

Aunty Cath wasn't a real aunty. She was a lady down the road, and Elda wasn't convinced that her flying visit was adequate care for her frail grandmother.

"How are you feeling, Mum? Have you seen the doctor?" Elda wanted to understand what had happened.

"The doctor came this morning. He said I need to rest and can't take on too much at home."

Elda was sure her mother would have spun the doctor a real yarn about the pressures of her caring role.

"I told him there's your nan to look after, but he was having none of it. He said I needed to stop doing all the lifting and all the running around shopping and cleaning."

This was pretty simple advice for someone who'd just had a heart attack. But her mother's words gnawed at her. *I'm never there. I don't help. I'm selfish.* Elda had a soundtrack in her own mind, and none of it was kind.

"You do need to ease off, Mum, if you're not well yourself. We'll have to look at what support we can get for you. I'll have to come home a bit more and take care of you both."

"Oh, Elda, you've got your own life to live. I don't want to burden you with all of this. It's enough for me, and you don't need to worry too."

Her mother's sing-song voice didn't ring true, and Elda remembered that beyond the curtain her fellow patients and the staff could hear everything.

Elda knew, deep in her stomach, that this was a moment that everything changed for their family. Her grandmother needed someone to look after her, full-time. She was dying, very slowly, of all sorts of things.

She rose to pull back the curtain at the other side of the bed and took in the ward. There were six beds in the room, each identical. Two elderly women were asleep. Their names were scrawled above their heads. Two more women were lying in bed, dozing in and out. One was reaching for her water jug and pulling her face into strange shapes.

The last patient was surrounded by family. More visitors than were allowed on the ward, but no one was complaining. They'd dragged plastic chairs up to the bed. Their voices mingled, and warm laughter erupted. The woman was being lifted from the bed and onto a comfortable foam chair. Her son was pouring fresh water and tidying away old snack wrappers. Her daughter, the elegant lady from the lift, was stroking her mum's arm and talking to her in a soft voice.

Elda turned back to her own mother, scowling at the other women.

"That one has done nothing but moan. And the other snores all night. She," pointing to the popular woman, "only came in this morning and she acts like she owns the place."

Elda bit down on her tongue and rubbed at the fabric of her trousers, trying not to absorb her mother's vitriol towards the world.

"When do you think you'll be ready to come home?" She smiled.

"I can't come home Elda, until they say so, and then there'll be rehab," her mum said with a fiery look in her eyes.

"Yeah, I know. I didn't mean it like that. I just meant it would be nice to get you home, where you're comfortable." Elda held out her hand and patted her mum's arm. It was cold underneath the thin cotton dressing gown.

"Your nan's getting worse. She's not well and not keeping much down now. She's been in here for all sorts and they sent off something for testing."

"What do you mean? What tests?" Elda's thoughts were spinning like a helicopter above her head.

"She was in last week, I told you. Up in the ward for prodding and probing. The poor love, she was full of holes by the time they were done with her."

Elda looked at the spotless floor and heard a siren somewhere outside. Her mother was still talking. She wished she was anywhere but here. She let the plastic chair take her weight, imagining she was still cocooned in her studio, sketching Charlie's jawline. She screwed her eyes shut, trying to dredge up an ounce of empathy for her mum. But none came. Her scattered thoughts landed on her nan, sat alone in the house waiting for someone, anyone, to come home.

CHAPTER TWENTY-FOUR

WHEN ELDA REACHED HER family home, she stood at the door for a moment. It was late, and she didn't want to worry her grandmother. She was also frightened of what she was going to face inside. As she turned the key, she called out.

"Nan, it's only me. I'm here now."

Her grandmother slumped in her usual spot, her neck disappearing into her shoulders. As she stirred from a doze, she lifted her head from her shrunken frame. Loose skin hung around her jowls. Elda reached around her, feeling the sharp bones of her shoulders.

Damp stagnated in the room, so Elda flicked on the heating.

"Have you had anything for your tea? Has Cath been up from number fifty?"

"No, love. She came this morning, but she had to go into town to pick her grandson up."

"Have you been on your own since this morning? What have you eaten?" Elda picked up discarded dishes and cups, clearing the carpet of tripping hazards.

"I'm not hungry, little one. You get something for yourself."

In the kitchen, Elda tried to assemble ingredients, but the cupboards were empty and thick grease covered the worktop. It was clear that her mum wasn't on top of things at home.

Elda screwed up her nose and stood back to take in the state of the place. She rubbed her cheeks and under her eyes. The room shifted in and out of focus. This was too much. A knot of guilt was gathering in her chest. She flicked on the kettle and faced the overflowing bin. The smell made her step back. *How have I missed this? I don't understand what's been going on.*

Tears sprang to her eyes as she started to understand how much her grandmother had done around the house. Only now, as it started to unravel, was it so obvious.

She took two hot cups of tea into the living room and plumped life into her nan's pillows. She couldn't rest yet. Elda could smell stale urine.

"Let's get you freshened up a bit before we settle down with our tea." With the supplies within reach, Elda lifted her nan to standing. She was much shorter than she remembered, and Elda towered above.

Elda began to play a tape in her head of what might have happened if she hadn't been able to get here tonight.

"It's only us, isn't it, Nan? We've got to look after ourselves." Elda filled the dead air with a one-way conversation. She'd heard her own mother do this many times, and thought she just enjoyed talking nonsense, but now she understood that the silence was unbearable.

"That's it, just lean against me." She pulled her grandmother towards her and supported her lower back. Elda shifted, easing her grandmother back into the chair. She drew a fleece blanket over her stone-cold feet.

"I think I'll go and see the doctor tomorrow myself. Or at least speak to them on the phone. Perhaps they can give us a better idea of when Mum might be home." She looked at her nan's face. It was covered in tiny lines and looked washed over with grey. "Are you feeling okay?"

"Yes, I'm all right. I'm glad your mum is feeling better. It was awful. She called the ambulance herself, you know? Clever thing. I'm not much help these days." Her voice was weak, and she closed her eyes with the effort.

Elda sat close and held her clammy hand. A few minutes passed. The clock on the cooker said seven o'clock. Her own skin crawled at the dirt she could see everywhere. She went to the kitchen and took out cloths and bleach.

The radio on the windowsill burst to life at her touch, but she hushed the volume so she could hear her nan call out. She worked her way through the kitchen, scraping at old grease and spraying away dust and mould. Elda wiped sweat from her forehead with the back of her arm, then vacuumed and mopped every floor in the house. In a frenzy, she sponged dirt from skirting boards, poked crevices, and dusted in corners.

By the time the nine o'clock news was playing out on the radio, Elda was dressing her nan for bed, with a fresh nightie and socks.

"You're a good girl, Elda. Thank you for looking after me."

Elda fought back a sob and squeezed her nan's hand. Her blotchy skin was paper thin, as if it would tear easily. She followed her shuffling grandmother into the downstairs bedroom. She was breathless, and the journey from one room to another had taken all of her energy.

"Will Cath be coming again tomorrow?"

"She might come and see you, Nan. But I'll be here to look after you. Don't worry about that now." Elda gave her an empty smile as her mind flicked through all the things she'd left abandoned at home. She wished she could fold into Charlie's lap right now.

She adjusted the pillows and quilted blanket and laid a fleece over her nan's feet. Elda closed the door behind her and turned her back to the room, struggling to breathe for a few seconds.

After she'd climbed into the spare bed, she studied the faint spots on the dark ceiling. The room was unfamiliar, but she could make out the shapes of the wardrobe and drawers in front of her. She reached to touch Charlie, but she wasn't there.

She began talking to herself, grasping at the meaning of words that were coming to her and then falling away. She counted her heartbeat in the silence, praying that sleep would rescue her from her thoughts.

It didn't. Rest was not coming in this house.

Elda swung her legs out of the bed, and the cool air hit her calves. She stepped out of the bedroom. Standing tall, she summoned every ounce of bravery and crept down to her grandmother's bedroom to listen at the door for any movement. If she could hear her nan sleeping from there, she'd walk away. She opened the door and leaned in. Her nan had slipped down into her pillows, her neck twisted into a fold.

Elda wedged the door open with a slipper and put her hands on her hips. She stood over the bed guard and traced her fingers along the crisscross seams of the quilt. She could smell her childhood. The quilt was big enough to throw over the backs of upturned chairs and hide underneath. Her grandmother would sit next to her, passing her toys. Safe inside, Elda would explore each diamond, following the story of the painted pictures.

Looking down at the quilt now, it was random and chaotic, but as a child, she'd found patterns and made sense of the stories.

"Linda?"

"It's me, Nan. I'm here." Elda took her hand and inched closer. "Hold on, I've got you. Let me move these pillows, and we'll sort you out." Elda hesitated, unsure what to do next, and petrified of hurting her nan's tiny body.

"Don't leave me, Elda." She was alert, reaching for Elda's hand. "You're the best thing that ever happened to me. You really are."

Her grandmother rested again. Elda's skin still tingled, and her heart boomed in her chest. She rooted herself to the spot and tried to slow down. Then she headed into the kitchen and flicked on the kettle.

As the boil became rapid, Elda picked at her dry lips. Her teeth ached from clenching them. This was going to be hard in so many ways. She hated her mum for being in hospital and leaving her alone to cope. But Elda also dreaded having to care for them both.

Why was this happening now? When all she wanted to do was spend every waking hour with Charlie. Was this punishment for finally finding a crumb of contentment in among all the shit she'd had to deal with?

The weight of her selfishness crushed her, and she burned with guilt. Her mind was telling her to be a grown-up and look after her nan. But every muscle twitched to run away, back to Charlie, back to everything she'd known twenty-four hours earlier.

CHAPTER TWENTY-FIVE

CHARLIE STUDIED HER SHOES on the doorstep and crinkled the plastic wrapping of the bouquets bursting from her grip.

Her pulse raced as the door opened, revealing a paler version of Elda. "Hello, you."

"Thanks for coming." Elda melted into Charlie's arms, and tears fell down her cheeks.

Her heart cracked seeing Elda so fragile.

Elda led her to the kitchen and took down some fresh mugs. "Nan hasn't been out of bed since I put her there last week. She's drifting in and out now."

"How's your mum doing? Are they discharging her today?" Charlie pulled out a wooden chair and sat down. She put her finger on a tiny crumb on the plastic tablecloth then flicked it away.

"I think so. She's waiting for a prescription and creating some drama, as usual." Elda tried to laugh, but she looked devastated. "I don't know how long this is all going to – " Elda choked back the words. "I can't even think about it."

Charlie stood and wrapped her arms around Elda's waist, pulling her close. "Tell me. It's okay," she whispered into Elda's neck.

"I'm awful. I feel like I want it to be over so we can get back to our own lives. But then I feel terrible for that." Her voice was thick with grief. "I'm not sure how much help Mum is going to need. She's been going on about rehab and resting."

Charlie tightened her grip. She stroked Elda's hair.

"Don't, Charlie, I'm filthy. My hair is a right mess."

Charlie cupped Elda's face in her hands and kissed her gently on the lips. She wanted to take all the pain away. "I know I'm a bit useless with all this, but this is what I can do. I can finish the tea while you shower. I promise not to come in." She winked and pecked Elda's cheek. "I'll look in on Nancy and sit with her. Take your time. And then, you can go and get your mum and try to pin the doctors down on what she needs at home."

Elda rubbed her bloodshot eyes. "You know where the milk is." She kissed Charlie on the lips.

***

Charlie rubbed sleep from her eyes and stretched the stiffness from her neck. The house had been restless overnight. They waited as the family doctor climbed two steps across the threshold. It had rained all morning, and the paving stones were slippery under foot.

Doctor Adams was weathered with age and wisdom, his face wrinkled in the right places. Charlie fidgeted in the hallway. Her thoughts were beginning to run away from her, and she needed to get a hold of something. The stairs creaked, and she followed Elda and Adams towards Linda's room and hovered on the landing.

"Linda, it's good to see you home. And with your daughter. Gosh, isn't she a grown-up, now? How is Nancy doing?"

"She's the same. We're both very worried about her," Elda said since her mother didn't respond.

"It's a difficult time, but I'm here now to help." He unclipped his briefcase and unfurled a pile of notes. "How are you feeling at the moment, Linda?"

"I'm very tired, doctor. The hospital gave me all sorts of instructions and exercises to do, but it's an awful lot."

"Yes, you've been through something very strenuous. That'll take some time to get over. You must do all the physio and take the exercise that the cardiac team have recommended."

"We're worried about caring for my nan. Mum needs some support with that," Elda said, her voice shaky.

"Yes. Have you spoken to the council?"

"It's a minefield. You're passed from one idiot to another."

Linda's outburst made Charlie examine the artexed ceiling, wishing she could escape.

"I'll make a referral today. Your spell in hospital changes the situation. I think we should also start to consider the end-of-life care that Nancy will need. I'll ask the team to come and talk to you about that."

Charlie spotted the panic flash in Elda's eyes. She placed her hand over Elda's as she gripped the edge of the banister. She wanted to fix all this, take it all away.

"I don't want to see her suffer, doctor. It's been awful. I'm sure it was what put me in hospital in the first place, and that's no place to be."

Linda was working herself up into a state.

"Mum, let's try to focus on what Nan needs."

"That's what I've been doing all these years. If you believe otherwise, you can think again."

Charlie dug her fingernails into her palms. Her jaw clamped, and she headed downstairs to avoid the rest of the conversation. This house was suffocating. Elda had warned her, but she was seeing it for herself. Charlie thought about her own parents, overflowing with kindness and love. She wished she could bring some of that here for Elda. She longed to be able to create safe spaces for her. For now, she had to protect her from Linda's bile.

Another restless night followed, and as the sky turned from black to grey behind the living room curtains, Charlie turned over, her bones creaking with fatigue. Her eyebrows pulsed, and she rubbed at the pressure across her forehead.

She eased her shoulder blades off the sofa, padded upstairs, and crawled back under the warm duvet. Elda reached behind her and pulled Charlie close into the curve of her spine.

"Here you are," Elda said.

"Just about." She nuzzled into Elda's neck and closed her eyes, enjoying the brief, unburdened moment.

"Where've you been?"

"I slept on the sofa, listening out for Nancy." *And now I feel like shit.*

"Thank you." Elda turned and planted kisses along Charlie's cheek.

It was enough for Charlie to unravel with lust. She'd missed Elda's body and wanted her. She couldn't shake the feeling of being out of place here, and maybe the distraction of a few minutes of bliss would do them both good. "Can I touch you?" Charlie waited for words, but Elda responded with a hard kiss. She placed her hand at the base of Charlie's neck and forced her hips against her.

"I'm yours. Of course, you can touch me." Elda smiled and pulled Charlie's T-shirt over her head.

They kissed again. A long, sleepy kiss that built with intensity until Elda leaned back, arching her neck for Charlie to devour. Elda shifted, edging down and kissing Charlie's supple skin and travelling further to take her nipple between her teeth.

Charlie was on fire. She wanted nothing less than loud, messy sex. Her lungs needed to be free, but she remembered Linda along the landing and bit down on her lip to stifle her moans. "I've missed you, so much." Her breath was shallow. Elda's hands were moving across her stomach, sending her boxers to the floor and her pelvis towards the ceiling. A dull ache spread between her legs, where she longed to be touched.

Elda flicked her tongue across her crease of soft skin. "You taste amazing." She covered her whole sex with her mouth.

Charlie tipped her head back and let the desire flood her entire frame. It was electric from the tips of her toes to the top of her scalp. Every cell simmered with energy. She forced her face into the pillow to dampen her own gasps as Elda teased her open, spreading her wide and kissing her deeply.

She wasn't used to giving up control, but she was weak and powerless under Elda's touch.

"I want you on me." Elda flipped her over so Charlie was on all fours, holding onto the headboard.

Elda shuffled underneath, bringing her face in line with Charlie's clit and eased her hips down over her mouth. Charlie thrust up and down on Elda's tongue, allowing her to fuck her with her mouth. Elda stroked her cheeks and touched her centre. Every nerve twitched in sync. Elda found a rhythm, and Charlie was losing control, aware of nothing but the sensation between her legs. She opened her eyes to take in Elda's control over her body. It was like nothing she'd ever experienced before. She was giving herself to this woman, allowing herself to be seen, touched, and undone.

Elda's eyes shone and filled with desire. They connected, silently declaring their need through their writhing, glistening bodies. Charlie's insides contracted, and she shattered into pieces, her arms and legs shaking. Her hips jerked as Elda's tongue drew in and out from underneath her. She was a goddess, riding her wave of pleasure, oblivious to everything around her. Seeing just Elda, feeling her touch, hearing her sighs. Tears sprang to Charlie's eyes, and she cried out, clasping her hand to her lips as she came, hard and heavy into Elda's mouth.

"Wow. You are something, Miss Brown." Charlie collapsed onto the bed and wrapped herself around Elda. She pulled her in close, kissing her own essence from Elda's lips.

"I wish we were anywhere but here. That's awful, isn't it?" Elda nestled into the crook of Charlie's neck.

"No, it's normal to want to escape hard things. Fight or flight." She stroked Elda's hair and inhaled her mint conditioner. "Where would you take me if we weren't here?"

Elda leaned back and stared towards the ceiling. "We'd take the river boat along the Seine to the Musée d'Orsay. It'd be late night opening on a Thursday. It's the best time to go, after they've kicked out all the tour groups." Elda leaned on her elbow and wrapped her legs around Charlie's hips. "We'd wander through the atrium. I've seen it twenty times or more, but it'd still take my breath away. I'd show you the Sappho sculptures, just for fun."

"I like this place already." Charlie brushed her lips across Elda's hairline. "Keep going."

"We'd get lost in the maze of corridors where they dim the lights. We'd huddle over a tiny sketch, one of the early masters, and I'd sneak a kiss, maybe more."

"Sounds dangerous. You know I have to follow the letter of the law, don't you, Miss Brown?"

"Absolutely. I'd never get you into any trouble."

"What next?"

"We'd sit too close together in a booth next to the gigantic clock for a glass of something French. It'd break the bank, but it'd be worth it for the view."

"The view's pretty nice here too." Charlie kissed Elda's cheek.

They both jumped when Nancy called out. Elda pulled the cover over her face and let out a low groan. Charlie squeezed her arm, rushing with adrenaline. For a moment, they'd both forgotten the weight of their responsibilities.

"Stay here. I'll go and check on Nancy and bring you some tea." Charlie climbed out of the bed and threw on the creased white T-shirt and Elda's joggers that were hanging on the edge of the bed. Her thighs were soaked and still tingling from her orgasm. She wriggled, enjoying the sensation of the heavy fabric against her raw skin.

Downstairs, Nancy's discomfort had been short-lived, and she'd fallen back to sleep. Charlie rested at the doorframe to make sure before she stepped into the kitchen and leaned against the worktop. Her thoughts slowed down, and she listened out for Nancy's breathing in the room next door.

Charlie made tea like a robot. Reaching without thinking into places that had become routine to her. Her few days with Elda were coming to an end, and she was dreading going back to work. An emptiness crept through her gut. She knew Elda needed her here, and the last thing she wanted was to abandon her. But she couldn't press pause on her job. People relied on her and needed her at court.

Tiptoeing back upstairs, she practiced the words she wanted to say next. She nudged the door open with her knee, walked across to the bed and put the mugs on the bedside table.

"Is she okay?" Elda stirred and lifted herself up.

"She's fine. She fell back to sleep, cheeky thing." Charlie left the door ajar, so they'd hear any more movement downstairs. They sat together for a few moments. Charlie took Elda's fingers in her hands. They were so delicate, she found it hard to believe they could wreak such heavenly havoc inside her. "I'm going to have to go back soon." Charlie hated herself.

"Really? Work stuff?" Elda asked.

"I don't want to. But the KC is putting pressure on..." The thought of her far-off promotion, which had consumed her a few weeks ago, seemed pointless here, in this house. Her head dropped, and her stomach swirled. "I wish I could stay with you. But I have a big case. If I go back for a few days and file some papers, I can get back here for the weekend."

"I know your work is important, and you can't just leave a case hanging." Elda stroked her arm and wore a smile that didn't quite reach her eyes.

Charlie's guilt hung in the air. She'd experienced grief first-hand and still knew its aftershocks. Leaving Elda to face Nancy's decline and Linda's inertia was heartbreaking. But there was something about being in their family home that was poisonous and unsettling for her, conjuring demons she thought she'd battled long ago. Despite the feeling of selfishness, she needed to breathe fresh air and pick up the pace for a few days before returning, refreshed, to be by Elda's side.

CHAPTER TWENTY-SIX

ELDA SNIFFED HER OWN armpit. She wasn't sure whether it was her who'd started to smell or the house. She was running on oven chips and sugary tea. Her teeth were furry, and she couldn't remember the last time she'd showered. The doorbell made her jump, and she dragged herself to open the door to another blue uniform.

"Hello, there. I'm Shirley, the district nurse," she said and smiled. "Where are we heading?"

Elda clapped her hands to her cheeks to wake herself up. Shirley seemed nice enough. "I'm Elda, Nancy's granddaughter. She's through here." Elda led Shirley through the short hallway and steeled herself to repeat their tale.

"Are you the primary carer, love?"

"Yeah. My mum's been unwell herself. She's in bed." She wasn't sure why she defended her.

"Is Nancy on any medication, my lovely?" Shirley's tone was like a warm hug.

"The doctor has taken her off most of it now. She has some morphine in the morning and at night."

They went into her nan's bedroom, where she'd shrunk further into the mattress. Shirley lifted her arm to take a pulse, and her thin skin sagged off the bone. Elda couldn't stomach it and studied Shirley's face. Blue eyeshadow was smeared across both eyelids, like she'd done it in the dark.

"Are you doing okay, on your own?" Shirley asked.

No, I'm not. I'm twenty-five years old caring for my dying grandmother and my pain-in-the-ass mother. She hadn't slept properly for a fortnight, and everything was fuzzy. "You've got to

keep going, haven't you?" Elda said. "Would you like a cup of tea?"
If only tea fixed everything like it was supposed to.

"That'd be a dream. I haven't stopped all morning."

Elda moved into the kitchen and after a few moments, Shirley
followed.

"It's the worst bit, this, Elda. But it's also time when you get to say
the things you need to...before someone goes," Shirley said quietly.

Elda knew, in the pit of her stomach, that they were on the final
countdown. Her shoulders ached with the burden. "What do you
think will happen?" She locked eyes with Shirley, sensing that she
might be the only person who would tell her the truth.

"From what I can see, Nancy is quite near the end of her life,
bless her. She's doing a lot more sleeping, isn't she? Well, that
might mean things are starting to shut down. The body starts to
prioritise what it keeps going."

Elda's thoughts were spinning, and she was grateful for the
brief silence Shirley left.

"We'll need to focus on keeping her comfy, warm, and with
enough morphine. It'll make her sleep, but that's for the best at this
stage."

Her mum appeared at the door, her grey hair thick with grease
and sleep. She reeked of booze. Elda wished she'd stayed out of
sight.

"How long will it take?" her mum asked in a harsh croak.

"I don't know, love," Shirley said. "It could be a few days. Or
she might rally for a bit. She's going to need you both around her
though, and you'll want to say goodbye."

"Bloody perfect timing, all this."

Who was her mum angry at this time? Her nan for dying, or
herself for not being strong enough to cope?

Shirley smiled and took her mum's hand. "It's okay to be angry
about losing your mum, love."

"Well, at least we're in it together, eh?"

Elda looked to the floor. They were anything but united in this.

"You must be very busy." Elda blinked away the shame and smiled at Shirley. "Will you come again tonight?" She thought about the sea of faces she'd opened the door to and wanted Shirley's to be the one she remembered.

"No, not me. Listen, don't try and do everything on your own. You'll make yourself ill and then where will everyone be?" Her eyes wrinkled as she laughed and collected her bags.

Elda closed the door behind her and stopped still. The house was silent again except for Nancy's rattling breath. All Elda wanted to do was scream.

***

Elda picked at skin on her thumb. She couldn't stop thoughts from whirring behind her eyes. Her phone pinged to indicate a text.

Just got to work. How are you feeling today?

The text messages from Charlie were short and scheduled. She was just a drive away, but that felt further than ever. Elda had withdrawn, not wanting to trouble her. Charlie had been busy with a case and hadn't been able to visit for more than a week, but Elda was relieved. She wasn't ready to put a face on for Charlie and pretend everything was bearable.

Her nan was barely conscious now, and Elda had fought to keep her at home. She didn't want her to wake up in the middle of the night in a place she didn't know, surrounded by weird noises and strange faces. She heard her mother's footsteps across the landing. She'd been spending her days in bed with the TV blasting, wasting away just the same.

The conversation in the house had run dry. She had long since understood that Nancy was the oil between her and her mother, and without her, there was only friction and discomfort. She thought about the next thing to do. Her tasks had been reduced to the most basic of human survival: food, water, clean clothes, and a warm bed. She walked across the hall to check on her nan.

Her phone rang, and she only half-smiled when she saw it was Charlie.

"Hello, you."

Elda checked the time. It was the middle of the afternoon. "You're early. What's wrong?"

"I'm between sessions and wanted to hear your voice. I miss you."

Elda heard the rumble of a truck and background voices, but she couldn't make out any words. Life was happening without her. Again.

"You okay?" Charlie asked.

"I feel hungover without having had the fun of drinking," said Elda, balancing the phone on her shoulder.

"That's sleep deprivation, angel. You need to get some rest." Charlie seemed further away than usual. "I wish I was there with you."

"I wouldn't want you here. Mum is acting like a pissed toddler most of the time. It's awful." It sounded like Charlie was crossing a road, and the strangeness of the conversation occurred to Elda. Everything had begun to feel surreal in the last few days. "I spoke with the nurse earlier and told her Nan isn't going to the hospice. I think she'd want to die here."

"I know. You don't have to do anything that you don't feel comfortable with. Don't let anyone force you to move her. If they think she needs more support, then they can provide that at home. She doesn't need medical care. Everyone is agreed on that."

"I wish you were here to talk to them. You sound much more convincing than me." Elda rested her eyes on the blank wall in front of her.

"Me too. If you need me, phone the office, and ask them to set up a call. I'll tell them that you're discharging Nancy's expressed wishes," Charlie said. "I'm going to try and come on Saturday. I'm hoping to get some of this work put to bed on Friday. Then I need to pop out with one of the KCs."

"Out where?" Elda frowned. She couldn't understand anything normal carrying on while this was happening to her.

"Just dinner somewhere. Not sure yet."

Elda snapped inside. So Charlie was happy going off for fancy dinners while she was left to watch her favourite person in the world slowly fade away. "Okay. Well, I'll let you get on."

"Hold on, I'm free now to talk to you. Don't rush off," Charlie said, a little breathless like she was jogging across another road.

"Charlie, things don't just happen on your schedule. I've got stuff to be getting on with too. There's lots to think about here. I have to go. Talk later if you have time." Elda put the phone down, and her heart raced. A wave of anger had come over her, and she'd been unable to keep it at bay. She sighed and regretted cutting Charlie down. Tears came to her eyes, and she let them fall.

Elda listened at the door of the upstairs bedroom. She could hear her mother's heavy breathing. She inched it open, expecting her to be asleep.

"What do you want, Elda?"

"Sorry, Mum, I thought you were asleep. I just came to check on you."

"I don't sleep."

Elda took a breath. She didn't want to get sucked into one of her mother's meltdowns. They were chaotic, and she ended up saying things she didn't mean. Or maybe she did mean them, but they were usually just hard to say. She gave a tight smile and walked across the room. Her mum was laid under the covers with her hair lank and hanging over the pillow. "Shall we open the curtains, Mum? Let some sunshine in. And maybe some air." The room was stagnant. Her mum had been confined to the room for days now, despite Elda's efforts to get her out. "Mum. I'm going to need you at some point. Come and see Nan."

"I don't want to see her. She's already gone."

Elda's ribs hurt. She could barely cope with her own grief but stepping over the messy feelings that her mum was spewing all over the house was worse. "She's not though. We need to look after her and make sure she knows we're there."

"I can't, Elda. I'm not strong enough. The doctor said I can't lift her anymore, and I have to be careful not to have another heart attack. That last one was just a warning."

Elda swallowed her impatience. "I know what the doctors said, Mum, I was there. But I'm not asking you to do anything physical. Just be there with her. Hold her hand. Talk to her... She can hear you." She struggled as the anguish snuffed out the oxygen in her lungs. "I just think you'll feel better if you spend time downstairs with us."

"Watching my own mother die isn't going to make me feel better."

"I'm not sure I can do all of this on my own." Elda turned her back. "Without us, she hasn't got anyone else, has she?"

"I've been here the whole time, Elda. You haven't. You've only just arrived. So please, don't try to tell me that I need to be there for my own mother. I know that." She shifted up the bed, blinking wildly and scratching at red blotches on her neck.

"Mum, don't get agitated. You need to rest."

"That's what I've been saying all this time, but you've come in here bothering me. What's she even doing? Sleeping. She only sleeps. She'll sleep until she slips away. What are you expecting me to do about it? If I come down there, she isn't suddenly going to wake up and say her fond goodbyes to us. She's bloody gone. It's just a shitting and pissing waiting game now."

Elda's stomach lurched with disgust. "This is so typical of you, Mum. This is all about how you feel. Can't you think for a moment about Nan and just being there with her? Or even me, and just being by my side through the next few hours or days?"

"You can try and pick a fight with me, Elda, and we both know you'll win because you've always got all the answers and all the words in the right order. Let's just face it. You love your nan more than me, and when she's gone, you'll have no reason to be here."

"Jesus, why does it always come back to how unloved you are? I can't even have this conversation with you right now." Elda clenched her mouth shut. "We do love you. We both love you, very much. But you're selfish, and you're hard to love." Elda forced every word out of her mouth. She was tired of having the same worn-out argument with her mother. She went to the window and threw the curtains back. The glare flooded the room, lifting dust off every surface. She raised her hands to block out the sun and blinked away her burning tears. Her nan was her guiding light. What was she supposed to do without her?

***

The house was silent. Elda's mum was sleeping after a cocktail of cider and anxiety meds. The rattle from her nan's bedroom was louder and irregular. There had been a stillness for days, but today she twitched. It was midnight when Elda began the night-time ritual of checking doors were locked and curtains were closed. She'd been at the bedside most of the day.

The silence was soul-destroying and lonely. She wondered about the other people who were dying across the world now, surrounded by their partners, friends, and children. She hoped they were held tight with the love in the room. She imagined voices were hushed and gazes met across the body of their loved one, a mutual understanding of the weight of what was happening in front of them too heavy to bear.

Elda had no one to share this with. Her mum had abandoned her. She craved someone to hold her hand and be in the room when she couldn't be. But there was no one. Her head hung like a dead weight.

In the early hours, Elda was hollow and hungry. Nurses had come and gone. When they tried to stay, she lied and said that her mum would be down soon. For some reason, she wanted to protect her mother from the shame.

She creaked with the slightest movement, and her stiff neck shot through with pain. Elda knelt at the side of the bed. She stroked her nan's hand and brushed her hair away from her face. "I hope you know you're loved." Her heart ached to say more, but she couldn't find the words without choking on her tears.

Time seemed to slow down. The thoughts inside her own head muted. She wondered if her grandmother was going to wait until she was alone to die. But all at once, there was movement, and she was strong and flustered for a few seconds. She moved her shoulders off the bed and back down again, looked at Elda, startled, as if death was a surprise. Elda held her nan's hand tightly as the life drained away from her piercing eyes.

Then, there was nothing.

Only Elda. And now she was alone; it was her versus the world. Her nan had been her shield against the many flaws of Elda's mum. She had fed her when she was hungry and clothed her when she had nothing in her own pocket. She had hidden the truths of her own daughter's selfishness, and now she was gone. Elda remembered being held by her. Loved by her. Who would she be without her?

All moisture drained from her mouth, and she grew breathless. She'd been expecting this for days, but the shock of it landed on her chest like a bowling ball. Winded, she rocked on the bedside chair, willing the air back into her lungs. Flashes of memory filled her vision. She saw herself as a child, being held in her grandmother's arms. She recalled being gently cradled to and fro while drifting off to sleep.

Echoes of what she'd lost burst before her, and tears sprang to her eyes. Brimming with the agony of fresh grief, she let them spill down her cheeks. Without censor, she screamed into the lonely, black night not caring who could hear her.

Her nan's death was the rawest abandonment of them all. It ripped a fresh wound in her fragile soul, breaking her. A numbness overcame Elda. Unaware of time passing, her limbs stiffened. They stung with the slightest movement as she kept a motionless vigil at her nan's bed.

Sat in the stench of her own anguish, the futility of it all tormented her. A terrible mix of rage and hopelessness rose inside her stomach, threatening to force its way to the surface. Unable to control her body, the bile surged, and she vomited in her mouth. She spat it into a nearby glass and wiped her mouth with the back of her hand before she stood.

The physical affliction of grief—her head pounding—was easier to handle. She welcomed feeling something rather than nothing. She stroked her nan's hand, her wafer skin already growing cold. Elda drew the quilt up around her collar as if that could keep her warm and put her hand to her cheek. "I love you, Nan. Sleep tight."

With that, she kissed her final goodbye and laid her head on her grandmother's shoulder, hoping for one last time she'd kiss away the tears.

CHAPTER TWENTY-SEVEN

CHARLIE TOSSED THE DUVET over her shoulder. She was turning over the same few thoughts. *When can I get to her? When will it end? I hope it's not tonight.*

Knocking hammered through the suffocating stillness. For a second, she thought she was dreaming. Confused, she opened her eyes. She jumped out of the bed, ran across the landing, and followed the noise. The knock continued, rapid and random. Sweat collected at the back of her neck and knees, the kind of sweat that comes with middle of the night panic.

She fumbled at the hooks on the wall and the keys clattered onto the floor tiles. "Hold on. Who is it?" Shivering, she jabbed at the lock and forced the heavy handle.

"It's me," Kim said.

Charlie dropped her head against the frame and braced herself. She opened the door, flooding the passage with the amber glow of the streetlights.

Kim carried Jacob in her arms, flanked by Chloe and Sam.

"You'd better get them inside. It's cold."

"I'm desperate. Darren kicked us out. He threatened me with all sorts." Kim stumbled into the house, words tumbling between her sobs.

Charlie saw the mark on her face. She took the weight of the sleepy Jacob and led them into the shadows of the living room. She cradled him and placed him on the sofa, stroking his hairline, then she flicked a lamp on. She struggled to find the words to relieve the fear hanging in the air. "This is an adventure, isn't it, guys? Come for a sleepover?" Charlie said.

"This is rubbish. Where are we going to sleep?" Sam took up space on the sofa and curled his legs beneath him.

"We'll think of something. Get comfy. There are blankets on the back of the sofa. I'll get us some warm drinks."

"Whatever."

"Shut up, Sam. It's not Charlie's fault," Chloe said.

Charlie gave her a quick squeeze on the way to the kitchen. Alone, she pressed her eye sockets, creating red patterns in the darkness. She craved control of the situation, but her thoughts whirled like a helicopter above her head. Hearing footsteps, she looked up to see the fresh torment in Kim's grey, tear-stained face.

"I'm so sorry for bringing them here." She could hardly catch her own breath. "I couldn't think of where to go."

"It's three a.m. The kids need some sleep." Charlie gripped the fridge door. "Hot chocolate and bed, if they'll go."

"I can't believe this is happening. I'm sorry. He was worse than I've ever seen him. I didn't know what to do." Kim steadied herself.

"Whatever's happening, you're safe now. Let's get the children settled." Charlie carried the steaming mugs back into the living room. "Sam, you can go in the spare room, and I'll put a fold-up at the foot of my bed for Chloe."

"Come on, kids, up you go. I'll stay here with Jacob. He's flat out now." Kim kneaded her temple, deep lines of worry gathering at her forehead.

When they were settled, Charlie came down the stairs and took stock. Jacob was on one half of the sofa and his mother was in a foetal position on the other half.

"I didn't mean to drag you into all this." Kim rubbed at her sore eyes.

"What's happening?" Charlie tried to keep her shit together. She didn't need this on top of everything with Elda. Her emotions were already wrung out, and she had no more to give.

"I couldn't stay in the flat. He threw us out." Kim fiddled with a loose thread.

"It's your flat, Kim. He can't throw you out of your own home."

"I had to protect the kids. He hurt me tonight, and I'm sure he was going to start on them." Kim's chest heaved up and down as she bowed her head. "I just wanted to feel safe."

Charlie perched on the arm of her sofa and took Kim's wrist. She stroked her flaking hand, feeling the work she'd put in to keep her children clean, safe, and fed. "I know. You're safe now. We'll sort something out." She flicked through a filing cabinet of memorised case law. "You need to be able to live in your own flat. We'll talk to the council and the police in the morning."

The pair sat in silence for a while, listening to Jacob's gentle snorts. His breaths were long, with huge gaps in between which made Charlie's heart jump. Eventually, Charlie rose, climbed the stairs, and dug out spare pyjamas for Kim. She took a deep breath before going back in. "Put these on. You and Jacob can stay in my room, and I'll sleep down here." Charlie nodded toward the door and lifted Jacob into her arms. His head lolled onto her bony shoulder, and it took all her strength to carry him up the steep stairs.

Halfway up, she heard her phone in the kitchen. Fear scrambled in her stomach, and she pictured Elda back home, alone. She quickened her pace and placed Jacob's sleepy frame into the king size bed, where he sprawled out on contact.

She jogged down the stairs and reached her phone just as it rang out. "Shit." Elda's missed call stared up at her from the counter.

The house was filled with a thumping, coming again from the hallway.

What the fuck now?

"Let me in, you bitch. I know you're in there."

Charlie took a breath and Kim came to her side, trembling with fear.

"It's him. He's found me."

"Let me in. You owe me that money, you thieving cow."

"Why has he followed you?" Charlie couldn't bear any more drama this evening. Torn between returning Elda's call and dealing with Kim's angry boyfriend, she chose to sort the crisis right in front of her first. Elda would have to wait. "Stay in the kitchen. I'll deal with this." She summoned the last shred of calm remaining in her body. The door shook at its hinges with another round of punches. She opened it to reveal the bulky frame of Kim's latest flame, Darren. His eyes were blazing with rage, and he showed no signs of moderating his behaviour.

"Please, I have neighbours. Could you lower your voice for me?" She spoke quietly and hoped that he'd mirror her.

"Fuck you. Where's Kim?"

She raised her eyebrow, not expecting such a vile greeting. "Nice to meet you. I'm Charlie."

"I know who you are. You're the posh bitch who thinks we need your charity."

Charlie's abdomen tensed like she'd taken a punch to the gut. "That's unkind. Kim and the children mean the world to me. They're like family. I don't offer them charity. I look after them when they need me." Her heart was pounding. "Which is more than you do."

"Piss off." He moved closer and leaned into her face. "They've taken everything I have, the greedy bastards. She owes me."

Charlie stepped further into his space, not giving in to his threatening leer. She met his glare with an icy scowl. The stench of his breath filled her nostrils, but she didn't pull back. "You need to leave before I call the police." She stilled the tremor in her hand.

"Kim, get out here."

He burst past Charlie, shouldering her into the doorframe. Her head bounced off the wall and pain shot through her neck. He'd done some damage, but she had no time to think about it. "Kim, call the police," she shouted. Her shoulder hung limp, sending jolts through her nerves with every step. Charlie ran after him. She had to get to Kim before Darren hurt her.

A scream echoed through the wall before Charlie made it. She thought of her phone on the kitchen counter, too far to reach. She bolted up the stairs two at a time to meet Sam and Chloe on the landing.

"What's going on?" Sam's mouth hung open.

"Who's screaming? Is that Mum?" Chloe asked.

"It's your mum's boyfriend."

"Darren?" Chloe began to sob.

"Call the police, Sam. Tell them where we are." Charlie gripped the banister. "Go into my room with Jacob, out of the way. Stay up here, all three of you."

Adrenaline pumped through Charlie's veins as she descended the stairs. She knew just two things. She had to keep the children safe, and she wanted that piece of shit out of her house.

"I didn't take anything, I swear!" Kim's screams burst through the kitchen door as Charlie swung it back on its hinges. She cowered at the table, with Darren looming over her tiny frame.

"You liar. There was five-hundred quid in that drawer, and it's not there now. So hand it over."

Charlie weighed it up. Blind fury was unpredictable, but she could work with threatening behaviour. She'd spent enough time in custody cells to know the difference. "I'll give you the money, Darren." She drew his gaze from Kim, maintaining eye contact. "I'll give you the cash. But you need to calm down and leave."

Her phone rang again. *Elda.*

"Shut that phone up. I can't think." He screwed up his face with anger and pushed Kim shoulders.

She shook with terror, sobs catching in her throat. "Darren. I know that you're angry right now, but you can't storm into my house in the middle of the night."

It was a gamble. He looked confused by her calm exterior, but it was enough for Charlie to position herself between him and Kim. "Let's talk about what you need so you can leave, and we can come back to this conversation when everyone has had some sleep."

"I want my five-hundred quid back. Every penny." His shoulders sagged. Without the volume to his voice, he sounded as defeated as he looked.

"Police! Can we come in?"

Charlie breathed again at the sound of a female officer, knowing that the situation didn't lie solely in her trembling hands anymore.

"You called the police?" He rushed at Charlie with his fist in the air.

She stepped back, sending a mug tumbling to the floor with a smash.

"We were called to a disturbance?" The officer came to the kitchen door. "Do you all live here?"

"I do." Charlie stepped forward, her legs shaking. "This is my friend Kim. She had to leave her home tonight. This is her boyfriend, Darren. He's threatening her and the children with violence."

"Right. Let's take some details." The officer shook her head and reached into her pocket. "Sir, can I ask you to accompany my colleague into another room while we get to the bottom of what's happening?"

"You sneaky bitch." Beads of sweat gathered at his brow.

Charlie gestured to the living room, and Darren was escorted through by another strapping female officer. She allowed herself to breathe and a sharp pain seared through her shoulder.

"You look like you need to sit down. Has he hurt you too?" The officer pulled a chair out from the kitchen table. "Let's put the kettle on and get some sugar into both of you. You're likely in a bit of shock."

"I'm fine. He hurt Kim." Charlie could barely speak through the spasms in her shoulder. "The kids are upstairs."

"We'll see they're all right. Might you need to see a doctor? You've gone very pale."

"Elda..."

"Charlie, are you okay, love?"

Kim's voice sounded small and far away. There was a rumble on the staircase as all three children burst into the room. Charlie opened her mouth to speak, but the words wouldn't come. She slumped and found the cold tile at her cheek. The heaviness of her eyelids overwhelmed her, and the noise drifted into the distance.

CHAPTER TWENTY-EIGHT

ELDA DRAGGED HER HEAVY feet to the door when it knocked, ready to fall into Charlie's arms. Jack stepped in, and she collapsed into his hard chest, sobbing.

"I'm so sorry," he said, holding her tight.

After the long, comforting hug, he came into the house and took off his shoes. Elda leaned into him.

"I know." He pulled her in, and her cheek brushed against his cold zip.

She ached. "I feel ill. I don't know if I'm ill."

"You might be. You've probably been holding it all in for a while. You can rest now."

He headed into the kitchen, and she heard the rumble of the kettle. It had been re-boiled four or five times this morning, and she still hadn't made tea.

Jack returned with two scalding mugs and put them on coasters on the mantelpiece. "Where's Linda?"

"She's upstairs in bed," said Elda. "She gets up for the loo but that's about it."

"Jesus. What should we do?"

"I'm not sure. I don't know how to manage her." Elda's head was foggy, but she couldn't rest. The pain of losing her grandmother was like a bad cold. Her muscles ached, and the space behind her forehead throbbed.

"Charlie is following me down. She'll be here soon." Jack touched Elda's hand.

"I know. She called from the police station. It sounds like she had her hands full last night."

"She phoned me after the X-ray. Nothing broken. What a piece of shit."

"Uh-huh." The distance between her and Charlie had stretched further than ever. She couldn't shake the sound of her phone ringing with no answer at the other end. "She might not make it today. She's got enough on with the police wanting witness statements and all that."

"Nothing is more important than being here, with you."

"I get that. She's just got to sort stuff back home after last night's heroics."

Charlie had had no choice, but it stung that she'd put Kim before Elda.

"Charlie did the only thing she could last night. It's not like she could ignore that brutish boyfriend threatening to knock her own front door down." Jack faced Elda. "Don't you want to see her?"

"Of course." It niggled that he could see straight through Elda's frustration. "But I can't bear the thought of her here in this house, with this mess and Mum upstairs acting like she does. It's awful."

"You're shattered, and you need looking after. Charlie will be here to support you. You don't need to be anyone else for her. And you certainly don't need to explain your mum's behaviour. We all know what's going on there. We're just here for you."

"She's not here though. She texts me when she can. And only calls me when she's between meetings. Last night I called her, over and over, but she was dealing with Kim's crisis. I don't know exactly what's going on there, but she isn't here. She's working, and she's got problems to solve. I'm just getting in the way." Elda's cheeks burned with the hurt, and tears fell once more down her neck. She knew she'd feel better when she cried, because holding it all in was unbearable.

Jack pulled her into his arms. "You need some sleep. Go and rest your eyes."

She stood and leaned into the strength of his wiry frame as he guided her up the stairs.

"I'll be here when you wake up."

In bed, Elda stared at the ceiling. She knew Charlie would have wanted to pick up the phone to her. The betrayal was all in her head. Her eyelids dipped.

She'd been stirring for a while before she heard the rapping of the door. Stumbling from the bed, she took the stairs and opened the door to Charlie.

"I'm sorry I'm late. I had to settle a few things to take a few days—"

"No, not inside." Elda yanked her arm, dragging them away from the house and towards Charlie's car. It was a freedom, walking out of the house on her own. She had craved it just a few days ago. Now she'd give anything to hold her nan's warm hand again.

"Elda, you haven't even got a proper jacket on. It's cold out here." Charlie held her shoulder. "Be careful of my arm."

"Sorry, I forgot." She swung around to inspect Charlie's injury. "Where are you hurt?"

"Don't worry, it's nothing serious. Just don't pull me around like a rag doll."

"I can't be in there anymore. I need to be somewhere else with you." She took the keys from Charlie and started the engine, crunching the gears into place.

"I'm worried about you. Can you just stop?"

"Not here." Elda shut the conversation down and drove towards the outskirts of town. She took a country lane, and silence filled the car as she navigated the road. The sky darkened, and the car groaned with speed, but Elda knew these roads well. She took a hidden turning and drove along a woodland track. In a small clearing, she cut the engine and the headlights, and her eyes adjusted to the dusk. She climbed over the middle of the two seats to get into the back.

"Elda, what are you doing?"

"I'm waiting for you."

Charlie sighed, opened the passenger door, and climbed into

the back. "Hey, what's going on?" She opened her arms.

Elda pulled Charlie towards her and kissed her. She needed to feel something other than the dead emptiness that followed her. She sat on Charlie's lap and tugged the zip of her jeans.

"Wait, Elda." Charlie pressed against Elda's shoulder. "What's happening here?"

Elda put her finger to Charlie's lips. Holding in tears, she silently begged Charlie to give in to her. Charlie's face softened. She took her cheeks between her palms and met Elda's lips with tenderness. Elda tasted the salty tears spilling down her face and pulled back.

"It's okay," Charlie said.

"I just need you." Elda softened into Charlie's arms and allowed her whole weight to lay in her lap. "I've been on my own with it all."

***

A long, black hearse approached the house.

Panic rose in Elda. "I don't think that car will be able to turn around." She looked at the cul-de-sac.

"Yes, it will. They do this every day." Charlie rubbed Elda's bare forearm.

Every single hair stood on end waiting for something to go wrong. In a semi-conscious state, Elda got into the car. She stared at the coffin through the windscreen. The sight of it dug at something inside her, and she held in her sobs with her hand.

A few minutes later, they approached the familiar church. This building had punctuated every big moment in Elda's life. It was the source of life and death. There was a collection of slight figures, hunched and cloaked in black coats.

"They look like a Lowry painting," she said to no one in particular.

A smile flickered at Charlie's lips.

"This is Father Andrew." Elda nodded towards the tall priest waiting to receive them into the church. "He's a good guy."

They filled just two benches in the cold, empty building.

"I'm sorry for your loss, Elda." A kind old lady took Elda's hands. "Nancy devoted herself to you and your mother."

That was the sad truth. She'd given her life for them both, sacrificing friendship, maybe even love, for the sake of their safety. There was much crossing and kneeling. Elda opened her mouth to sing, but nothing came out. Charlie gripped her shoulders, and she leaned against her.

When it was over, they drove to a nearby cemetery, and her nan was laid to rest. The sun was shining on her and warming the ground. Tears soaked Elda's collar, and she fought to keep her frame from shaking.

She turned away from the open grave, and Jack approached. "How're you doing, Elderflower?"

"Thank you for coming." She knew that was what she should say to people.

"I know you must miss her so much; she was everything." Jack wiped his eyes. "She was the kindest person I ever knew."

They walked a few paces to the shade beneath an oak tree.

"It'll take some time to figure all of this out," Jack said.

"I don't know what I'm doing."

"We'll work it out. Be careful with your mum. Don't let her take your life too."

Elda looked up at Jack. His face was serious, and she could see new frown lines. She trusted him. He'd been by her side through good times and bad. She thought that Charlie would be there for her but doubted whether she'd ever come before work or someone else's problems. Her gut wrenched at the question, but it had been churning for the last few days, and she'd been powerless to stop it. Was Jack the only person she could rely on?

CHAPTER TWENTY-NINE

CHARLIE STOOD FOR A few moments at the door, shuffling from side to side. The name on the intercom was fading, but still there. A.J. Hartwheel. She'd always thought it was a made-up name. When she went through the door, it was like entering a fantasy world where she could be someone else for an hour. She pressed the button and noticed her skin peeling at the side of her short nail, betraying her anxieties.

Her boots clicked across the tiled floor, and she slowed down. She wasn't ready to face her old therapist yet. She raised her phone's camera screen to her face and examined the dark shadows beneath her eyes. Her lips were turned down, so she plucked at her cheeks and tried to make a smile. The face looking back was drained of blood and had a yellow and grey hue.

Charlie made her way to the familiar office, following the smell of aromatherapy oils floating through the air.

"Charlotte, it's good to see you." A.J. stood and held out her arms.

"Thank you for seeing me at such short notice." Charlie exhaled. This was a safe space.

"Of course. My door is always open to you."

The lamp on the side table was on despite it being light outside, and two sofas sat at either end of the room. Cushions were scattered on each, and as Charlie reached behind to adjust them, she remembered how they were too soft and offered no support. It was typical of a place that was supposed to make you at ease to be so uncomfortable. She sat opposite A.J. and sank further into the sofa to reach the floor with her toes.

"It's been a while. How are you today?"

A.J. was old enough to be Charlie's mum. She had a short bob, dyed brown with grey at the roots. Her round face was soft, creased, and kind.

Charlie's throat closed.

"It's okay. Take your time." A.J. held still. "Let's start with today. What's brought you here?"

They knew each other well enough for this opening number not to last too long. But it had been more than two years since Charlie had seen her therapist, and she was out of practice.

"Everything's too hard. And I know what to do now when I feel like that." Charlie looked everywhere but directly ahead. The curtain quivered in the morning breeze, and she stared at a box of tissues at the edge of the coffee table. She looked down at her arms folded across her, keeping her upright. If she let go, she'd crumble.

"I'm glad you've come. Tell me more about the hard things."

"My girlfriend, Elda, went home to care for her dying grandmother. She passed away." Charlie's voice broke. "I should've been there with her. But Kim came to the house that night with the children and needed my help."

"Kim needed your help?"

"She turned up at my office a few months ago. It was just money at first, but then her boyfriend got violent. She thought he was going to hurt the kids, and she had to leave her flat. She's desperate, and I'm the only one she's got really."

A.J. sat still and silent.

"You know. I'm the only person. I feel responsible for her. And the children."

"Yes. I know this is something that you keep coming back to, Charlotte. That you feel responsible for Kim. Tell me why."

"You know why." She scraped her fingernails at her palms. She thought she'd left all this behind her, but here she was, unpacking her guilt in this room again. "Because I let Theresa die."

"Did you?"

"I wasn't there for her. I saw what was happening and didn't do anything about it." Charlie had said these words so many times, they were second nature.

"You've said that to yourself before. We've talked about it here. Let's go back over the power that you feel you had over that situation back then." A.J. shifted on her sofa. "Remind me how old you were back then?"

"I was fourteen when we met. I was seventeen when she died."

"What do you think seventeen-year-old you should have done differently?"

"I should've seen what was happening and told her not to do it. I should've taken away the pain. I should've loved her more. I should've kept her safe."

"Could you have done that, Charlotte?"

Charlie fell silent and heard her breath catching on its way in and out of her lungs. She recalled all the previous times in this office, going over the same arguments. The wave of relief hit her in the chest. She knew the answer by heart. "No. I couldn't have. We've been over this before. I know." She laughed at the absurdity of paying someone to tell you truths that she already knew. "I know I was a child. A powerless child. I had no weight with anyone around us at the time. I know all of this now, but that doesn't stop me feeling so responsible."

"You feel responsible for a lot of things."

"People look to me to fix things. I look for things to fix. I sometimes think I attract people with broken bits."

"What if you don't fix things? What happens if people have to rely on themselves?"

"Kim is chaotic, and there will be all kinds of drama if she's left to handle it." Charlie tugged at the hair near her temples. "But I know I need to break this habit of her coming to me for money and for help. I know that it started because I was so ashamed of what happened."

"Shame is a big feeling." A.J. left a gap, but Charlie said nothing. "Who else needs fixing?"

"Elda. She's a bit broken too, I think. Her family dynamic is so fucked up."

"How do you feel about that?

Charlie rubbed at her fingers. If she couldn't say the words aloud here, where could she? "I love Elda. I've never met anyone who has filled in parts of me. In a way, she's fixed *me*."

"Maybe." A.J. crossed her legs. "Why did you need to see me today?"

"I know when I'm starting to feel unwell now. I can recognise feeling out of control, getting angry out of nowhere, and feeling so tired but not being able to sleep. And I've started to detach again. Like I'm watching myself." She looked towards the corner of the room. "I said I'd come back if that happened again."

"I'm glad you're aware of those things happening to you. That's real progress. What do you think you want to work on?"

"I want to get control. I want to feel more like myself. I want to be able to tell Kim she can't rely on me anymore without feeling a tidal wave of guilt."

"It's okay to feel guilty for disappointing someone. That's a normal response," A.J. said.

Charlie squinted. She couldn't make sense of all this.

"You might need to feel guilty for a bit, for it to pass."

"I feel like I've not been there enough for Elda. She's dealing with all the shit on her own, and I've been here, working."

A.J. held the silence.

"I feel a bit guilty about that too."

"A bit guilty?" A.J. tilted her head slightly.

"A lot guilty. I feel like I'm just expected to be there at her side, and I can't really handle it. It's too much."

"That's you trying to fix things again. Do you really need to be there? Has she asked you to fix it?"

"Not really. I just want to be." Charlie's stomach churned with confusion.

"You can't fix everyone, Charlotte. You want to because you couldn't fix Theresa and you lost her. But your job is not to solve all the problems for all the people you love. Sometimes they need to work things out by themselves. Sometimes it'll be hard for them, and it'll feel hard for you." A.J. folded her hands together.

"I know. You've told me before." A single tear fell down Charlie's cheek and onto her bottom lip. She had shared her darkest thoughts with A.J., and each time she returned, they came back to the same truths. Charlie wasn't responsible for Theresa taking her own life, and she couldn't fix everyone she loved.

Kim's trouble wasn't hers to fix, but she could do her best to help. She'd call Joshua and get him to work his brilliant mind on Kim's lease and the restraining order for the creep she was living with.

But right now, she had to get to Elda—not to fix everything or take anything away. She just had to stand by her side and love her. She hoped she hadn't already messed everything up.

CHAPTER THIRTY

THE DEATH ADMIN WAS finally done. Elda was proud of herself. Somehow, she'd made decisions about caskets and hymns and only paused momentarily to wonder why she hadn't thought to ask her nan what she'd wanted just a few weeks ago. They weren't that kind of family. Death was a ritual that burdened the living.

Today, there was more tidying up to do. She had to close her nan's bank account and needed papers from the attic. Elda heaved the bottom rung and the weight of the ladders unfolded. She climbed each step steadily, adjusting the spread of her feet to get her balance. She didn't like heights and wondered whether she should have asked Charlie or Jack to help. Braving the dark, she patted her hand on the dusty floorboards for a switch. It clicked, and the attic was flooded with light.

There were boxes piled from corner to corner. An old rocking horse stood in the middle. She touched the wood, remembering its shape cradling her. Her heart ached with the memory of her nan standing next to her. She dusted off a pine chest and sat down. She'd never really been allowed in the attic as a child. It was baffling how her mum and nan managed to climb the ladders, though they clearly hadn't been up here for years.

Elda tipped her head back and looked up at the beams above her head. She marvelled at how they had kept the roof up all these years. How do things remain constant, keep going, and stay strong when the world around them is crumbling?

She opened a box to find two vases and a candle holder wrapped in browning newspaper. She could see them on the shelves of her childhood. She turned to a maroon shoe box, peeling at the corners. Inside, she discovered a pair of bulky leather boots, weathered at the toes. They looked familiar, but she couldn't place them. They were large, far too big for the women in their house.

Elda's lips parted and the dryness of the attic air clung to the roof of her mouth. Underneath the boots, she uncovered a bundle of brittle photographs. She recognised herself and the man holding her as her father. She stroked the flat outline of his shape, a faint memory stirring at this fresh evidence of their co-existence.

It had been two decades since his name was spoken in the house.

She stood up and lost her footing, and the angle of the roof tilted towards her. Steadying herself, she swallowed back stale air, then began to take in the enormity of the gaping hole in her life. For years, she had been numb to her father's rejection of her. Deep down, Elda had known all along that her mother was capable of such a hateful distortion of the truth, she'd often questioned whether he really walked away or if he'd been pushed.

But the reminder that he had held her once, cradled her like a normal dad, and that she missed his presence, was ripping her fragile heart in two. She inched down the ladders, and her legs shook as she walked into her mother's bedroom. She was awake, leaning against propped up pillows, biting her nails.

Elda raised her chin, hoping her mother didn't mistake her anger as fear. "Why didn't you tell me you had photos of my dad?"

Her mum's eyes flared with rage. A cigarette balanced between her fingers and a plume of smoke erupted from her thin, twisted lips. "Get out, Elda. You've no business snooping up there."

Elda's skin stretched around her knuckles as she fought to stay calm. "You told me he burned all the photos. You lied. Why?" The words had cracks between them, like the pieces of her life.

"Elda, you're dragging up stuff that you don't know about. If your nan was here, she'd tell you that he was a waste of time. We were all better off, girl, I promise you that."

Elda wasn't about to be dismissed so easily. She doubted that her nan would corroborate her mum's lies, but she had to accept that they had both kept her father from her. It shook her to think that her nan would do anything to cause hurt. "You said he'd gone without a word and that he didn't want me. But he was up in the loft the whole time. I wanted to see him." Tears fell. Elda pushed them to her ears and stayed fixed to the door frame.

"You think you're seeing something in those photos? It's bullshit, Elda. He was a conman. He made me believe that he loved me too." Spittle gathered at the corners of her cracked lips. "He didn't love you. He hated both of us. He didn't love you on a Friday night, a Saturday night, or a Sunday night when he was drunk at the club or touching up barmaids." She stabbed the air with her pointed finger.

Elda nodded at the ceiling, bit her lip, and tasted her salty tears. She was breaking inside. Every truth she'd ever known about herself was being hurled across the room.

"He thought you were a burden, lady. And eventually, he hated me because I had you." Her mum stubbed her cigarette into an overflowing ashtray. "How dare you come in here attacking me when my own mother has just dropped dead. You selfish little bitch." Her mum swung her feet onto the floor and rose.

"Okay, Mum. That'll do." Elda raised a hand. Inside, her skinny, six-year-old self stood in the doorway as her mother's anger unfolded. She remembered the bedroom had always been a frantic place, words and objects launched like cannonballs. She had the sense of a man's shadow at her shoulder, pushing Elda behind him. He had a large, calloused hand and rough, splintered nails. She'd been frightened, and her cries caught in her chest. She was remembering her dad, protecting her from her rampaging mother.

"Put this behind you, Elda. Your nan's gone. We need to move on with our lives now," her mum said, dragging Elda back to the present.

"That's all we are to you, isn't it? Just emotional crutches keeping you going. You don't love any of us." Elda grabbed the hair at the back of her neck. "I don't think I can do this anymore." She turned and slammed the door behind her.

"Elda, don't make threats you can't keep, my love." Her mum laughed.

Elda choked back her fury. She had to leave this toxic house. There was nothing here for her except her mother's deception. She wondered whether anything in her life was truly hers. She'd been tormented by Charlie's distance and was furious with her for carrying on with her life while Elda was stuck on pause waiting for her grandmother to die.

She was torn between wanting Charlie so much it hurt and wanting to run away from everything, and she battled with the voice inside her head telling her that no one loved her now. Even Charlie wasn't really there when she needed her most. She'd put Kim and the children before Elda on the night her nan had died.

Anger smouldered beneath her skin, and she craved the contentment she'd had a few short months ago. Before everyone she loved had deserted her, one way or another.

CHAPTER THIRTY-ONE

CHARLIE HELD THE CORNER of the car door and popped her hand over the sharp edge to protect Sam's head as he got out. Chloe followed him.

"Stay with me, guys, until I can get Jacob out." He was sleepy but unclipped himself, and she reached for his hand. "Here, little man. Let's go and see the sea."

Her mother walked down the crunchy gravel drive towards her, arms open wide.

"Look at you four. What a sight," she shouted, clearly bursting with joy at having her daughter and new people to fuss over. "Let me help you, Charlie. Give me that bag. You take your time. You dad's got the kettle on. Isn't it a gorgeous day?"

"Chloe, Sam, take your bags in and follow Mum. This is Mandy, everyone." She bent down to Jacob. "She lives here by the sea, and we're going to have a little holiday here."

"Where is the sea? Is it in the back garden? Is Mummy coming too?" Jacob pawed at Charlie's leg.

"The sea is just behind the house, sweetheart. Not quite in the garden but nearly. And yes, your mummy is coming tomorrow. She's going to get the train to the big town that we passed on the way, and we're going to pick her up."

"When's she coming, love?"

"Not sure of timing yet, Mum." Charlie threw a look which begged her not to pursue the details with the children in earshot. "Let's get in, and we can get a bit more settled."

The group walked into a shadow spreading from the doorway, and Charlie's dad stepped across the threshold.

"My goodness, what a troop we have here," he bellowed, even though they were within earshot. "You'd better not have come here to eat all my party food."

Charlie grinned. Her parents were signalling their generous welcome to the children in the only way they knew, loud and proud hospitality.

"Party food?" Jacob tugged at Charlie's pocket and then jumped forward to fall in line with Mandy. "Are you having a party?"

"I should think so. A right old welcome party for you three, our special guests for the weekend." Her mum hooked his hand and led him into the hallway, where he pushed off both trainers with his toes and continued to natter.

Sam shrugged off his rucksack and dithered, waiting for instruction.

"Would you like a drink, Sam? I have something for you." Her mum led him inside. "I need your help to set up the gaming room. I borrowed a Nintendo from my friend Jim, who lives down the road."

Her mum had thought of everything when Charlie had no room for anything else in her head. She looked back at Chloe, hesitating, her nails digging into the strap of her bag. Charlie put a free hand on Chloe's back and rubbed it. "It's okay. You're safe here with me. Plus, they've got great Wi-Fi." She squeezed her shoulder and guided her inside.

It didn't take too long for the teenagers to lose themselves in their screens, and Jacob to become engrossed in a game of snakes and ladders with Charlie's dad. The knot of unease inside her chest loosened just an inch or two and she took her eyes off them, following her mum into the kitchen.

"Well, love, you didn't say much on the phone. What's going on? Two teens and a little one is an awful lot to handle on your own." Her mum scrubbed at a saucepan lid and rinsed it under running water as she cleared up after breakfast.

"I know, that's why I'm here. I need help. This has just sort of...

unravelled." Charlie was out of breath, trying to say everything at once and keep her volume down. "I couldn't speak properly on the phone. The kids were hanging around, and Kim was with me. She's going to the flat this weekend to pack up Darren's stuff. He's not there. There's a restraining order in place, so she knows to call the police if anything's awry."

"And he'll be gone, will he? Just like that?" Her mum's back straightened.

"Not quite. It's taken quite a bit of wrangling over the last few days, but we're there now. He backed down in the end because Kim has the better legal team."

"Was he a swine?" Her face wrinkled in disgust.

"Yes, he was." Charlie held onto the worktop, not wanting to revisit any of the horrors. "They were very frightened."

"And what about you? Are you recovering? We were very worried about you taking the brunt of it all like that."

"I'm fine. Don't worry about me."

"Well, I'm sorry you've been embroiled in all this. But at least it's sorted. You must've been such a help for Kim, sweetheart. The children clearly trust you."

"Don't," Charlie said. "I'm trying not to get too attached, Mum, because they'll be going back home soon, and then I can get on with my own life." Her chin dropped, and she looked away. "They've been a bit of a distraction really."

"From Elda?"

Charlie couldn't answer.

"Where is she now?"

"She's at home sorting stuff out. I asked her to come back to mine, but she needed space, apparently."

They danced around in silence for a while, clearing up and drying the crockery stacked on the draining board.

"How's she doing with it all? Must've been so hard for her to have to care for someone in their final days," her mum said.

Charlie leaned against the countertop. "I think she's lost more than just her grandmother this month."

"Why don't you go and stay with her?"

"How can I? With all this going on?" She gestured towards the hubbub of the living room, her dad's voice ringing through to the hallway. "To be honest, I'm no good at grief. I clam up when I'm there."

"You're not seventeen anymore, Charlotte. You've a lot more to give than you think." She rubbed Charlie's back and kissed the top of her shoulder. "Don't keep Elda at arm's length, she needs you."

Charlie pushed away the guilt. It would overcome her if she let it.

"Sherbert," her dad shouted. "Get your kickers on. We're off to the beach."

"It's kicks, Dad." She smiled faintly at her mum.

A cackle of laughter escaped from the living room and a half-dressed Jacob burst into the kitchen with a spade. "We can dig!"

Fifteen minutes later, Jacob was hopping at the bubbling shoreline. He took her mum's hand without looking and dragged her further into the water. They both shrieked with joy.

Chloe sat at Charlie's side, poking at the sand.

"Have you been to the beach before, Chloe?" Charlie tilted her head and blocked the sun with her hand.

"Yeah, when we were little. Before Jacob." She appeared hypnotised by her own finger, spelling her name in an invisible ink as the sand disappeared into itself.

Jacob ran towards them, and Charlie scooped him up and flipped him onto her back. The warm air caressed her shoulders. "More sun cream for you." He wriggled from her arms and jogged around the moat that Charlie had built. "Hat on too."

"The beach isn't as relaxing when you have a moving object to keep an eye on." Charlie stood with her back to the sun, observing her little warrior as her dad watched on from his worn-out deck chair.

"No, darling, it's relentless." His belly laugh caught on the breeze, and he lifted a flask of tea from a picnic basket.

Charlie knelt on a blanket next to Jacob and kept her hands busy.

"How are you feeling, Dad?"

"Perfect, Sherbert. Never better."

"The doctor still keeping an eye on you?" Charlie slipped her sunglasses down the bridge of her nose to peer at him.

"Absolutely. Heart, lungs, sugar, and mind. All in check." He leaned back into the sagging canvas. "You don't need to worry. Your mother does enough of that for all three of us."

"Chloe, come and see the rocks." Jacob jumped up and dragged his sister to the water's edge.

"Off they go." Her dad nodded towards their silhouettes.

Sam was strolling further along the beach, alone in his own world with his headphones on. Charlie frowned and settled into the matching deck chair next to her father. She grabbed at the sand with her toes. "I worry about Chloe and Sam. They've disappeared into themselves."

"They're good kids."

"That's what worries me. They're so compliant. It's not normal for teenagers." Charlie folded her arms and let the canvas support her neck. "They've seen a lot of horrible things. They should be angry. But they just do whatever's asked of them."

"I forget you're a grown-up sometimes. You've had a hell of a time. It's not like a usual case that you can let go when you take your robes off. Are you sure about all of this?"

Charlie took a deep breath. The breeze made her eyes sting. "I don't know what I'm doing, Dad. I'm drifting away from Elda while I'm picking up pieces for a woman I barely know and for children I have no responsibility for."

"Yes, it's all a bit complicated, isn't it, Sherbert?" Her father's gaze fixed on the horizon, but he gave her arm a squeeze. "You'll work it out though; you always do."

Charlie was safe and whole in the scale of her father's presence.

Her thoughts drifted to Elda, sitting alone in Linda's acrid house. She swallowed. *Fuck. I have everything, and she has nothing. And I've left her to it.*

"Dad." Charlie stood. "I think I've messed everything up a bit."

"Maybe, Sherbert. One step at a time though. Let's get these kiddos back to base for lunch."

The walk back along the dunes was harder than ever. Charlie sank further into the sand with every step. Forcing her way out only served to dig deeper. She was frustrated. Life was crammed with other people's problems, and she was trying to troubleshoot everything all at once. She had to get back to Elda before it was too late. She had to repair the rift she'd torn between them the night that Nancy died. Before all this, they'd been inseparable, maybe even indestructible. Was it too late to get back to what they'd had?

CHAPTER THIRTY-TWO

ELDA COULD FEEL CHARLIE'S presence behind her. She flicked her thin jacket collar up and marched on. Charlie jogged to catch up. They were walking in the woods. The sunlight dappled onto a bed of leaves under their feet. It was mid-morning, and the air was beginning to warm around them, but the atmosphere between them was frosty.

Charlie grabbed her arm. "Elda, wait. I want to talk about this."

"There's nothing more to talk about. I've heard what you've said, and I know you think I'm an idiot." Elda wasn't ready for Charlie to expose her erratic behaviour. "Do you know how many times I've wished I could be held by my dad?"

Charlie sighed as she caught up.

"I've wanted to be loved by him forever. Once I cut out an advert in the back of a pink paper for a private investigator."

"What happened?" Charlie asked.

"I got cold feet and threw the ad in the bin, but that's not the point." She ran her hands through her hair. "I don't have anyone. Not anymore."

"Please. You have me. Running away isn't the answer." She held the soft part of Elda's upper arm and she turned. "Are you going to look for your dad? Is that what this is about?"

"No. That's not what I'm doing."

They stood for a moment, daring the other to move first.

"I know you think I'm wrong. But you're not me. You can't feel what I'm feeling. I'm suffocating. I need to be alone to work some of this out," Elda said.

"Why are you going to Paris of all places?" Charlie asked.

"Everything went to shit last time, and you came home miserable."

Elda understood Charlie's angry desperation, but it made her all the more determined to carve her own path out of this mess. "Well, everything's gone to shit here too, Charlie. So I've got nothing to lose."

A stillness fell between them.

"Nothing to lose? What about us?"

Elda took a step back, unable to look Charlie in the face. She stamped at the soft ground underfoot and dug her heel into the mud, rooting herself so she could stand up to her. They were everything together. But Charlie hadn't been around for half of the anguish that Elda had faced over the past few weeks. Charlie was a good time girl who lost her courage when the hard stuff came knocking. "I need some space for a while. What we had was great. It was fun." She couldn't stomach hurting Charlie but pushing her away was the right thing to do.

"You're throwing away what we have. Listen, I've always supported your decisions..." Charlie touched her hand. "But you can't quit on us. I'm here for you."

Elda closed her eyelids and saw circles in the darkness. She wished everything would be quiet. "You've barely been here for me at all. You're obsessed with work. You have friends to help out. I just want to work out who I am and where I fit."

Charlie's shoulders sagged. "I'm sorry, Elda. I know I've been shit. Work has been too much. And this stuff with Kim and the children has been a nightmare."

"I don't care about Kim and her fucking kids." Elda's rage exploded between them.

"Okay. I'm making you feel worse." Charlie held her hands up.

"I'm not sure I can feel much worse. I'm beaten by all this. I've failed. I need to step off this conveyor belt and see what's next." Elda saw Charlie's frown, convinced she was right to walk away.

"Where are you going to go?"

"I don't know yet." She faltered. "My train is booked for Saturday morning. I've got an overnight stay in Paris and then I'll go from there. I might head south."

"Will you see Francis?"

"No, why would I?"

"Is it a holiday?" Charlie stopped, holding the silence between them.

"I don't know. Probably."

Charlie stopped walking. "Please don't go, Elda."

Elda kept moving. She couldn't look back. It was too much.

***

Elda stood at the check-in desk. Someone was playing the piano on the concourse of St Pancras. It was a delightful, complicated melody, and a crowd had gathered to listen. She knew that if she looked back, she wouldn't leave.

When the agent called her forward, a knot tightened in her chest. She pictured Charlie's face and imagined her velvet skin and forced herself to lift one foot and then the other. Through passport control, her breathing calmed. She focused on counting seconds. She looked up towards an advert on the wall. Perfume and a picture of the Eiffel Tower. That was the escape she needed. Glamour, fun, and charm. Her head ached with exhaustion, and she rubbed her puffy eyes.

She'd slipped away that morning without saying goodbye. She thought she'd be able to leave her mum's spite at the door, but realised she was still carrying it with her through the departure lounge, their hurtful exchanges echoing inside her head. She looked across at a man opposite her, tapping on a laptop. She wished she could busy herself. She wanted anything but to be in freefall.

Her platform was announced, and she gathered her bags. There was a chill in the air, and a grey hue that matched her mood. She looked at the tall carriages, wanting to remember them. She resolved not to return until she was ready.

"Miss, are you getting on board?" the man with the laptop asked from a polite distance.

She realised she was holding up the line of passengers. Without a word, she embarked and settled into a leather seat. It was too early for alcohol to numb her anxiety, but her bones were heavy with sleep, and she hoped to switch her brain off.

As a carefree tourist, Elda could just about pretend she was okay. She could play the part of an independent young woman travelling Europe. She could order in her best French, sip house wine, and drink strong coffee late into the evening. And maybe, just maybe, she could forget about the shitstorm her life had become.

A few hours later, Elda arrived at the front door of her hotel in a pretty area of the city. The main café, Arts et Metiers, was named after the area, and its tables spilled out onto the pavement. Mopeds skirted at the edges, and the waiter balanced trays of espresso cups. This was the Paris she dreamed of.

Elda found a table inside, and her eyes wandered over a catalogue of framed memories on the café walls. The waiter was impatient with her stuttering French, but she managed to order a glass of wine. She was on a holiday of sorts, after all. She sat back to take in the world around her. It was a million miles away from the stale air she'd left at home. Life was happening outside. Pedestrians threaded their way across pavements. Children scurried home from school. Workers huddled, talking fast over coffee and cigarettes. Shoppers carried posh paper bags. The city was alive.

Elda registered that, for the first time in weeks, the racing thoughts in her mind had slowed down. *I can hear myself.* Breathing came easily. The solitude of travelling alone wasn't lonely; it was liberating.

She opened the blank sketch book she had bought at St Pancras. Her finger cramped around the pen. It had been a while since she'd sat drawing, but it brought her the peace she'd been searching for. She sketched hastily. First, the outline of the table in front of her, then details in the background, and a woman outside a shop. She disappeared into the movement of her pen across the paper.

She looked up, and there had been a changeover of people around her at the little tables. Two women were deep in conversation, their voices low. The way they gazed and held the other's space made Elda think of Charlie. *Yes. I wish you were bloody here.* She pushed the image from her mind and gulped her wine. It burned the back of her throat.

As her mask slipped, she longed to be next to Charlie, cocooned in her arms and legs. She wished she'd had the courage to return to their home, put her silver key back in the lock and work out what happened next for them both. She had run away from the hard questions. She was overcome with fear and shame, and she no longer liked who she was.

CHAPTER THIRTY-THREE

CHARLIE'S FINGER HOVERED OVER the doorbell. She'd thought twice about making the journey, but decided she needed to distract her mind, and her body, from missing Elda.

Jude opened the door and held out her arms. She flashed a smile just as wide. "Hello, darling. Get inside. I've missed you."

Charlie shrugged off the nagging feeling that this was a bad idea. She took the glass of wine that Jude offered and sat at the edge of the curved velvet sofa. Jude's living room was decadent and ridiculous, like the basement of a Berlin cabaret. A place where anything could happen in the middle of the night.

There was no denying Jude was attractive. Here, in her own space, with her hair down and the straps of her bra just visible under a fitted shirt, she was hot.

"I was surprised when you called. You've been keeping your head down in chambers. I thought you'd shacked up with that woman from Paris, never to be seen again."

"Not quite. It didn't go entirely to plan." Charlie laughed.

"No?" Jude winked. "Didn't she fall for your charms? Not like you."

"She did. Briefly. I fell harder for hers if you really want to know."

"I'm not surprised. You were smitten the last time I saw you. What was her name?"

Charlie took a breath. "Elda."

Jude smiled.

"Don't pity me, Jude." Charlie poked her in the ribs playfully.

"Anyway, I've had a run of cases and I needed to have some fun. I thought of you." Charlie skipped the part where she couldn't get out of bed for three days and missed a court appearance.

"That's nice to hear." Jude's furrowed brow was just perceptible beneath her chunky fringe. "Drink up, and we'll hit Lock's for a cocktail or two."

Charlie leaned back and flicked her legs up onto the sofa. The depth of the sofa was absurd, even for her tall frame. She shuffled closer and met Jude's gaze. "Let's hang around here for a while, like old times."

"Charlie." Jude laughed and turned away. "It's been ages since we had old times together, I wouldn't know where to start."

"I would." Charlie caught hold of Jude's chin. She traced her thumb across her lips and pushed away the thought of Elda. She stroked the back of Jude's neck and moved in, tasting her earlobe. The sharpness on her tongue made her sit back. "I'm sorry, I'm not sure I can do this." This was wrong.

"Of course you can't," Jude whispered, taking Charlie's hand and rubbing the back of it. "You know this isn't what you want."

"I'm such an idiot. I'm so sorry, Jude, I never wanted to use you." Tears fell down her cheeks, and she looked away, ashamed of herself.

"Sweetheart, you are dear to me. So when I tell you this, know it's coming from a place of love and respect." Jude's hands steadied Charlie's shoulders and she withdrew, creating space between them. "There's nothing I'd like more than to rip your clothes off here, take you to bed, and touch every inch of you. Of course I would—look at you. But you're hurting. You're deeply in love with Elda what's-her-face. We both know this. Chances are, she's still in love with you too, and you'll be back together before you know it. So, let's drink up, and you can tell me all about it."

Charlie slumped, forcing a breath in and out, spinning with confusion. She'd always been in control of her interactions with Jude. They were playmates, and they both liked it. Now she found herself being read like a book. "Am I that obvious? I shouldn't have come." She squirmed but was grateful to Jude for calling her out.

"Nonsense. Here." She put the glass back in Charlie's hand. "Let's crack this together. Tell me the facts of the case."

Charlie filled in the blanks, and Jude supplied booze and tissues all night. In the end, she proved herself as wonderful a friend as she was a shit-hot lawyer. Charlie stayed the night on the round sofa and drifted in and out of sleep, thinking about where in the world Elda was. Charlie had hit rock bottom, and the desperation clung to her like a bad smell. But that meant whatever happened next had to be an improvement.

***

Charlie examined her pores in the bathroom mirror. Pink veins had burst in her eyes and her bones were weary. She went into a toilet cubicle to use as her makeshift dressing room. She unzipped a long, dress bag revealing the delicate black dress that had made an appearance at every formal dinner for the last ten years.

She thumbed the silk then took out a strapless bra. It was awkward and tight in the cubicle, and everything was grabbing at her skin. She pulled the flimsy, spaghetti straps over her shoulders and threw everything else in the bag before exiting the toilet stall.

She paused at the mirror for a quick check under the blue hue and applied a layer of red lipstick, while praying that the venue lighting would be much more forgiving. Her clown face looked like a stranger's: interesting but odd. She bared her teeth to check for crisps and tried to practice a smile. *This is going to be a nightmare.*

Playing nice at chambers' dinners was not Charlie's favourite thing. It took all her energy to act the extrovert for the evening. A cab was waiting outside the building, and Charlie climbed in, scooping her dress behind her. She fiddled with her neckline. It was a bit low, even for her small breasts.

As the car pulled up to the city hall, she regretted accepting the invitation and almost bolted. Without Elda, work was the only thing keeping her going, and she had to be seen at this event if she was ever going to make it anywhere near KC.

Charlie considered the six pillars ahead, each dressed in fairy lights that wound from bottom to top. The hall's entrance had been softened by swirls of chiffon. In the daylight, they would have been garish and tacky, but lit by a thousand soft bulbs the size of ladybirds, they looked like a dream.

She pulled up the front of her dress, every step pinching her toes, and walked to the main doors, where hollow laughter spilled out. With one final check of her neckline, she tilted her chin, pressed her lips, and marched in.

"Charlotte, you look wonderful tonight." Edward Foster, KC, put his arm around her waist and claimed her. He reeked of stale alcohol and sweat.

"Mr Foster, thank you for the kind invitation," she said.

"Not at all. You deserve a place at the table. It'll be yours soon, after all." He winked.

Charlie swallowed her own saliva and plucked a glass of champagne from a passing tray. As they were led to the table, Charlie realised that she would be the only woman present. She became more conscious of her dress clinging at her waist and the cold air at her bare chest. She found herself sandwiched between the head of litigation and a retired professor.

"Of course, we attract cheap young graduates and squeeze them for every billable hour. We're off to see the Vice Chancellor next week, aren't we, Bob? Get our next batch lined up." The professor was in full swing. He eyed Charlie from the side and lifted his glass to acknowledge her presence.

"Quite right, Maurice. Get them while they're yet to ripen," Bob said.

He had the emotional intelligence of a house brick. Charlie blinked. *Disgusting.*

"They don't know what work-life balance is at that age. Eh, Charlotte, remember those days?" Bob asked.

She forced a laugh and gripped her champagne flute. She was

so far down the chain, late nights and early starts were still very much her thing. "Sadly, Bob, I'm yet to achieve the Friday afternoon golf swing." *Please laugh.*

The men frowned and turned away, while a young waitress served a prawn mousse. Charlie became aware of someone on the stage, recognising him from TV re-runs. Underneath his warm-up act, there was a rumble of conversation, clanking of cutlery, and the odd shriek of laughter. It was a collection of old professionals with more money than sense, flirting over lukewarm food and bad shiraz.

Over the tail end of the braised beef, Charlie would've eaten her own foot just to get away.

"Miss Charlotte Mason, how wonderful to see you again."

Her heart bounced a little at the familiar voice. She turned to see Jack at her shoulder, grinning. The men flanking her took no notice when she was swept off by an unfamiliar man in a dinner suit. He demanded her attention and looked part-client, part-lover.

"Jack, what are you doing here?" She guided him to a botanical plant house in the centre of the venue.

"The corporates bought us a table as a reward for hitting sales targets or some shit. I don't know. I just organised the taxis. Anyway, you look completely different. What are you doing in that dress? I didn't even know you owned one."

"Don't. I hate these things. But I have to look the part." She looked down at her black heels and didn't recognise her own feet.

"Do you?" Jack challenged. "That's not like you, Charlie."

"Nothing is like me at the moment, Jack." She faltered and didn't want to say more but couldn't stop herself. "I'm a wreck. Have you heard from her?"

"Yes. She's in Paris. She's trying to find herself and failing miserably—because she left half of herself here."

Charlie's heart pounded, and she held her breath. "What do you mean? Elda left a lot behind when she ran off."

"She left you behind, Charlie. You know that. She's a dick, and she's trying to fill a gap in her life, somehow not realising that she left you here." He touched her hand. "I think you should go and get her back."

Charlie tried to push back the tears with a wipe of her hand. "She doesn't want me. She made that clear. We didn't just break up like normal people. She went so far away."

Jack looked up at the ceiling and sighed. "Charlie, she wasn't running away from you. Or even sad, old Linda. She was running away from herself and dealing with shit that she still can't handle. But Elda needs you, and me, for that matter. She doesn't know how bloody lucky she is." He laughed and nudged Charlie gently in the ribs. "Go and get her."

"I can't go back in there. Those men are so awful." Charlie looked past him at the vast room of round white tablecloths. She laughed through her tears.

"Let's go back to mine and get *Beaches* on." He grabbed her hand, and Charlie followed him through the heavy double doors.

Outside in the cool air, she held Jack's sleeve and came to a halt. "Where *exactly* is she, Jack?"

"I have the address at home. Let's go."

Her head was swimming, but she knew one thing. Elda needed her, and she'd do anything to bring her home.

CHAPTER THIRTY-FOUR

ELDA REMAINED IN PARIS. She had stood, thirteen days ago, at the Gare de Lyon as the departure board to Avignon ticked over. She'd seen her platform number and hesitated a moment too long at the sing-song voice of the announcer. It was enough to know she wasn't going to leave. She might even have wanted to go home. Fuelled by coffee and fresh pastry, she had made a plan. Without uttering a word, she made her way across the city to the outskirts, where the real people lived, and to the apartment of her only French friend, Sylvie.

"Oui." Sylvie's tone had been sharper than knives when Elda pressed her intercom.

Within a few moments, the ancient double doors flung open, and Sylvie stood back to let Elda into the cool foyer.

Two weeks later, Elda laid on a rigid futon bed in the living area of Sylvie's flat, counting the sections of the wicker blind at the window. Elda sketched in her book with both legs outstretched. Her muscles were tired, and she craved more sugar.

"Are you sick? What is wrong with you?" Sylvie looked up from the textbooks piled on her kitchen table. There were six empty bottles of Kronenbourg on the floor.

"Nothing. What do you mean?" Elda dragged herself across the tiled floor to close the shutters.

"Walks by the river. The same songs on repeat. Sketching in your book non-stop. Eating every time I look at you. Are you sick?"

As ever, Sylvie shone a light on Elda's worst attributes. She was lost. At first, Paris had been a distraction. Elda was seeing out her mourning period in a magnificent city, and she had plenty to keep her busy. She devoured the exhibitions, sat at the back of churches with a rosary, ate from patisseries on street corners, and listened to accordion music without throwing money in the hat.

And she found comfort in long, meandering conversations in the flat, shifting between her bad French and Sylvie's rude English.

But there was a different emptiness emerging. Something was pulling at her thoughts and her body every day. She couldn't shake the thought of Charlie and what she was doing back home.

"Why are you still here?" Sylvie asked as she fried onions and courgettes.

Elda had missed the frankness of Parisians. She smiled and tried to answer simply. "I don't want to go home, and I don't want to move on. I'm stuck."

"Meaning, *I* am stuck with *you*. You feel like Paris owes you an explanation?"

"Maybe. That's a curious question." They both laughed. "I do actually. This place has done me over every time I've been here. It's about time it served up some excitement and adventure."

"Why?"

"Because it's supposed to be a magical place. People come here to fall in love and find their artistic purpose. I've only ever fallen out of love and lost everything."

Sylvie made a sound that meant something in French but just sounded like a big wheeze to Elda.

"Paris owes you nothing. You brought terrible people with you, and you gave up your painting. Face it; you're to blame."

Sylvie pulled a cigarette from her pack of Gauloises and lit a match. She blew smoke across the small kitchen table and picked at her red lip. Elda considered whether Sylvie might be right. She shuffled the memories around in her mind. Her shoulders sank as she remembered her own part in the chaos and how powerless she'd been in her life. "What can I do? What the hell am I doing?"

"Ah, well, that is the question, darling."

"I'm serious. I don't know what I'm doing." Elda sighed, holding a cushion to her chest.

"You don't have a rudder." Sylvie flicked her cigarette into an ashtray.

Elda bit back a comment about how close it was to the food. "Yep. Rudderless."

"Your mother is a shit. Useless." Sylvie's expression was dead serious.

"Well, I wouldn't put it exactly in those terms, but yeah. She's done bugger all with the funeral or the admin. There's tonnes still to do when I get back."

"So you are going back." Sylvie peered through the steam. "What is bugger all?"

"It means *nothing*." Elda pushed the image of mounting paperwork from her mind. "Plus, Jack is being a constant nag and worrier. His heart is in the right place, and I do love him, but I can't stand any more questions. It was bad enough when I was at home, now he's just texting me every day."

"And Charlie? Where are we today with Charlie?" Sylvie held a glass of wine at her lips.

"I told you. Charlie is obsessed with becoming a silk or whatever at work, something I cannot even comprehend because it looks to me like it takes twenty years to even get a promotion, and you just stay locked at the same firm forever. She couldn't spare the time for me when I was caring for my dying grandmother, so what hope have I got any other time?" Elda knew, deep down, that Charlie's distance wasn't about work, but she couldn't put words around what was happening between them. "I've put her out of my mind."

"So, you're in Paris. Again." Sylvie had a slug of wine.

"It's lovelier than I remember. Paris is miserable when you're an outsider but charming when you're a tourist," Elda said, trying to convince them both.

***

The river swelled at Pont Neuf. On the right, the blunt towers of Notre Dame touched the sky. On the left, a web of streets led deep into the city. Elda had taken this route many times and she let her memory guide her while she was deep in thought.

She was on her way to meet Francis. Something was pulling her back into his orbit. She'd tried to ignore it, but she was curious about what he was doing. Elda crossed a cobbled path and turned left onto a tiny backstreet. Bistro tables nestled on the pavement, and Francis occupied one at the back, twisting a napkin ring in his fingers. He wore sunglasses and his hair was swept back higher than ever.

He stood to greet her and opened his arms. "Elda, my sweet. You look wonderful. Here, take this seat."

Confidence leaked from every pore. Francis's ability to manoeuvre her where he wanted her was well honed.

"Thank you for seeing me." She scolded herself for sounding too formal. *This isn't a bloody job interview.*

"Well, I've forgiven you for walking out on me and the department if that's what you're asking. You left me in quite the lurch. But at least there's enough room in the apartment now." A smile teased at his lips. "You're in Paris. Of course I want to see you. Tell me how you are."

"I'm okay. It's been a hard few weeks looking after my grandmother. But I'm healing. Grateful for the break." Elda held back. She omitted the parts where she'd fallen straight into Charlie's arms and failed to get a permanent job. "I'm sorry that I ran out on you. It wasn't fair to leave like that, but I didn't know what else to do."

"I've been successful at the university."

She smiled as he took over the narrative.

"I'm going to New York in September for a secondment. They're asking me to run a show there." Francis flicked his hand through his floppy hair. "It'll be hard work. Some sort of digital installation using new things. Nothing traditional. That's all gone."

Litter tumbled down the street and got caught at the downpipe next to their table. Elda noticed how filthy the pavement was around her.

"You want to come to New York with me?"

Elda raised her eyebrows, amused by his direct question. "No. But thank you for the offer."

"You've been painting, no?"

His question was innocent, and she'd expected it. But it gnawed at her confidence. *No, I have not been painting. I'm not the artist you thought I was.* "Not really. Looking after my grandmother has been a bit full-on." *Understatement of the fucking year.*

"Of course. Family is everything, Elda. I know that."

Elda wriggled beneath Francis's constant gaze. She tried to relax, remembering that she'd set up the meeting, and he wouldn't have agreed if he was still angry with her. The strangeness of the situation sent her heart racing. This wasn't how she'd seen the reunion play out. She'd imagined feeling something for Francis, just a hint of the mentor he'd been, but there was nothing. Instead, she was defensive, guarded, and wary.

"It's a shame, Elda. There is space in the world for your take on it." Francis sipped at a tiny cup of black, thick coffee.

Her neck stiffened. He was patronising her. When the waiter came, she waved him on. She wasn't going to prolong the exchange. "I'm glad you're happy, Francis. It's very good to see you. I came back to Paris to see whether I missed it."

"And?"

"I don't. It's been a good reminder of what I have at home, waiting for me." Elda stood and patted her shirt down. Francis rose to his feet and put his arms around her. He kissed her on both cheeks and put his finger on her nose. Elda didn't need his permission to leave, but she smiled. She walked back towards the river and squinted at the glass-domed boats floating away. Her mind was back in England on the semi-detached opposite the green.

She was glad she'd seen Francis. It crystallised in her mind what she'd already known. She hadn't made a mistake going home, and Paris *wasn't* the place for her to create or to thrive. She was loved at home, and she deserved that love.

Tears sprang to her eyes. She missed Charlie more than anything. It was Charlie who held her in the light and showed her how beautiful she was. It was Charlie who made her feel alive every day they were together.

Elda's heart raced, and she tried to piece together the fragments of her scattered thinking. Charlie hadn't abandoned her at all. Elda had been the one to turn away.

CHAPTER THIRTY-FIVE

THE TOP FLOOR OF the chambers was a stark contrast to the rabbit warren below. Charlie shielded her eyes from the shards of sunlight which were flooding the space and walked towards Maureen's office. She knocked harder than she meant to. She'd wanted to appear assertive and unwavering but feared she'd overplayed it.

"Enter." Maureen beckoned her into the room.

There was a richness to it: mahogany accents, plush carpets, and matching accessories. Charlie thought about the track she was on. If she kept her head down and waited long enough, eventually all the old farts would die off, and this office would be hers. But she wasn't going to wait for things to come her way. She'd made her mind up and needed to take charge of her own happiness. First step was telling Maureen to keep her career advice.

"Charlotte. I'm glad you came." Maureen stood to greet her.

Charlie waved away the formality. She wanted this to be over with. "Thank you for seeing me without an appointment."

"Not at all. I will always make time for you. Now, what is it?"

Charlie's toes curled in her shoes. She hoped her nerves weren't on show. "I'd like to take a break. A couple of weeks at least. Joshua is able to sort my current brief. It's so early in the proceedings, someone else can take over."

Maureen adjusted her spectacles, and there was a glimpse of a frown across her brow. "I see. This is unexpected, Charlotte. I must say, I'm disappointed."

"I'm sorry," Charlie said, infusing the words with a sincerity she didn't feel. "But this is a matter of personal well-being. I won't go into detail, but if I'm not able to take a couple of weeks, I will have no choice but to leave the chambers."

"I don't think that's necessary. Let's not get emotional."

Charlie took stock, pinching her lips together so she wouldn't be tempted to fill the void in the conversation. Maureen was underplaying her hand, but she wasn't going to let her walk away completely. That was a good sign.

"I've heard your request. We'll need to talk to the chief clerk and make arrangements. When did you want this break to start?"

"Tomorrow. My case is ready to hand over. Joshua's on top of everything."

"As always." Maureen sat down, and Charlie sensed a hint of defeat. "I'm not going to attempt to dissuade you. Clearly, you have given this much thought. It's unconventional, and I do not want to set a precedent for barristers to take time off, willy-nilly. You shouldn't have any problems being discreet, I trust?"

"Not at all." Charlie ignored the jab at her personal life. It was the least of her worries if she was able to skip out of the door tonight and get to Elda. "I'm very grateful for this, Maureen. It means a lot."

"I have a clue, Charlotte. I'm not a robot, despite what people think of me." Maureen smiled. "Now, please leave, and let the fine Joshua do what he needs to do. You're good, Charlotte. You could be brilliant. Do what you need to do and come back. Keep in touch. I want to know exactly when you're due to return so we can schedule your next brief."

***

Charlie thought of herself as a pretty independent woman. There wasn't much she hadn't done by herself. But walking up to the Eurostar check-in desk, she wavered. She cleared her throat and reached for her passport, but her hand shook. *Get a grip. You're thirty-two. You can travel on a train by yourself.* But this wasn't a commute to London. Her stomach flipped another somersault. Every time she sat down, she needed a wee, and her mouth was like sawdust.

She settled into the train seat and replayed the last conversation she'd had with Elda. She'd let her go. She hadn't fought hard enough for her. It was no wonder that Elda had felt abandoned. Charlie had spent the last two weeks going over what she had done wrong and what she had not done at all. Too much work, not enough time off. Rescuing Kim and the kids without telling Elda exactly what was happening. She hadn't been at Elda's side when she was battling one of the hardest fights of her life.

"Bonjour," a man said as he sat opposite and stretched his legs beside hers.

"Bonjour."

"You are English?"

"Is it that obvious?" She closed her eyes. The last thing she wanted was company.

"Yes, it is. Is your trip for work or play?"

Charlie held her breath for a moment. She could brush this off and ignore this guy for three hours, or she could be honest and he might leave her alone. "A couple of weeks ago, I let my girlfriend leave for Paris. I thought she needed space to grieve, but I think I let her go because it was easier than fighting with her. And I don't really like dealing with loss, so it was simpler to turn away from the whole thing." She grinned at her elevator pitch. "Now, I'm going to get her back."

"So, not Disneyland." He raised his eyebrow and smirked.

"No. Not yet." Charlie laughed for the first time in weeks.

"I'm Vincent." He extended his hand.

"Charlie." She shook it then settled back into the seat. Maybe this journey wouldn't be so awful.

"I'm going home. My brother had a baby, and the whole family is celebrating like he's a king. I'm bringing bad habits from England, and no offspring. So, no Disneyland for me either."

"Oh, disappointing your parents is so cliché. You can do better than that." Charlie's eyes were stinging from lack of sleep. She leaned against the head rest and surrendered to the rhythm of the train.

When she opened her eyes, they were in the tunnel, and it was black outside. A tiny bottle of red wine sat in front of her. Vincent looked up from the pages of his book and caught her eye. Without speaking, she twisted the cap and poured half into the plastic glass. She sipped, and the wine loosened her tongue from the roof of her mouth with a tingle.

"Tell me more," said Vincent. "Who are you going after?"

Charlie raised her glass to her lips. "Her name is Elda. I nearly ran her over once. And I've loved her pretty much ever since."

Sunlight flooded the carriage and once her vision adjusted, Charlie could see fields stretching out beyond them. She focused on the smooth grinding of the train's wheels against the tracks and her heart rate slowed.

"We'll be there in a couple of hours." Vincent topped up her glass.

The time passed slowly, despite Vincent's best efforts to entertain her. By the time her carriage pulled into the station, Charlie was already on her feet ready to disembark.

She had been to Paris as a child but hadn't prepared herself for the noise, dirt, and attitude. The Gare du Nord spat her onto a pavement to join an impatient queue of people for taxis.

She looked at Jack's drunken scrawl and when the driver repeated it back to her, she had no idea whether she'd end up at the right place. The car spluttered across the city, swerving across wide roads and down narrow streets. Shops were tiny and shabby, and then tall and elegant. Charlie could smell the stench of rumbling engines and the distance between shops got further. The signs got tattier, and the people looked less like tourists.

They came to a stop, and she stepped out onto the pavement. Charlie stared up at the imposing apartment block, and her heart raced. She wasn't ready. She scurried to the nearest cluster of shops and peered into the window of a tiny café. Her skin crawled.

She pushed the door open, and the warm air hit her cheeks. Blood rushed to her face. This wasn't like her. She had to get a grip.

Charlie wasn't sure whether to sit or queue, so she did a bit of both until a kind waiter waved at a spare stool in the window. When she was sat, the ground firmed up. Her breath steadied, and by the time the waiter returned to take an order, she was able to speak.

She started to rehearse while waiting for her coffee. She opened her lips and released a long breath. *Well, this is pointless.* A fun-size coffee arrived, and the door chimed as someone entered. Charlie jumped. What if Elda just turned up? Not being in control was sending her into another tailspin. Her stomach growled with anxiety, and the combined aroma of croissants and pizzas was making her sick.

She thought back to her last therapy session. She didn't need to fix anything. She could make amends for something she had done wrong. She could apologise. But she wasn't in charge of anyone else's actions. Charlie had loved two people more than she thought was possible. The first was taken from her, and she had never forgiven herself. She was determined not to let the other slip away without fighting for what they had.

It was dark by the time Charlie wheeled her suitcase up and over the buckled tree roots. She was conscious of every heavy step and the noise she was making. Back at the front door, she stroked her finger up and down the list of names, until she found one that matched Jack's scrap of paper.

"Allo." The greeting was razor-sharp.

"Oui, bonjour. Je cherche Elda, elle est là?" Charlie cringed, and there was a buzzing sound.

"Venez, deuxième étage."

She wasn't sure what that meant but kept climbing until she saw an open door. The light inside was warm and music flooded the stairwell.

"You're Charlie?" A woman poked her head out the door.

"I am. Are you Sylvie? Thank you so much for letting me in." Charlie almost laughed at her ever-so-British introduction. "I'm looking for Elda." Her hand raised to her chest to keep her from exploding and running down the stairs and out of the door.

"Come in." Sylvie led the way into the kitchen.

Charlie scanned the room, looking for signs of Elda.

"She's not here."

Charlie's cheeks flushed. She'd spent so long fretting over knocking on the door, she hadn't stopped to think about Elda not being there. "When will she be back?"

"Why do you want to know? You let her come here. You didn't stop her."

Wait. She thinks I abandoned her. "I didn't leave her if that's what you're saying. Elda was grieving and needed space. She said she needed time to be alone." Charlie stopped talking. She had no reason to explain herself to this stranger.

"Yes, she's been alone these past few weeks. She has lost everyone around her, except her useless mother of course," Sylvie said and dismissed her with a wave. "She was vulnerable and needed someone to gather her up and keep her safe. But you let her pack her bags and travel alone. She was heading to Avignon after spending a day here. My God."

Charlie retreated. "When she's back, I'll be happy to discuss this with Elda, but for now, perhaps it's best if I wait outside."

"Sit down, please." Sylvie walked to the counter and poured two small glasses of red wine. She looked less furious. "I don't hate you. I'm angry that Elda has been hurt."

Charlie's cheeks burned, and she couldn't swallow the lump in her throat.

"She went to see Francis."

"Really? Why?"

"God knows. She has been all over the place these past few days. I don't know what is in her head."

"Elda's head is a difficult place to navigate." Charlie's hands shook as she tipped the glass and gulped the wine. The smooth alcohol warmed her throat. "Sorry, this is a bit much. I've come all this way and need to find her. Where might she be?"

"Where do you think?"

"Honestly, I don't know. Please help me out here." Charlie considered the farce of chasing Elda around Paris. "I love her."

"Of course you do. You have come all the way to Paris on a Thursday night to tell her. Where do you think she's hanging out, all by herself?"

Of course. Charlie finished the glass of wine in one, thanked Sylvie for the welcome, and stepped out of the apartment. The ancient, uneven concrete steps were a blur as she raced towards her destination.

"The Métro is two blocks away. Enjoy," Sylvie called from her window.

Charlie spun around to face the final leg of her journey. She braced herself against the chill and forgot the weight of her suitcase. Desperate to reach Elda and tell her how much she loved her, Charlie hoped the adrenaline pumping through her veins would be enough to carry her across the city. She tripped on a flagstone and gathered herself. This last-chance attempt to reach Elda was worth every painful step.

CHAPTER THIRTY-SIX

THE LAST OF THE guided groups was leaving the atrium. Elda nodded to one of the guards she'd gotten to know over the past few weeks. Her late-night trips to the Musée d'Orsay had become a kind of therapy.

In the wide-open heart of the building, she could stretch her lungs and admire the sculptured giants around her. But tonight, she sought out the dark corners of the museum and followed the twisting corridors until she could smell the musty age of forgotten masterpieces. Here in the bowels of the old train station, she would stumble upon an early work or a rough sketch. She needed to know the imperfections of the masters and their work in progress. She wanted to understand their faults and corrections, so that she might comprehend her own mistakes.

Resting on a polished stone bench, the cold crept beneath her skin. She shut her eyes, planning her next move. Going home was easy. She could afford the fare, and she could be there tomorrow morning. Returning was harder. What would she say to Charlie? The bitterness of her anger lingered, even though she was desperate to feel Charlie's arms around her. Charlie had let her down when she needed her most.

She looked across at the brown walls cocooning her. Tiny, framed pieces hung on display. They were the kind she had to peer at to discover their meaning. She knew the feeling. She'd had to get close to her own emotions this week to reveal her truth as well as her flaws.

A tear dropped onto her cheek, and she wiped at it with her fingertips. She was so alone. She'd ruined the best thing that had ever happened to her. She'd run away from Charlie, giving her no chance of being there for her. She'd left before she could be abandoned.

The paintings blurred, and she pressed her eyelids, wishing the pain would go away. Somewhere down the corridor, there were footsteps, and she hoped that her solitude would remain unbroken for a few more moments.

A silence followed, and Elda suspended her thoughts inside it, caught in the void. It was threatening and peaceful at the same time.

"Here you are."

For the briefest moment, Elda thought it was Charlie, and she smiled at the power of her imagination. At the touch on her arm, her eyes sprang open to see it really was Charlie. She wasn't dreaming.

"Charlie—"

"Please, hear what I have to say. I just want to tell you something." Charlie held her hands out.

Elda had missed her face so much, she was using all her strength not to pull her against her. "How did you know I was here?"

Charlie kneeled at the stone bench, her hands wringing. "It doesn't matter. I wasn't there for you. I haven't put you first. And that was wrong. You are first. You are *everything*."

"But how?" Elda's mind was frantic, piecing together the parts that had brought her here.

"It's late-night opening at your favourite museum. I knew you'd be here." Charlie looked away. "I've already been chewed up by your friend Sylvie. She seems lovely, by the way."

"She's a Rottweiler. Heart of gold but very protective." Every inch of Elda wanted to collapse into Charlie, but something inside her needed more. "Why did you come though?"

"To find you. To tell you that you're the most important person to me." Charlie took Elda's hand, and the fire between them roared back to life. "I love you."

A drum thundered in Elda's ears. The words she longed to hear. Could they be real?

"I've taken a break from work. I want to show you that you come first. We can stay here for as long as you like. You can paint, and we can be together."

The booming got louder. Charlie wasn't just telling her that she was loved; she was showing her. "You took a break from work, for me? What about becoming KC?" Elda pulled away from Charlie and tucked her shaking hands beneath her legs.

"It can wait. Everything can wait. I was an idiot to not understand what was happening. That night, when you jumped in front of my car, everything changed. I changed. I've never felt this way about anyone." Charlie laughed through her tears and grasped Elda's knee, sending shockwaves through her body. "Elda, speak to me."

"I've never been truly loved by anyone but you. I've not really been able to trust anyone. But I think I want to trust you." Elda brought her palm to Charlie's cheek and wiped the tears away. "I'm sorry I ran away from you. You didn't deserve that."

Their gaze met, and so many unsaid words passed between them.

"You need to kiss me now," Elda whispered. She froze with anticipation. When Charlie brought her lips to her cheek, Elda shifted and met her with a hungry, hard kiss. She bit down, craving every part of Charlie's body against her.

***

"Those ceiling roses are fuzzy. Or is it me?" Elda closed her eyes against her blurred vision and the dawn breaking through the bedroom's linen drapes. They had spent the night entangled in each other's arms.

"No. They're layered with paint. They must be so old." Charlie nestled into her neck and kissed her collarbone.

"I feel brand new."

They hadn't made it back to Sylvie's apartment. Elda walked Charlie through her favourite parts of the Orsay, but they couldn't keep their hands off each other, so they booked a romantic hotel room in the Latin Quarter.

"I feel like I could run through this city with my clothes off. It's exhilarating, isn't it?" Charlie kissed Elda's ear, and a shiver curled across her front.

"Really? I'm not letting you out of this room. We have all day. Let's not waste it."

There was a knock at the door, and Charlie got up, wrapping a towel around herself. She returned with a breakfast tray.

"Get back into bed. I missed you." Elda lifted the sheet and pulled Charlie on top of her, enjoying the heavy weight crushing her.

"I only went to the door." Charlie laughed.

"I mean, I missed you these past few weeks. I'm sorry. I shouldn't have run away from you. It was just all too hard." Elda traced her fingers across the ridges of Charlie's shoulder blades, her skin responding to her touch. She was struggling to put into words the emptiness that had appeared in her world without Charlie.

"Me too. I'm sorry I let you walk away."

"You couldn't have stopped me. I had to work things out on my own." Elda pinched the bridge of her nose. "I'm still furious with my mum, but I'll have to sort that out too eventually."

"You will. It'll take some time. She has her own grief to work through." Charlie caressed Elda's cheek.

"You know what? You know what my nan would want me to do? Live my life. Live it until I die. That's what she'd want, and that's what I'll do." Elda gripped Charlie's arms. "Yes, I'll paint. We'll be together. And I will adore you forever."

"Are we going to stay here forever?"

"You weren't serious about staying in Paris, were you?" Elda turned to face her.

"Of course." Charlie sat up and relaxed into the feather pillows, revealing her breasts. "I've taken a couple of weeks off. If you want to stay here for a while, or for longer, then we will."

Elda flipped the sheet, straddled Charlie's waist, and ran her hands through Charlie's bed hair. "I love you, Charlotte Mason." She kissed her forehead. "But no, I'm not going to shatter your dream of becoming a top KC. I don't want you to give anything up. You don't need to. And finally, I've had the romantic night in Paris I've always dreamed of. But I want to go home with you."

"Not yet though, eh? Let's stay here for a while." Charlie arched her back to reach Elda's lips, and their bodies met as they kissed.

CHAPTER THIRTY-SEVEN

A TREMOR COURSED THROUGH Charlie. It wasn't like her to feel nervous, but this was so far from her usual courtroom performance. The next conversation promised to be raw for both of them. "Hi." She opened her arms wide, and Kim accepted the hug. "How're you doing?"

"This week has been a good one. Thanks to you."

"You've done all the hard work," Charlie said. "How are the kids?"

"Settling back home now Darren has cleared off for good. Jacob's oblivious, but Chloe has been quiet for a few days. She takes everything in."

"Yeah, I noticed that. Keep an eye on her. How's Sam?"

"Angry. Taking it out on the football pitch. His coach called me after the match last night and said he was a bit full-on with the referee. I filled him in on what's gone on. I had to speak to the school as well because the police will be in touch. They need to make sure they're safe."

"Good. I'm worried about Sam. He must've been frightened that night."

"Don't remind me. They were terrified." Kim's head dropped.

"Thanks for meeting me." Charlie stood aside, allowing a couple of dog walkers to pass them at the entrance to the park. "Shall we walk?"

"If you like. It's been ages since I've been down here. I used to bring Sam and Chloe when they were little."

The scratch of the gravel beneath their footsteps filled the silence. Charlie ran through the script she'd prepared in her head in the early hours. Tossing and turning, she'd almost woken Elda with her restlessness. It hadn't helped one bit. She still struggled to find the words.

"Did you want to talk through the police report or something?" Kim glanced at her. "It's not like you to invite me out for the afternoon. You're usually up to your eyes at work."

"I know. I've got a couple of weeks off. Sorry, you must be curious about what I needed to speak to you about." Charlie kicked her boot against the path. "The truth is, I've been meaning to talk to you for a while about..." She wasn't sure how to describe their relationship. The last few weeks had catapulted Charlie to Kim's go-to person. "About our friendship. I need to reset some expectations."

"Charlie, I know what you're going to say." Kim held her hands up. "I've thought about it too. I've relied too hard on you, and I can't come begging for any more money."

The harsh sunshine caught Kim's cheek, highlighting the lines between her eyebrows and at her lips. It made Charlie think of how flawless Theresa's skin was as a teenager. She stopped herself. It was her constant comparison of the two women that pulled Kim closer to her every time she tried to break away.

Charlie looked to the heavens for a beat, taking in the wide expanse of the blue sky above her. The world was so open to them all. Anything was possible if they allowed it.

"Am I right then?" Kim asked, drawing her back down to earth.

"Sort of. Although I wouldn't have put it as bluntly as that." Charlie touched Kim's arm, craving her understanding. "This last couple of weeks have been horrible for you and the children. I don't want you to think I've abandoned you if you need my help again. I will be there for you. But before the chaos with Darren, I wanted to redraw the boundaries between us. The only way I can do that is by being completely honest with you about how I'm feeling."

"Go on. I'm listening." Kim stopped walking. "Don't worry about offending me if that's on your mind. I've got pretty thick skin, even if it does bruise easily."

Charlie grimaced, recalling the inky, yellow stains on Kim's body after Darren was done with her. She pointed to a bench, and they strolled across to sit down. "This is so hard. I don't want to push you away when you need me most." Charlie closed her eyes against building tears.

Kim mirrored her angst. "You've done enough for me, Charlie. I've leaned on you when I really shouldn't have. If I'm being honest with myself, I liked having you close because you're the only living reminder that Theresa was ever happy in the world. That she ever breathed, and laughed, and loved someone. You were hers, and I wanted to have you around. It's selfish of me. You're just a child yourself."

"I'd never thought of it like that." Charlie picked at her thumbnail. "It's not how I see it. I was the one who needed you in my life. When you found me, you were the first person who ever believed how much I loved Theresa. I hadn't ever told anyone else. So, don't think you've done me any harm. Being with you has helped me grieve."

"Ditto."

Charlie swallowed back a lump of fear. "I still want to see you. I want to see the children."

"Of course. They think the world of you."

"But you can't turn up at work."

"No. That was a one-off mistake. I know that."

"And if you need me in the middle of the night, you need to call first."

"I'll try not to. Darren's out of my hair, and I just want a quiet life for me and the kids. They're too important to me." Kim blew out her cheeks. "I won't be asking for money either. Now that he's not pissing it up the wall, I can manage. I promise."

"You don't need to make promises to me. Make them to yourself."

"Good thinking. You always did have the brains." Kim winked, lightening the despair between them. "You've got your own life to be getting on with too, haven't you? You and Elda?"

"Yeah. We're going to make a go of it." Charlie hesitated. "I love her, you know? It's a strange feeling to move on, after all this time. From someone who was so significant but so fleeting."

"She was only here a short time, but she made it count. Theresa would want this for you. Don't ever doubt that." Kim squeezed her hand. "I want it for you. You deserve everything that makes you happy."

"Thank you. You mean the world to me, too, you know?"

"I know. Your actions speak louder than your words, Charlotte Mason. You've always been there for us." Kim planted a kiss on her cheek and brushed away her teardrops.

Charlie rested her head against Kim's shoulder, finding instant comfort and relief.

***

Charlie hesitated at the entrance to Elda's studio. The first time she'd stood on this threshold, she was edgy. Now, it was a place of calm. Anywhere Elda was, Charlie was restored.

Hanging back, she took in the scene from the doorway: Elda held her brush between her teeth while Jack leafed through the pages of a magazine. They both looked content.

"How was it?" Elda looked up from her canvas, her face screwed up with concern.

"It was a good conversation. Kim understood." Charlie ruffled Jack's hair as he sat on the sofa. "You're quiet, mister."

"I am bathing in Elda's creativity. She doesn't usually let me into her inner sanctum."

"He's behaving himself." Elda threw a rag at Jack's head. "If he doesn't, I've threatened to chuck him out. I'm on a deadline for that exhibition in Manchester next month."

Charlie kissed Elda on the lips, leaning into the flare of desire.

"Cut it out, you two." Jack yawned. "You have your whole, love-struck lives to get it on. You can at least wait until I've gone to work."

"What time does your shift start?" Charlie asked, and he threw the rag back in their direction.

"Not 'til two, you cheeky cow. Plenty of time to enjoy an early lunch with my two favourite people."

"Well, if you put it like that. Grab your coat, and we'll wander."

"I'll follow you down." Elda turned back to her canvas. "I just want to finish this section. Order for me?"

"Absolutely." Charlie slipped her arm around her waist and pulled her in for a goodbye kiss.

"She'll only be ten minutes." Jack yanked her hand.

"Make that twenty," Elda called after them.

Charlie settled into Jack's relaxed pace. The glow of contentment followed her out of the mill building and across the street. She chuckled to herself. She had no idea that she was lacking until Elda had stumbled into her life. Elda filled up parts of Charlie that she hadn't ever known were empty.

She looked across the canal towards the imposing mill. Once, she'd have blustered her way through life, shrugging off the emotional ties which came with physical pleasures. Now she knew that real strength came from being known, and being loved, unconditionally.

CHAPTER THIRTY-EIGHT

Elda looked out onto the green from Charlie's bedroom window. Her thoughts drifted as a couple pushed their toddler on the swing. She shook away the nagging doubts. Perfection wasn't something she should aim for and comparing her family with others hadn't done her any good in the past.

The door creaked and she turned, full of joy at the sight of Charlie balancing two mugs of tea and a packet of chocolate biscuits.

"Too early for snacks?" Charlie asked.

"Never." Elda rescued the toppling packet and knelt onto the creased sheets.

They laid back against the headboard, watching clouds floating across the two windows. A silver birch swayed in the park. "I could stay here forever," Elda said, pushing crumbs into her mouth.

"You should." Charlie set down her mug and kissed her neck softly.

Elda wriggled from underneath. "Don't start, Miss Mason. We need to get ready soon. I don't want to be late for your parents."

Charlie crashed back on the pillows with a groan.

"Drink up, and we can jump in the shower." Elda raised her mug, while Charlie shot her a hopeful look. "Together, yes." Elda smiled.

"Nice compromise agreement. You should be a lawyer." Charlie took her in her arms, kissed her deeply, and nipped at her bottom lip, which made Elda squeal with anticipation.

The doorbell rang as Elda rolled out of bed.

"I'll go." Charlie kissed her shoulder and left the room.

Elda flicked the curtain to see a taxi pulling away. She listened for the click of the front door and heard muffled voices at the foot of the stairs.

"Elda, can you come down?"

By the time she'd pulled her jeans and a jumper on and taken the stairs two at a time, Charlie was boiling the kettle with fierce concentration on her face.

"Hello, Elda." Her mum sat at the table, clutching her handbag.

"Mum." Elda stood fixed to the spot. "What are you doing here?"

It had been a month since she'd left their family home. She'd called the house twice, but her mum had put the phone down. After a while, she'd put it all to the back of her mind. But now, in Charlie's kitchen, her temper reignited.

"I came here to see you," her mum said to the floor tiles, as if she couldn't bear to look Elda in the eye.

"Did you have breakfast, Linda? Would you like some toast?" Charlie moved around the kitchen, trying to make everything normal.

"No, love, you're all right."

"Mum survives on fags and vodka. Don't fuss over her, Charlie," Elda said.

"Don't." Charlie placed her hand on Elda's arm and squeezed. "Your mum's travelled a long way this morning. Did you get the train, Linda?"

"Yes, I did. Thank you for thinking of me, but don't worry about Elda. I've heard it all before. I deserve most of it," her mum said calmly. "Can we have a minute, do you think?"

Charlie looked at Elda and waited for her signal. She nodded, and they were left alone.

"Why have you come? It must've been a nightmare on the train. Did you have to get a taxi to the station?" Elda asked.

"I wanted to give you this." She extended her arm, holding a brown envelope. "And this." She handed her a white piece of folded paper.

"What is it?" Elda took the items and tried to slow down her thoughts.

"The envelope has some money that your nan saved for you. It's not much, but she was putting it away so you could have it."

Elda stepped back, bringing the envelope to her chest. She was surprised her mum hadn't spent it down the club, but she kept that to herself. She unfurled the note and stared at the London address. Elda narrowed her eyes as she tried to read her mother's expression. "I haven't got time for riddles, Mum." Elda set the paper down on the side and began to clean the countertop.

"Please stop," her mum said gently. "That's your dad's address."

Elda froze, gripping the wet cloth. She studied the flecks in the worktop and tried to steady her heartbeat. "You know his address? Why are you giving it to me now?"

"Because you were right. You deserve to make your own mind up about him. He might have changed."

"What about you? Have you changed?" She let her tears fall.

"I thought you were better off with a clean break. I did okay without my dad around. I thought you'd be all right with me and your nan." Her mum's face was grey. "Maybe I was wrong. I haven't been up to it, have I?"

Elda's mind was flooded with sadness. She was grieving the loss of her grandmother, as well as the mother she'd never had. "You did your best." It was all she could say. A numbness crept over her chest and down her arms.

Her mum sat still for a few moments, rolling a coaster between her fingers. "I've stopped drinking."

"Have you really?" Elda focused through her glassy tears.

"Yeah. About time, really. I'm going to the meetings now. It's early days, but it helps."

Elda took her hand and wrapped her mum's cold fingers in her own.

"I'll leave you." Her mum stood and gathered her bag.

"Where will you go?" Elda didn't want to see her wandering the streets. "We'll drop you somewhere. We're heading to Charlie's parents for the night."

They both had much to say, but neither had the words today. Resentment bubbled in Elda's chest. She wasn't sure if she was still angry with her mum or herself.

"I'll just get the next train back, love. I've seen you now."

It wasn't enough. Elda wanted more time to think about what was happening. She didn't want her mum to leave with everything unsaid and unresolved. She wondered what Charlie would do.

"We'll drop you in town on the way, and we can get a coffee or something." Elda put her hand on her mum's shoulder. "Just wait here while we finish getting ready." Elda turned to face her, relaxing her jaw. "I'm glad you came over. Maybe next time you could stay for a bit."

***

The dining chair cradled Elda's body. She spread her fingers and counted her breathing, still reeling from this morning. Her mum's visit had lifted the lid on emotions she'd buried for years.

She looked across to Charlie's parents, cherishing the ease with which they moved. She recognised the battle of envy and hope inside her. She'd always dreamed of a family where each member was loved for who they were. But she'd been dealt one that smothered and lied just to keep everyone in their place.

"Elda, would you like some potatoes, sweetheart?" Mandy passed a ceramic pot with both hands.

"So, girls, what's next? Any adventures?" Harry's cheerful voice boomed around the room. He looked delighted to have Charlie beside him and basked in her happiness.

"We're going to Denmark this summer," Charlie said, setting down her fork.

"Good for you, Sherbert." He turned to Elda. "You're a marvellous influence on my daughter. She's been overworked by those chambers for years."

"We've booked a cabin on the coast. No one around. Just peace and quiet. And a bit of painting," Elda said.

"Now, talking of which. I hope you don't mind, but I've dragged out the old easel from the garage. You can take it down to the beach this evening and have a go at the sunset if you like." Mandy gestured to the corner of the room. "I've saved your bits and bobs from the last time you were here too. So you've got everything you need."

"That's right. Your mother's been fussing down there all morning, setting you up a nice little area with the deck chairs and what not." Harry raised his flute in a toast. "What would we do without her?"

"Thank you so much. That sounds amazing." Elda joined the toast. She took Charlie's hand under the table and squeezed tight, trying to work out what was washing over her.

They met each other's gaze, and she felt blessed. She was entirely loved by Charlie and part of a wonderful, connected family who loved her for who she was. There was just one thing missing in her life.

CHAPTER THIRTY-NINE

ELDA BALANCED HER WEIGHT on the rumbling underground train. She'd always hated the tunnels. Sweaty, suffocating passages that threatened to collapse, trapping her beneath the ground.

Today, she was filled with even more dread. She bore the weight of impossible expectation on her shoulders. She had waved Charlie off at the station with a brave smile, passing her trepidation off as excitement. Now, in the belly of London's Undergound, fear threatened to subsume her entirely. She had no idea what would face her on the other end of the line, the other side of the door on which she intended to knock.

She alighted at Seven Sisters and blinked into the glare bouncing off the car windscreens as four lanes of traffic crawled along the road. She smiled at the familiarity. So common, yet so alien.

Just like her father. Such an ordinary thing, to go and see your dad. *Not if it's for the first time in twenty years.* Panic rose in her chest, and she almost turned back for the ninth time that morning. *Get a grip, Elda. What's the worst that could happen?* She'd already examined every possible outcome from this adventure. She'd imagined her dad as a recluse, unwilling to open the door to her, and as a psychopath, who might lock her in his basement for three years. She wondered for a long time whether he might be a drunk like her mother. That would be a bitter disappointment. It wasn't all bleak. Her fantasies had taken her on glorious family holidays. Her dad might want to make up for lost years.

Her phone buzzed in her hand, telling her to take the next left. She paused at a striking building on the corner. A stunning art gallery had grown from the ashes of hunger and misery in this impoverished borough. She saluted the artists streaming through its doors and took it as a sign she was in a good place, even if she wasn't about to receive the welcome she ached for.

She rounded the corner and came face-to-face with the street name which had been seared on the back of her eyes since her mum had passed her the folded piece of paper in Charlie's kitchen. There was no turning back now. Number eighteen came too soon, and she checked herself. Before she had time to second-guess the next move, the door swung open just a few feet from where she stood.

"Can I help you?" the man asked, turning to lock the door behind him. "I don't need any circulars if that's what you've got. I've still got last week's charity bag too."

His voice was warm and pleasant. Elda hadn't thought about how he might sound. Her breath caught in her throat, unable to respond.

"Are you okay?" He adjusted his glasses.

She coughed, begging the words to come out. "You don't recognise me."

He peered a little closer at her then his eyes widened. "Yes! Yes, I do. Elda. Of course I do."

"I'm sorry to come out of the blue."

"Wow. It's so good to see you. Look at you." He stepped toward her. "You're so grown up. And beautiful."

"Hi." She swallowed.

"Hi." He fidgeted with his keys. "Would you come in, for a cup of tea?"

"Yes. I'd like that." She followed him inside the narrow hallway and into the living room. It was old fashioned, scuffed at the edges. But it was clean and tidy, just like him. She sighed, drinking in the relief that her dad might just be normal.

"Please, sit down." He stared and said nothing for a long moment. "I don't know where to start."

Elda perched on the low sofa and set her bag on the floor. "No. I don't really, either. But Mum gave me your address, and I would like to talk, if that's okay?"

"I'd really like that, Elda." He hesitated and closed his eyes. "I owe you a thousand apologies."

She saw her own reflection in his agonised expression. "We'll get to that." Elda put on a brave face. She really wanted to hear what he had to say. "I just came to see if you were here."

"Yes, okay. I'll put the kettle on."

He scuttled out, leaving her alone with her thoughts. For the first time in the week since her mum's visit, Elda's heart rate slowed. The man before her had left her younger self. He had abandoned her when she needed him most. But he had once been her protector, and she felt that now, sitting in his living room. She was shielded by the same force that had stood between her and her frenzied mother so many years ago.

She couldn't fathom why he hadn't had the strength to stay, or why he hadn't taken her with him when he'd fled. But she had the time and patience to discover all these truths now that she had found him. She was willing to listen with an open mind and an open heart. She desperately wanted to forgive him if only he could explain what happened. So, this was the start of a conversation.

He returned and set down a tray with a teapot and a plate of biscuits before sitting beside her.

She smiled at the touching and welcoming hospitality. "Why did you leave me?" The question popped out before she'd had time to swirl the words around her head once more.

He stared at the teapot and swallowed, the silence between them agonising.

"It doesn't matter. It's all in the past." Elda filled the dead air, cringing with every fibre of her body and not meaning a word of what she said.

"It does. You deserve answers." He scratched at his palm. "I'm sorry. You were so little when I left, and you didn't deserve it."

Elda held her breath, forcing herself not to speak into the void.

"You know your mother struggled, but she hasn't always been that way. She loved you. She still does, I'm sure of it. I wouldn't have left if I thought otherwise." He looked down at the fraying carpet.

"This isn't about Mum though, is it? Please tell me. I just want to know why you went that day and never came home?" Elda bit back the rising anger, not wanting to spoil this chance now she had it. "I don't need any more apologies, just an explanation."

His eyes widened with what looked like fear. "I had a breakdown. I was basically useless—paralysed, mentally but also physically, in a way. I'm not blaming your mother, but her behaviour was hard to live with. It got too much, and I couldn't cope. I ended up losing my job and then, well, everything fell apart. Your mother threatened to kick me out, and your grandmother took her side. Of course she did, I don't blame her."

Elda breathed through the realisation that her father had suffered, and she'd known nothing about it. "But why? What happened?"

He moved to touch her hand then withdrew quickly. "I know you're looking for that one reason I left you, but I don't have it. I've looked inside myself so many times. I've stared at some dark places in my head. The answers won't come." He sighed. "All I can tell you is that we know more about our own minds now, don't we? Doctors and smart people, they've figured it all out. Sick people get treatment and support. But in those days, these things happened, and they were hushed up. Blokes couldn't fall apart. If you pulled a sickie at work, your bloody arm better be falling off."

"Yeah, I suppose." Elda's gaze darted around the room, still searching for firm foundations. "But why did you leave me with Mum? She never really got over it." Elda held back the worst details of her mother's behaviour.

"Kids stayed with their mothers back then, no matter how chaotic the home was. It would've been an impossible fight to try and keep you. And I would've been no use to you anyway, Elda, in the state I was in. No job. No place to sleep."

"Mum said you didn't love us."

He coughed, and his jaw fell slack with obvious disbelief. "I loved you more than anything. I just had nothing for you. I was stuck on friends' sofas for well over a year before I made it to London. By that time, you were settled. It would've been confusing for you, me flitting in and out of your life. You'd almost got over it all." He pinched his eyebrows.

"I hadn't, Dad." Tears sprang to Elda's eyes. "I never got over it." She hesitantly took his hand in hers and stared at it. The touch felt so familiar and yet not. These were the hands she'd needed holding her for her whole life: supporting, helping, just being there would have made so much difference. She glanced up at him and saw his tears mirroring her own, saw his own grief and regret at the years he'd lost too. Elda had to stop thinking about the past and look to her future, but did he want to be part of it? "But maybe, I could get over it now..."

His expression brightened, and he grasped her hands tightly. "I would love to be a part of your life." He swallowed hard, looked up at the ceiling, and blinked back his tears. "I never thought you could possibly forgive me, Elda."

She gave a tight smile and nodded. She wasn't sure that she could either, but he was the only one with the ability to repair the last remaining hole in her heart. And for that reason alone, she had to try.

EPILOGUE

Five years later

"I'VE GOT TO GO, Dad. I'm being pulled." Elda struggled to keep the phone to her ear.

"Right-oh. I just wanted to check you're coming on Wednesday for the gallery. Shall I make up the beds for the three of you?"

"Yes, please, that would be great. Charlie will work from yours for the day. It'll be the last one for a while though."

"I guessed that. You'll need to slow down and get some rest."

"Chance will be a fine thing."

"And will Mister want his tea as usual?"

"Yeah, but he's gone off peas this week. So you might need to play it by ear." Elda climbed on the wooden frame and pushed her hips into the steel slide. The curved, metal edge was cold against her warm skin.

"Where are you, Elda? You sound like you're in a tunnel."

"I'm at the park, chasing your grandson around. I'd better go. See you Wednesday."

"You will do. Bye, love."

Elda put the phone in her pocket and looked up towards the sky. She saw nothing but blue. The air touched her skin, and she released her breath, enjoying the moment to herself. "Is anyone down there?" she shouted down the pipe, sending her voice rumbling through the tunnel.

"Come down, come down."

She shuffled forward and pushed off with her palms. Her jeans caught at the slide's metal seams, and in the middle, her weight slowed her down, but she made it to the bottom with laughing tears streaming down her face.

She popped into the light, and Elijah screeched with joy as she caught his soft, stocky frame between her arms. He wriggled out of her reach, and Elda was stuck at the bottom of the slide, her quads no longer strong enough to force her pregnant frame to full height.

"Mama caught me." He bounced off Charlie and ran in circles around the park.

Charlie pulled Elda to her feet. They locked lips and Elda melted underneath the embrace, forgetting their hosts.

"Come on, you two. We've got lunch to eat." Chloe spread a rug across the warm grass. She and Jacob bumped heads and emptied a picnic basket.

Elda set after Elijah and he rushed at her, giggling with joy as she raised him to her chest and planted kisses along his downy hairline.

"Chloe, will you grab Eli?" Charlie put her hand across her eyes to block out the sun. "Elda shouldn't be carrying him; he's too heavy for her."

Chloe bounced towards the pair with her long limbs outstretched. She scooped the two-year-old into her arms and blew raspberries into his jumper.

"Chloe, I'm fine!" Elda said as she reached the picnic rug. "Charlie worries about me too much. She's turning into her mum."

"You shouldn't have been going down that slide either. You need to take it easy." Charlie rested her hand on Elda's bump and kissed her cheek.

"I've done this before, Charlie. I'm listening to my body, and it's telling me to move." Elda grabbed a sandwich. "And eat."

They each took a space, and Jacob handed out plastic plates and overfilled glasses.

"Ice cream?" Elijah pulled at Charlie's jeans.

"We'll have ice cream after our sandwiches, Eli." Charlie sat him down behind a plate of crisps. "What time will Sam finish work? I want to see him before we go."

"He's on shift 'til four. Then he'll be home. Mum's making him sausage and mash," Chloe said.

"We'll see him and your mum, then, when we drop you off," Elda said.

"If he doesn't stay late. He loves a bit of overtime." Jacob shoved a handful of crisps in his mouth and created a volcano of crumbs.

"Well, that's good for him. A bit of extra money. He'll have that car before he knows it." Elda smiled across at her makeshift family.

"Has your mum been working long hours at the pharmacy?" Charlie asked.

"Yeah, she's a supervisor now. Not sure what they'd do without her."

"She deserves it. Good on her." Elda broke her bread in half and handed a piece to Elijah. "How's uni, Chloe?"

"It's good. I'm trying to get my dissertation finished. Which is, you know, a pain in the tits."

Both women nodded with their mouths full.

"Did you get that bio-science placement?" Elda adjusted herself to make room for her bump.

"Yeah, the letter came through last week. I haven't told Mum yet. I don't think she's going to love that I'll be in London for a year."

"She'll be proud of you, Chloe. It's such an achievement. Plus, we'll look after you when Elda's down there working." Charlie picked up some discarded crusts. "Eli, don't throw, darling. Jacob, don't let him do that, sweetheart. He's making a mess."

"I can't stop him trashing the place. He's a liability!" Jacob laughed.

"So were you at that age, you cheeky monkey." Charlie nudged him in the ribs. "We can tell you all the stories, if you like?"

"No thanks, you lot." Jacob grinned.

Elda considered her strange little family. The joyful possibilities of her life stretched out in front of her. She counted her blessings around the picnic rug; she'd been showered with unconditional love and acceptance and had learned what it was to be part of something. She was cared for, nurtured, and cherished in a way she'd never known.

While they ate, Charlie hugged Elda closer and put their hands together in her lap. She leaned across and nuzzled into her neck.

"Here you are."

"Here we are." Elda put her hand on the baby growing inside her and leaned to kiss Charlie's sticky lips. Love, unrivalled.

Hi there, I just wanted to say a big thank you for checking out Elda and Charlie's story.

Did you enjoy it? If so, I'd be thrilled if you could leave a quick review on Amazon or Goodreads. Reviews mean everything to us new writers. They help us find our footing and become better at our craft.

If you're hungry for more stories, why not sign up for my newsletter? Find out more at jofletcher.com. It's totally free, and you'll get a cheeky little prequel to Elda and Charlie's story along with a sneak peek of my upcoming novel.

And if you're on the hunt for more indie authors, be sure to check out Butterworth Books.

Thanks again for your support, and happy reading!

www.jofletcher.com
Follow me on Instagram and TikTok at JoFletcherWrites

Other Great Butterworth Books

Stunted Heart by Helena Harte
A stunt rider who lives in the fast lane. An ER doctor who can't take chances. A passion that could turn their worlds upside down.
Available on Amazon (ASIN B0C78GSWBV)

Dark Haven by Brey Willows
Even vampires get tired of playing with their food...
Available on Amazon (ASIN B0C5P1HJXC)

Green for Love by E.V. Bancroft
All's fair in love and eco-war.
Available from Amazon (ASIN B0C28F7PX5)

Call of Love by Lee Haven
Separated by fear. Reunited by fate. Will they get a second chance at life and love?
Available from Amazon (ASIN B09CLK91N5)

Where the Heart Leads by Ally McGuire
A writer. A celebrity. And a secret that could break their hearts.
Available on Amazon (ASIN B0BWFX5W9L)

Stolen Ambition by Robyn Nyx
Daughters of two worlds collide in a dangerous game of ambition and love.
Available on Amazon (ASIN B09QRSKBVP)

Cabin Fever by Addison M Conley
She goes for the money, but will she stay for something deeper?
Available on Amazon (ASIN B0BQWY45GH)

Zamira Saliev: A Dept. 6 Operation by Valden Bush
They're both running from their pasts. Together, they might make a new future.
Available from Amazon (ASIN B0BHJKHK6S)

The Helion Band by AJ Mason
Rose's only crime was to show kindness to her royal mistress...
Available from Amazon (ASIN B09YM6TYFQ)

What's Your Story?

Global Wordsmiths, CIC, provides an all-encompassing service for all writers, ranging from basic proofreading and cover design to development editing, typesetting, and eBook services. A major part of our work is charity and community focused, delivering writing projects to under-served and under-represented groups across Nottinghamshire, giving voice to the voiceless and visibility to the unseen.

To learn more about what we offer, visit: www.globalwords.co.uk

A selection of books by Global Words Press:
Desire, Love, Identity: with the National Justice Museum
Aventuras en México: Farmilo Primary School
Times Past: with The Workhouse, National Trust
Young at Heart with AGE UK
In Different Shoes: Stories of Trans Lives

Self-published authors working with Global Wordsmiths:
Steve Bailey
Ravenna Castle
Jackie D
CJ DeBarra
Dee Griffiths
Iona Kane
Maggie McIntyre
Emma Nichols
Dani Lovelady Ryan
Erin Zak

Milton Keynes UK
Ingram Content Group UK Ltd.
UKHW020612010823
426133UK00011B/316

9 781915 009449